RUNNING TOWARDS DANGER

SECOND EDITION

TINA CLOUGH

RUNNING TOWARDS DANGER

A catalogue record of this book is available from the National Library of New Zealand

Lightpool Publishing

www.lightpoolpublishing.com

Cover Photo: Tina Clough

THE DANGER DREAM

I can no longer stay - he knows where I am. Whatever is about to *happen I can't bear to think that I will die cowering on the wet ground. I push off and leap up the slope, toes digging in for better grip, arms bent and pumping, slightly hunched in instinctive concealment mode. I run toward a cluster of dark trees further down the riverbank in the direction that will take me away from the road and danger. The trees are a long way off, but the only thing that offers possible shelter.*

I run so fast I can hear the water being sucked out of the wet ground as each foot lifts off. I reach the trees unharmed and stop, trying hard to suppress my panting breaths, lean against a tree trunk and try to blend in with its shape. Gradually my heartbeat slows, my breathing becomes calmer and I move slowly away from the tree to look back to where I have come from. And as I stand there listening, searching the shades of grey and black for any sign of movement, arms grab me from behind.

A hand comes round my head and clamps hard over my mouth, the other arm clasps me tightly round the rib cage, locking my arms to my body. I freeze in the position I am in, one foot slightly raised, consider fighting, kicking back into the shins of the person holding me or biting the hand over my mouth. My heart is pounding; this is the danger dream. It is like re-living a past event. I am waiting for what must come, for the harm or the threat. We stand silently and very still for what seems like an age. His head moves closer, warm breath brushes the side of my head and a nearly soundless whisper reaches me through the sound of the wind in the trees. "No noise! Don't move."

I slowly lower my foot to the ground and nod my head against the hand over my mouth, indicating that I will obey.

1

Until that spring day I had never seen anyone die. I was walking home from the bus stop at a leisurely pace, enjoying the spring weather and planning a quiet evening watching a film on TV. I was only a hundred meters from my apartment building when I heard footsteps running behind me and someone called my name. I turned and saw Nick about twenty meters behind me, out of breath and running hard. Then two shots rang out in close succession and Nick fell to the ground, in a sort of slow-motion movement that left him lying, slightly skewed, at the edge of the sidewalk.

I stood as if paralysed; for a moment my mind did not connect the sound of the shots and Nick falling to the ground, then realisation hit me, and I ran towards him. He was badly hurt; his head was angled to one side and blood was pooling under his neck and shoulder. When I knelt beside him, he lifted a trembling hand and his voice came out in a panting whisper, "Help me!" His eyes closed but his hand was still raised just above his chest, clenched and shaking.

I was vaguely aware that a car had drawn up alongside

us, but I did not look up. There was a burst of three rapid shots, and I flinched with shocked surprise as Nick's head seemed to disintegrate. My head snapped up and I just caught an impression of a dark car accelerating away; sound seemed muffled and muted. I looked down at Nick again and knew that there was nothing I could do to help him now.

His hand that had reached out towards me was resting on the ground, as if tossed aside. I lifted the limp hand and put it on his chest; it was a shock that it felt so warm when I knew Nick was dead. There was a key on the sidewalk beside his legs and I picked it up as I rose. Three people ran towards me, one of them was shouting something but I could not hear the words.

A middle-aged man got there first and looked down at Nick in horror. "My God! That's awful!" I felt oddly removed from the scene, as if I was observing it and myself from a distance, as if this was not happening in real time.

"We must call the police," I said to the man. I hesitated, unsure of quite what was needed. "Or an ambulance?"

"I'll do it." He pulled out a cell phone and I watched him without moving. The other two had reached us now; one of them was an older woman carrying a guitar. She looked at Nick and then at me and put the guitar case on the ground, pulled a tissue from her pocket.

"Oh, you poor thing – let's get some of that blood off your face."

I stood quietly while she dabbed at my forehead and cheeks. I knew I was unhurt so it must be Nick's blood, but somehow it didn't concern me. Everything seemed unreal and remote still. While the stranger cleaned me up, I tried to think of what I must do next, but my mind was blank.

The man tucked his phone in his pocket and looked

down at Nick again. "Should we cover him up with something? It doesn't seem right to leave him like this."

He looked round as if expecting someone to hand him a blanket, but what he got, held out at arm's length, was a shawl clutched in the hand of a young girl. I had not really noticed her till now; her face was white and shocked, and her lips were trembling. "Here, take this – oh, the poor man!"

She took a step backwards, her eyes still on Nick. The man bent down and covered Nick's shattered head with the shawl. As he straightened up we heard sirens and I turned towards the sound. A crowd had gathered, some on our side and a bigger group on the other side of the street, staring across at us.

And that was how it started. Sudden and horrifying, but with no indication that it would soon change my entire life and make me do things that I would never have thought myself capable of until circumstances forced me to confront violence and danger.

A police car came to a halt right beside us and two men jumped out. "What happened?"

The man who had called the emergency services replied. "This guy was shot by someone who followed him in a car."

One policeman lifted the shawl that covered Nick's head. "Definitely dead," he said and straightened up. He went to the car and we heard him talking over the police radio. They moved everyone, who had not been an eyewitness away from the scene, telling the rest of us to stay where we were. We stood a slight distance from Nick's body, a little clump of white-faced people, not talking or even looking at each other, just waiting.

Within minutes the place was a hive of controlled chaos:

more police officers, an ambulance, 'police incident' tape, more calls on the police radio and more people. A van arrived with a PVC structure like a square tent that was immediately erected over Nick's body.

I stood there, watching with a kind of detached fascination as the scene was quickly transformed into an organised and tidy operation by people who knew exactly what to do. A chubby man in plain clothes appeared in front of me, studying my face as if he thought I might suddenly faint or burst into tears.

"I am Detective Sergeant Benson. I believe you were first on the scene? Do you mind telling me what you saw?"

I hesitated, not quite knowing where to start. "Well, I was on my way home - I was coming from the bus stop, from that direction. I heard someone shouting my name and I turned round and saw Nick running towards me."

His eyes narrowed slightly. "So, you know him?"

"Yes, he's my boarder. I thought he was out of town - I didn't know he was back."

"Tell me what you saw."

"I heard him calling and turned round. Then there were two shots and Nick fell, so I ran up to him and knelt beside him. I thought I might be able to help him. A car came alongside us and they shot him again, three times in the head – and face."

I shuddered at the memory and for the first time I realised I could have been killed myself. "And then the car sped away."

"Did you see what kind of car it was? Did you get a look at who was in it?"

"I didn't see anyone. I didn't look up until they had fired those shots and all I saw was a dark, medium-sized car driving away. I don't know what make it was. There must have been two people in it because I saw the arm of someone on the passenger side windowsill as it drove off."

The man, who had called the police, interrupted. "I've just told the constable here that it was a dark blue or black Honda Accord, a fairly recent model. I think the registration plate started with GF or GE."

Benson turned back to me. "I would like to talk a bit more with you. Would you prefer to come to the station, or can we come to your place? This is probably not the best place for you right now."

"I think I'd like to get home and get cleaned up. I live just a few doors down the street." I knew from the way Benson's eyes were roving over my face that I still had at least smears of blood on me.

"OK, let me write down your name and address and phone number. I'll come and see you a bit later. Just give me Nick's full name before you go."

"His name is Nick Cheviot." I gave him my details and turned to go, but he was not quite finished.

"Is there anyone at home at your place? No? We can get Victim Support to send someone over to be with you."

I shook my head. "No thanks. I'll be better on my own. At least for now." I gave him the PIN code for the street door, and he wrote it down in his notebook.

"All right - I'll be with you as soon as I can. Half an hour max."

As I walked the short distance to the entrance of the block of flats where I lived, I was hoping that I wouldn't meet any of my neighbours. I had lived there for two years, and Nick had rented my spare bedroom for a year and a half. He was on the road for his job nearly every week and when he returned to town, he spent very little time at home.

A look in the hall mirror showed me a distressing reflection; streaks of smeared blood on one cheek and splatters in my hair and on my neck. Suddenly some primitive urge gripped me, and I couldn't bear having a dead person's blood on me for one moment longer. If Benson turned up too soon, he would just have to wait. I dropped my bag in the hall, tore my clothes off in the bathroom and stepped into the shower. I scrubbed my face and neck and shampooed my hair twice before finally turning the water off. As I stood there letting water run down my body a sudden brief fit of shivering travelled through me. I think I realised even then, at that very early stage, that I was more resilient than I had known. I was upset and shocked by what had happened, but I was not going to break down and cry or need someone to hold my hand; I was surprised by the discovery.

Benson rang the doorbell about five minutes after I had dried myself and got into clean clothes. He did't introduce the young, uniformed man who was with him as I showed them into the living room. We sat down and the constable got a notepad out ready to take notes while Benson explained that it was important that I tried to be as accurate and descriptive as possible even if some details might seem unrelated or unimportant.

"So, let's start at the beginning" said Benson. "How long have you known Nick? And what was your relationship?"

Already at that stage I knew instinctively that I had to make it clear that I had no 'relationship' with Nick. I could tell that Benson had reservations about me, that I had been moved from 'witness' to 'potentially involved' when I told him that I knew Nick. Now I wanted to put a distance between Nick and myself, to ensure that his murder was not seen to be part of my life in any way apart from by circumstance.

"He replied to an advertisement I put in the paper for a boarder, about eighteen months ago."

"Did you have a relationship with him?" Benson was not letting go of the relationship angle. Perhaps him it seemed unusual that a man and a woman could share a flat and not have some sort of involvement.

I kept my voice neutral and friendly. "Not apart from the fact that he rented a room from me. He had a girlfriend of long standing, since before he came to live here."

He was like a dog with a bone, refusing to give it up. "Why didn't he live with her?"

I did not reply straight away, just looked at him, hoping to convey that I found him a bit ridiculous now. "I didn't think it was any of my business, so I didn't ask him."

"Can you give me her contact details?"

"I've never met her. He used to go to her place; he often stayed overnight and sometimes the whole weekend. I don't think he ever mentioned her name - he'd just say 'I'm off to see my girlfriend' or something similar. He never brought any of his friends here at all, at least not when I was at home."

The constable was writing busily, and Benson paused for a moment. "But you do know where he worked and where he was from?"

"Yes, I do. He was a salesman, or perhaps he was the sales manager, for a printing company. They make customized stationery and brochures. He travelled nearly constantly - I think he covered about half of the North Island."

"And the name of the company?"

I had to stop and think: had Nick ever told me? But a vague memory from when he first answered the advertisement surfaced. "I think they're called Goodwin or Goodson or something similar – I asked him when he came to look at the room. He said he had been there for two or three years and intended to stay there."

"What sort of car did he drive? I have his wallet with his driver's licence, but there's no next of kin listed and we can't find him in the vehicle registration database."

"Well, he had a company car of course, but that's all I know for sure. I don't think he had a car of his own; he never mentioned a car."

"Do you know where he was from and how to get hold of his family?"

"No, I've never had reason to find out. He mentioned a brother a couple of times; I think he lives somewhere near Palmerston North."

I could see that my sparse information was raising further doubts in Benson's mind, and I must make him understand that I was not being evasive. I said in my most reasonable voice, "I know it must sound odd to you that I don't know more about Nick. But he spent so little time here and he was a very private person - I imagine this was his private space, and his life involving others was elsewhere. He never once cooked a meal in the kitchen here and he never spent a whole evening with me watching TV or talking, not once. For me it was the perfect arrangement - he paid rent for his room, but he didn't interfere in my personal life in any way at all."

Benson studied his fingernails for a moment and frowned; was he thinking or was he trying to put me on edge? Then he looked up, eyes sharp and alert. "But didn't you think that it was a bit strange? That he might be using this place as a bolthole?" He studied my face as he asked the question and I thought he was hoping to catch some unguarded reaction.

"No, I never thought of it that way. I just felt lucky to have such a quiet – and often absent – boarder. We got along fine when he was here. He was a nice person, very calm and cheerful. Sometimes I made him a cup of tea and very occasionally he sat down for half an hour in the living room to watch the news with me. But mostly he was in his room when he was here. He has a TV there and I think he liked to watch it in bed. And as I said, his social life seemed to be either out on the town or with his girlfriend."

The constable cleared his throat and looked at Benson. "Sir, can I interrupt?"

"Go ahead" said Benson and the young constable looked at me with great curiosity. "Why do you think someone saw fit to shoot him? I know it's just happened, but it must have occurred to you to wonder?"

"Yes, of course I'm thinking of it - I can think of little else at the moment! He must have upset someone very badly for them to come after him with a gun. It's not what you expect to happen to a normal person, is it? He must have been involved in something illegal."

The men looked at each other for a brief moment and Benson replied. "Yes, you're probably right. It's either that or someone wanted to punish him for something, maybe even something as trivial as stealing their girl friend to use the popular phrase."

He stood up abruptly and stretched. "I think that's all for now, but we might want to talk to you again. Can we have a look at his room please?"

I hesitated for a moment, not sure if I was being a bit over-the-top detail conscious. "I need to tell you something first - I don't know if someone else told you, but those shots - they were very close together. They sounded a bit like in the movies when they fire machine guns."

It was clear from Benson's face that nobody had told him this and his eyes sharpened. "Could you demonstrate how close together?"

I thought for a moment and then I said "bang, bang, bang" very fast. But even as I said it I knew it was not fast enough. "No sorry, that's far too slow - it was more like this I think, nearly one continuous noise." And I did it again much faster: "bangbangbang".

Benson's face had a thoughtful look now. "Mm, that's rapid fire. We'll find out from forensics, but thanks for telling me - it's always useful to have a bit of advance information."

We went out into the hall where the door to Nick's room was half-open as it usually was when he was away. I took a step inside and looked around. "I don't think he's been back here since he returned from his sales trip, it looks exactly the same as it has for the last couple of days. He must have just got back."

Benson glanced around the room. "We're going to have to seal the door until we have time to go through his things. We have no explanation for why he was killed so this isn't only a murder investigation, but it's potentially about some other criminal activity as well."

"Of course, that's fine. I have no reason to go into his room anyway."

The constable was sent down to the car to get whatever they needed to seal the door and while he was gone Benson and I stood in silence until a thought struck me.

"Would you allow me to have that table under the

window? It's mine – I lent it to him when he moved in, and I have often regretted it. It was useful in the hall, and it might as well be back there. Unless it's against the rules?"

"No, not at all. There's no reason why you can't have it back. We can move it out now, before Bart seals the door."

Together we lifted the table out from Nick's room and pushed it up against the wall under the mirror in the hall. Bart returned,d Benson and I watched him seal the door and then they left.

It was half past seven now and once I was alone, I felt restless and unsettled. I rang my friend Lorraine and talked to her for half an hour with a glass of wine in one hand and a sandwich on a plate beside me. Lorraine is a few years younger than I am and just qualified as a lawyer after working and studying alternate years to pay her way through law school. She's very funny and smart and her partner is a middle-aged police officer, so talking to her was very enlightening. She told me about things that might happen during the next stage of the investigation and made sure I knew what my rights were.

"You do realise, don't you, that if he was involved in something criminal you're going to have to be very careful that you don't appear to have had any involvement with him. I mean apart from being his landlady?"

"Yes, I know - I thought of that when Benson was asking me about Nick. He kept using the word 'relationship' so I tried to make it clear that Nick never involved himself in my life at all, he never brought any of his friends here. I hope he believed me!"

. . .

Settling down to watch the film now would have been impossible so when we finished the phone call, I wandered round the flat trying to think of something to do.

I went into the hall and looked at the seal on Nick's door and tried to imagine what they might find in there and noticed that the table was the wrong way around with the drawers facing the wall. It was an old-fashioned hall table, long and narrow with two wide drawers, side by side; I had stripped it back and oiled it after I bought it and I was pleased to have it back in the hall. Now I dragged it out from the wall and swung it around and thought that it must have had the drawers facing the wall in Nick's room too, or Benson would surely have checked them before letting me have it back. I pulled out one drawer and to my surprise it was full of bank statements. I pulled out the other one and that too was full. Why did Nick have so many bank statements in the era of online banking?

Either Benson or Nick's family should have these, so I fetched a carton and started taking untidy bunches of papers out of the drawers. As I straightened the edges and I noticed that there were bank statements from different banks. I flicked through them again and became increasingly puzzled. They were for half a dozen different accounts and only one in Nick's name, but they were all addressed to the same Post Office box. Intrigued now I looked more closely, and my interest grew. I sorted them into separate piles on the hall table which was soon too small to hold them.

In the living room I sorted the statements into piles, one for each account, on the dining table. I picked out statements for the last four months for each account and put them in date order to have a closer look. It wasn't long before I had to get a pad and a pencil to keep track of the emerging pattern. An hour later I had a rough analysis of the way money moved through the accounts and I knew what I was looking at, though I had never seen it before – this was money laundering.

The whole thing was very cleverly constructed. One of the accounts was for a business called "White's Farmers Market" and had quite large cash deposits at irregular intervals, then money was transferred from there to the other accounts, on the same date each month, but there were also random amounts moving between banks.

I could trace payments from one account to another and the illusion those movements created was brilliant. Most of the accounts received regular income and could have passed as someone's only bank account; salary going in, expenses and bill payments going out, occasional cheques. It was magnificent and mind-boggling. Nick must have had an extensive record keeping system to be able to juggle so many bank cards and create the ongoing debits for this number of accounts. But why would he do it instead of just spending cash? And how could he possible use so much money?

I made a cup of coffee and drank it standing beside the table looking down at the piles of papers, trying to find a rational explanation. But there was no denying it – the total coming in, discounting the sums transferred between banks, was astounding. I did some mental arithmetic, extrapolated it to cover a year and decided that the money fed into the accounts must account to more than four hundred thousand dollars over a year, possibly more than half a million. I imagined Nick regularly going to different banks and different branches and using his many identities to deposit cash, which would then filter through in an orderly fashion into those other accounts. It would require meticulous planning and recording to work well, and it must have taken up a lot of time. Maybe this was what he did when he was at my place; maybe he spent his evenings working on this scheme when I thought he was watching TV? And what did he spend the money on?

By looking for the largest debits I found where the money went. There were payments from all the accounts to a company of sharebrokers. Now I knew what he was doing; he filtered illegal cash through many accounts and invested considerable sums in shares, the perfect retirement fund. I tried to imagine how he had organised it. Presumably he had multiple identities with the sharebroker, using the names on the bank accounts, which seemed logical, but how did he cope with the Inland Revenue department? He must have registered these imaginary people with the tax department somehow. It was hard to reconcile the cheerful young man, who had been living in my flat, with the clever criminal mind I had now discovered.

By now I was starving and highly energized, so I made another sandwich and sat down to watch the late news. The leading news story was Nick's murder, presented in typical tabloid style; close-up shots of blood in the gutter and the canvas 'tent' over the body, an interview with the middle-aged male who had been the first to reach me and a statement from the police. There was no mention of names; just a rather exaggerated and dramatic account of 'a woman kneeling in the victim's blood when he was shot a second time'.

While I ate my snack meal I planned. I had to make sure the police got the bank statements, but I would be safer if I didn't to mention money laundering. If I admitted that I had been snooping Benson would become even more suspicious. Keeping a low profile seemed the safest option to avoid anyone thinking I was part of Nick's activities. I would leave the bank statements sorted into their separate bundles, so that anyone looking at them would straight away see that there were many accounts from different banks and in different names. The natural conclusion would be that Nick had kept them tidy and removed me from the equation. I put them back in the drawers in tidy piles with alternating bunches lying crossed. Now someone who tried to fit them into a normal document box would need to turn them the same way round; another way of making sure that the many identities were obvious.

I was getting ready for bed when I remembered the clothes that I had dumped into the washing machine when I got dressed in a hurry after my shower. I checked the pockets before turning the machine on and felt something hard in the pocket of the jacket I had worn. It was the key that I had picked up from the sidewalk. I started the wash and went to bed with a book until I could hang things up in the bathroom.

When I was finally ready to call it quits for the day, I noticed the key again on my bedside table. I sat on the edge of the bed and looked more closely at it, trying to imagine what it might fit. It wasn't like any key I had ever seen before. Compared to normal keys it seemed very flat and un-detailed. The end you hold on to was just a flat disc with the letter C on one side and 9 printed in blue on the other side. Was it Nick's or had it already been on the footpath, and he just happened to fall next to it? I put it back on the bedside table and got into bed.

2

After waking very early, I lay in bed thinking of all that had happened the previous day and decided it might be better not to tell anyone at work that my boarder had been murdered. I could imagine the endless questions and the huge interest this would generate. Even if the police released Nick's name there was no reason why anybody at work would connect me with his name. It would be much easier not having to recount the same gory details to one person after another. I knew that Lorraine would not talk about it; she and John know how to keep things to themselves.

Much later I would think back on this early focus on keeping my name out of the media. What was it that made me so careful? Something apart from Benson's suspicion that I was involved made me feel I must not draw attention to myself.

· · ·

I spent a busy morning at work trying to sort out a client's messy GST problems, while in the back of my mind thoughts of Nick revolved endlessly. The money laundering, the source of the money in the first place, the way he had deceived me – what had he been involved in? I could only think of drugs and gangs, but Nick seemed such an unlikely candidate, fond of trendy clothes and so normal and well-mannered. Not that a good façade was any guarantee of honesty or integrity, but it was still hard to reconcile my memory of Nick with what was coming to light now. The police called just after lunch and asked me to come and unlock the flat, so they could examine Nick's room. I was glad to leave early; it was hard to concentrate on work. I had no client meetings that day, so I told the receptionist I had an unforeseen appointment and went home.

This time Benson had another man with him, a thin middle-aged man who sniffled continuously. "This is DC Grant; he's going to help me go through the room. I hope we won't disturb you for too long."

He removed the seal from the door, and they went to work while I retreated to the living room. I left the door to the hall half-open as a compromise between being accessible but not overly curious. An hour later Benson tapped on the living room door and came in. "We're nearly finished. We are taking a few things away for testing. Is it OK if we leave the rest here until someone can come and pick everything up? His brother is going to come up from Fielding in a couple of days."

"Of course, that's fine. Will he come on his own or will you come with him?" Not that I was worried about having Nick's brother there with me, but I wanted to know when I should stage the "finding" of the bank statement collection.

It seemed important that Benson found them himself to maintain the impression that I had nothing to hide. It was ironic that I had never had anything to do with Nick's life, but now I was busy planning devious ways of creating proof of this to keep Benson at a safe distance.

"I won't come over with him myself, but somebody will. If you're OK with that?"

"That's fine." We went into the hall, and I made a sudden gesture, as if I'd just noticed something. "Hey, wait a minute, did you check those drawers?"

Benson followed my glance, and I could tell from his voice that he was intensely irritated with himself for having missed something. "I didn't notice those yesterday. I'd better have a look."

He opened one drawer, frowned and pulled out the other one. He took out a thick stack of bank statements and flicked through them. He was putting them down on the table when he paused and started looking through them more slowly. He looked up at me, his face a mask of professional discretion. "Do you know anyone called Martin Hislop?" I shook my head. He flipped through another few pages. "Or someone called Ryder?"

"No," I said, pretending surprise. "Why?"

"Just wondered," said Benson at his very blandest. "It seems that some of these belong to someone else." He shuffled the pages together again and put them on the table. "You wouldn't have a box of some kind we could borrow, do you? I need to take all this stuff away for a closer look."

"I'll get a carton." I knew from Benson's reaction that those bank statements would soon become a vital part of the investigation into the reasons for Nick's death. I was very satisfied with my new-found talent, making things happen without apparently doing anything at all.

.   .   .

They were gone by ten to five and I was just about to make a cup of coffee when Lorraine rang. "Hi honey, how are you today? Are you feeling OK after all that ghastly drama yesterday?"

"I'm fine, but I'm sad for Nick of course - such a waste of a life. I had to come home early from work to let the police in and they've just left with some of Nick's things. His brother will pick up the rest when he gets here - from Fielding I think."

"OK, I suppose it's better to get it all sorted. We saw it on TV last night - John knows the chap in charge of the investigation, Benson. Have you heard anything new?"

"Well, I haven't heard the news since first thing this morning. I left work early to come home to let the police in and they've only just gone, but they didn't tell me anything."

"Do you want to come over for dinner? Mia and Thomas are coming, and a bit of company might be better than being at home on your own."

"I'd love to - can I bring something?"

"We have everything we need, or at least we will when John gets home. Why don't you come over right away?"

John and Lorraine live in a townhouse in a little street that is so narrow there's hardly any parking. I circled their block in Parnell twice and ended up parking three blocks away.

Lorraine opened the door with a tea towel over her shoulder and a knife in her hand. We have known each other for years and anyone less domesticated would be hard to find. She laughed when she saw my face. "Don't worry - I'm not doing anything in the kitchen, not food anyway. I am just unloading the dish washer and putting things away. John's due home about six and he'll do the cooking."

By the time John arrived, we had set the table and could

leave him in charge of the kitchen, which is the way he prefers it. "Why don't you give Karen a glass of wine, Lorraine? And one for me, please. Karen, I can't remember if you have met Mia and Thomas?"

"I've met Mia a couple of times, but not Thomas."

"You're in for a treat," said Lorraine. "Thomas is a treasure. Did I ever tell you about his scar? No? Well, don't be put off when you first meet him. He looks like a thug from one side and like the lovely man he really is from the other side. But it takes a bit of getting used to."

She had no sooner stopped talking than the doorbell went, and Mia and Thomas walked in, and I was glad I'd been warned about the scar, it was very hard to keep your eyes off it. Over dinner John told us that he and Lorraine were planning a week away 'somewhere exotic' as he put it, and this prompted Thomas to tell us about an interesting situation he had come up against the previous week. I knew he was an accountant, but I soon realised that his firm mainly deal with international tax law. The story he told us was about a new client, who had asked the firm to front a trust, and in return Thomas would be able to use the client's beach house in the Bahamas for two weeks every year with house staff and a boat thrown in for good measure.

"Oh my God," said Mia, "You didn't tell me - what an offer! Anyone else would have accepted it, whatever they thought he's going to use that trust for."

Thomas looked at her with a straight face. "It's a great offer - all we have to do is tell him when we want it."

Mia choked on her wine. "You can't have, it must be something ..."

And then she saw the look on his face and laughed. "For a moment I thought you'd lost the plot completely."

"So, what do you think he is going to use that trust for, Thomas?' I asked. 'I suppose Mia is right and it would be something illegal or at least borderline. Do you think he's a criminal?"

Thomas grinned. "I have no idea – not yet. He's engaged us to structure his investments and properties. He has houses on three countries and a lot of money invested all over the place. He wants to know if we can do anything more to minimise his tax liabilities. It's what we do."

Mia interrupted him. "So, you don't know how he made his money?"

"No, I don't, but we usually find out. If we think someone's trying to hide something criminal like drug trading or if they're involved in the illegal weapons trade, then we give them the report they've paid for and decline to do any further work for them. Once when we had specific and serious doubts about a client, we declined to do anything at all and gave his deposit back."

"What is the process if you agree to help them further? Do you actually mastermind creating companies and trusts? It's funny, I've never asked you before." Lorraine was curious too.

"Yes, we do. My two partners are lawyers who specialise in international law and unfortunately or fortunately – depending on which side you are on – our company laws and trust laws used to make New Zealand a pretty good place for all sorts of hide-and-seek ways of managing money. It was well known among the kind of people who need these things, or who think they do. But that's all changed now – after the Panama paper scandal the laws were all changed."

Lorraine was thoughtful. "It's amazing that those who have the most money are always the ones who try and avoid paying tax and doing their duty, isn't it? And then they say that if everyone takes personal responsibility and looks after themselves there's no need for a welfare system – I mean that's what the reactionary wealthy say. Bonkers!"

Thomas stood up to take a couple of plates to the kitchen and said over his shoulder. "But we do have principles, Lorraine, I promise. I meant it when I said we never get involved in anything we think is suspect, we only take on things that will never come back and bite us."

I drove home at the end of a pleasant evening, thinking of the next day at work and what I might do in the weekend, and parked the car a few blocks away where there are no restrictions on parking. Walking back to my street I glanced across as I exited the alleyway, but nothing could be seen of yesterday's drama. I wondered vaguely if someone had washed the blood stains off the sidewalk or if they would be there until nature took care of them.

I had left before the TV news and now I had just missed the late news, so I went online to see if there had been any new developments about Nick's murder. And it was a lucky I did because it prepared me for the possibility that I would have to reconsider my anonymity. Someone had given a cell phone video clip to the news services. It was filmed from the other side of the street and not quite steady, but clear enough. You could see Nick's legs with a man and a girl standing between his body and the camera. I was standing just beside his head and that helpful woman was dabbing away at my face. My profile was clearly visible and when I turned toward the approaching sirens there was a full-face shot of me before a police car interrupted the view.

My first reaction was irritation; there went my privacy.

Not that anyone apart from the police knew my name, but whoever had held that phone might well have been watching to see where I went. The last thing I wanted was reporters looking for eyewitness interviews, and I particularly didn't want it to be known that Nick had been my boarder.

I sat there in the living room with the laptop on my knees trying to figure out why I felt so angry. Did it really matter that people found out I had been present? All it meant was that there would be questions at work the next day and I needed to prepare myself. Trying to avoid talking about it would be useless now, so I might as well have a planned response. The best approach might be to tell people whatever they asked me, but not to mention that Nick had been my boarder. Some people at work knew that I had a boarder, but I never really talked about him, and they would not know his name.

The next day nearly everyone at work came into my office to commiserate about my bad luck and to ask how frightening it had been to nearly be shot myself. I replied in the way they expected, said that I had friends to support me, that the police had taken a statement and that it had been very scary and left it at that. Lorraine called late in the afternoon and suggested a movie that evening with her and Mia.

"The guys won't come, but Mia and I felt like going out. It's just a silly romantic comedy, but probably quite funny."

The romantic comedy we saw was predictable, clichéd and amusing. We went to a bar just down the street that Lorraine recommended and ordered tapas and wine. The conversation touched briefly on the film and then it became an all-out question and answer session about the events on Tuesday. For some reason they were more curious now that the men were not with us. Lorraine is as sharp as a tack and

Mia has been through her own drama; both of them have experience of things that I had not. I trusted them enough to tell them about the bank statements I had found and my conclusions about the money laundering.

"That sounds weird. Where do you think he got all the money? Must have been crime," said Mia.

Lorraine's take on it was more personal. "Let's keep this a secret between us three and not tell anyone else. If the police have the bank statements, they'll investigate it. Isn't it better that nobody else knows that you worked out it was money laundering?"

However we much we tried to come up with theories we always came back to gangs and drugs. Lorraine had no doubts at all. "It has to be drugs! What other form of crime involves such huge amounts of cash? Perhaps he was a drug courier, or someone who brokered drug deals. They do exist, you know – drug brokers, the illegal version of share brokers."

"Well, I don't believe he was a drug courier. I thought of that at first," I said. "But he only took holidays once or twice a year."

"But Karen, he might not have been a sales rep at all. How do we know he was even employed? Does that company exist?" Mia was really interested now. "His whole life, as you thought you knew it, might have been a front for something very different."

Lorraine interrupted. "Were there wage payments into his own account?"

"Yes, I think so," I said, "but they might have been faked as well. I mean, he might have set them up from one of the other accounts. I couldn't tell you how it all was structured in detail unless I sat down and spent hours analysing it. It was incredibly elaborate - so many different identities with separate accounts in different banks. I figured out how things were moved from one account to the next and did some rough estimates. Bur you could be right, maybe he just made up the sales job to have a cover."

"OK, so when you thought he was on the road or at his girlfriend's place for a few days he might have made a quick trip to Asia or South America or somewhere. You'd never have known." Mia looked thoughtful now. "It sounds like a TV drama, but the drug trade involves huge money so people take big risks - it's a dangerous game."

"I know anyone can be a criminal and you can't tell by how they look, but if you had met Nick you would be a puzzled as I am. He was your original nice young guy without a bad bone in his body – or so I thought. Polite and really easy to get on with."

Lorraine laughed at the thought that I might have found a well-mannered drug dealer. "And think of that TV series about people who get caught by the Customs; all those people who look pretty ordinary and then it turns out they have drugs concealed in their luggage or in their shoes or even worse places. I bet there are lots who don't get caught at all."

"Well, whatever he was up to it would certainly be interesting to find out what it was. So long as I don't get dragged into it by association – that Benson chap doesn't quite trust me, I could tell. He kept harping on a about my supposed relationship with Nick."

"I suppose he must have had fake passports, if he made frequent trips to the same places or it would have alerted customs," said Mia. "But we might never know, of course." She looked at me and could tell she was choosing her words carefully. "You want to be careful about publicity, Karen. The less visible you are in this business the safer you are. As long as the cops have no idea that you looked through those bank statements you can genuinely act innocent. We want no trouble for you if they get it wrong and think you're involved – or if someone else thinks you are."

Lorraine nodded in agreement. "She's right, Karen. One thing Mia and I have learnt from past experience is that the fewer people know things, the less likely it is that there will be trouble. That old caution about only telling those who need to know is probably best in most contexts."

"I'm not telling anybody else about it – not a single soul. I even managed to make Benson think I hadn't looked in those drawers. Which I'm sure you shouldn't 't tell John, Lorraine – he'd be horrified."

Lorraine tipped her wineglass upside down and looked sadly at the single drop that fell out. "Ah well, this excitement is all very well, but I've got to work tomorrow and it's after midnight – time to go home."

It was an unusually warm evening for so early in the season. On the way home I walked around the block after parking the car instead of going through the alley. A couple walking their little dog said "Lovely evening" in greeting as they passed, a car drove leisurely past, and life felt quite normal again.

Before I went to bed, I sat down to write an email to my parents. Their current jobs were in the Bangladesh outback working at a UNICEF clinic. They had to travel miles into the nearest town over terrible roads to check their emails, so occasional delays were the norm in our correspondence. I mentioned Nick's death, but I said nothing about the bank accounts or my suspicions about what he had been involved with. My parents are very good parents, but their focus has always been on their work and on humanity at large. Laura is a doctor and Steven is a theatre nurse and before they worked for the UN they worked for charities and did voluntary work. I love them dearly, but somehow, we never had the kind of 'arguments-and-hugs' relationship that my friends had with their parents. As a result, I became very self-sufficient at an early age, which was a good thing, but the other side of the coin is that I rarely confide in them if I have a problem. It always feels as if they already shoulder so many of humanity's overall problems that it would be petty to add my little worries to their burden.

Having dealt with that, I scrolled down the messages in the Inbox and found one from my ex-boyfriend that was nearly a month old. As always, I hesitated; the relationship had broken up several months ago with no hard feelings on either side. We never lived together and though we were great in bed together I always felt there was something missing. Out of bed we never seemed to want to do the same things and we had shared no interests apart from liking the same music. I broke it off when I suddenly realised one day, that when he was away for a long weekend fishing with his mates I felt as if I'd been given a holiday. Not good enough to build a long-term relationship on. I missed the spectacular sex, but apart from that he had left no gaps in my life. He continued to send occasional messages and I usually replied later rather than sooner.

Lorraine sometimes suggested potential partners for me, but she invariably picked someone I would never fall for. The truth was that having someone just for the sake of it held no appeal for me. I was fine on my own and I had plenty of pleasant things to do in my spare time without trying to fit in with someone else's demands.

Once I said to Lorraine, "But why would I go hunting for love unless it pops up right in front of me and biffs me on the nose? I'm very happy with my life and I do get asked out, you know. I don't want a permanent man in my life just for the sake of it. You never used to be a matchmaker till you met John. Before that you always said having a permanent boyfriend was a waste of time - you've gone soft."

The truth was I was not prepared to cut down on things that I loved doing just to please someone else, who wanted to do different things. I had never met anyone who made that change worthwhile. Now I spent a couple of hours each week swimming and went to Tae Kwando once a week. There was barely time for all the movies and exhibitions I wanted to see, not to mention reading. I was very happy with my solo status.

3

———

A day later things conspired to delay me and I was late leaving for work. I hurried across the street towards the shortcut to the bus stop and a car braked hard to let me cross. I smiled apologetically and ran the last few steps. The car was quite like the one that had cruised past last night, a late model silver-grey Mercedes. Must be someone who's moved in nearby, I thought, as the bus pulled up, a lot classier than most cars around here.

Later that morning I was focused on a complex spreadsheet when the phone rang. I picked it up while still studying the figures on my screen, so at first the male voice made no sense.

"Sorry," I said. "I think you have the wrong person. I don't know what you're talking about."

"OK, take that line if you like." He had a quiet voice but there was no mistaking the menace in it. "We know Nick spent a lot of time at your place and we want what's ours. Just have a look through his things and find the bag and give it back to us."

"What on earth are you talking about? Of course, he

spent time at my flat, he lived there. And I've no idea what he might have had that belongs to you."

My mind was assessing options as I spoke. If this was connected to all the money that filtered through Nick's bank accounts, I must be very careful.

"Don't be stupid! You know he didn't live with you. We've looked everywhere and the bag is missing. Go through whatever he left at your place and I'll call tomorrow."

"What am I supposed to look for? I still don't know what you're talking about."

"Never mind - all you need to do is find a dark blue satchel with a zip and a padlock. We know he had it, he left a meeting with it and it's missing."

"Maybe the police took it. They took some of his things away the day he was killed."

"No, don't try that one - we have our contacts, and we know the cops don't have it. It must be somewhere in the flat, we know they only searched his room. I'll call you again. And don't call the cops - we know where you are, we can come and visit any time." The line went dead.

I sat very still and tried to figure out what this meant. Nick must have been involved in drugs in some way, either as a middleman or as an importer, or perhaps he had been manufacturing drugs. It was clear that he had more strands to his life than I had been aware of. These people were looking for money or drugs that Nick had left somewhere, and they thought I knew.

That evening the silver Mercedes once again cruised past as I crossed the street from the bus stop to the alley. When I emerged into my own street there it was again, slowly coming towards me with tinted windows concealing the occupants. A cold shiver of fear ran down my spine, and I walked very fast the rest of the way and punched in the door code as quickly as I could.

I searched Nick's room and found no bag, but I was surprised at how few clothes and possessions he had kept there. In the back of my mind, I was beginning to accept that he had not really lived in my flat at all. Somewhere in the city he had another home or maybe more than one. I considered his pattern of being away 'on the road' as he called it, his brief spells with me, then moving on to spend a couple of nights at his girl-friend's place. I had to accept that my flat had been his secret place where he might well have kept things that he didn't want to be found. Or perhaps where he just took time out and did things quietly on his own. I wondered where all those ATM cards were, and maybe multiple passports and whatever else I knew nothing about.

I searched the whole flat, but there were few places where he could have hidden a bag and I found nothing. I pulled the kitchen drawers right out and looked behind them and poked my arm in behind his bedhead and found nothing but dust. Had he realised that someone was trying to get the blue bag off him? Had he left it somewhere before he came back to my flat? And why had they killed him before they found the bag? Who had killed him; the man who had called me or someone from a competing drug gang?

My mind was in turmoil as I stood at the window of his room and tried to work out what my options were. If my caller had contacts inside the police, it might make things worse if I reported the threats. But what protection did I have if I didn't report it? And if I didn't report it, would the man who had called take that as an indication that I knew something and was trying to stay under the radar? The kitchen window overlooked the street, and I found myself watching for the Mercedes while I was making dinner, and then he called again. "Look out the window. We're watching you."

I stood well back from the window, but even from there I could see the Mercedes parked on the opposite side of the street. The back of my neck prickled as I realised I was talking to someone in that car, someone I couldn't see.

"I've searched the whole flat and the bag isn't here – I have looked everywhere." My voice came out tense with fear.

That calm, hard voice responded. "That's better – now you're taking this seriously. Check for anything that points to another bolt hole or a hiding place. Like an address or a receipt - or a bunch of keys. The cops didn't find anything of that kind."

It was frightening to think that this awful man knew so much about what the police had or did not have. All I could do was try to appease him for a while to give myself time to think. "OK, I'll go through his stuff again."

All he said was, "I'll be in touch." Then he broke the connection.

I sat down to eat, but after a few mouthfuls I gave up. Tension and fear made eating impossible, I felt as if I was chewing concrete. I got up and wandered around the flat, wondering what I could do and how to protect myself. No answers presented themselves and all I could do was worry about what would happen the next day, when I had to tell them I had found nothing.

The next morning was beyond me. I had a cup of tea while I dressed and when I put the mug on the bench, I saw the Mercedes on the other side of the street again. By the time I got to the street door my nerves were jangling and I couldn't bear to look straight at the car. It slid quietly away from the kerb as I walked towards the alleyway, and I knew without looking around that it would be there when I emerged at the other end. Of course, they would drive around the block to terrorise me further. It was parked so close to the bus stop that I had to walk within a couple of meters of it when I crossed the street, but it gave me a boost of confidence to realise that I could choose to ignore it. They could look at me, but as I could not see them through the tinted glass, I preferred to not acknowledge them in any way and kept my face turned towards the bus that had just pulled up. I refused to turn my head to see if the Mercedes drove away when the bus pulled out, but when I got off a block from the office the Mercedes drove slowly past me.

I was now so intimidated that concentrating on work was nearly impossible. By the end of the morning my head was pounding, and I knew I would get nothing done that day. I checked my diary, picked up my bag and I went to tell reception that I had to go home.

There was no sign of the Mercedes when I got off the bus and a weight lifted from my shoulders. At this time of the day the alleyway empty and there was no inkling of threat until I heard quick footsteps behind me. I started running, but a man appeared at that end and came towards me, and I was trapped. One of them grabbed my arm and pushed me hard against the wall, nearly lifting me off my feet. The other man moved in and stood very close in front of me. "Any progress? What have you found?"

My voice came out in a squeak. "Nothing - there's *nothing* in the flat!"

He looked at me for a short moment, his eyes a pale metal grey and then he swung his fist at the side of my head. The impact was shocking, my head bounced off the wall behind me and rebounded to meet his fist as he swung again and connected with my cheekbone. For a second the world went dark, and I slumped against the hard hand gripping my upper arm. When I could focus again, the look on his face was a mask of fury.

"OK, in that case we'll have to come and help you look, won't we?" It was obviously not a question.

He hit me hard in the solar plexus. I bent double, gasping for air. If one of them hadn't been holding my upper arm I would have fallen to the ground. I tried to suck air into my lungs and fought nausea, straightened up slowly. My voice was hoarse and laboured. "I don't know what you're talking about. I had nothing to do with Nick's stuff!"

Suddenly they both looked towards the far end of the alley. A middle-aged couple with shopping bags were walking quickly towards us. The man was pulling a mobile phone out of his pocket, he shouted something. The grip on my arm loosened and both my attackers ran; they were out of the alley before the couple reached me. The relief made me weak at the knees. "Perfect timing - thank God you turned up."

They both spoke at once. "Are you hurt? Did they mug you?" and "I'll call the police right away."

"No, no! Don't worry, I'll report it when I get home - they didn't take anything. You came just in time." All I could think of was to get to my flat safely. "I live really close. Do you think we could walk along together, please?"

"Of course." The man was all for a quick solution, but his wife had her own concerns. "Are you sure you're not hurt? It looked as if he had just hit you, that man."

It was a relief to realise that nothing showed on my face, or not yet. My head was pounding, and I felt nauseated, but getting home safely was my first objective. "No, I'm OK - truly, but it would be nice to have company."

We walked together to the end of the alley and out into the sunshine, but there was no sign of the men or the Mercedes. The couple walked with me to my door, waited while I punched in the code and said goodbye. I made sure the street door had locked behind me before I went upstairs, but I had a moment of sheer panic when I put the key in my apartment door. What if they had got into the building somehow and were now inside waiting for me?

Cautiously I swung the door wide open, not entering just standing still and listening carefully, before I went in and closed the door behind me. I put down my bag and walked quickly through the rooms making sure there was nobody there. I went back to the hall, put the chain on the door and leaned back against it and exhaled. I felt as if I had held my breath since first putting the key in the lock. I promised myself that even though I knew the bag was not in Nick's room I would search minutely for anything else that might be a clue, however small.

First, though, I had to calm down. I washed my face, changed out of my skirt and high heels, and swallowed a couple of pain killers before I made a cup of coffee. The side of my face was aching, and a bruise was appearing on my temple and across the cheekbone. The other side of my head had a painful lump where it had bounced off the wall. I walked around holding a tea towel with ice cubes alternately against the two places, hoping to lessen the pain and the swelling.

After an hour's thorough search, I picked up the phone to call the police despite their warning, and it rang just as I put my hand on it and nearly made me jump out of my skin.

"Enough!" There was no doubt about who it was. His voice told me everything; he was furious and out of patience, no longer quietly threatening. "Now you're in serious trouble. We know the police haven't got a clue – they think that Nick had a lot of drugs or cash, and they think he got done because of it, but they don't know why. You and I both know he had that cash and I think you know where it is."

"But I don't! I didn't know anything about him. I thought he was who he said he was. I've no idea where that money is."

"Listen bitch - we know the cops are wondering if you have the money, so whichever way you turn someone's going to get it off you. You won't be able to spend it without us knowing, so let's do a deal. You give us the money and we let you keep ten thousand - call it a finder's fee. And just to make sure that you understand that we mean business, check out the papers from November 2018. Search for an article about a woman who caught fire in her back yard, and when you read it, remember it could happen to you."

He cut the connection and I stood frozen to the spot trying to take in what he had just said. Who could help me now? Would the police even believe me if I went to them? How could I possibly clear my name or stay safe?

I powered up my laptop and went to the Herald's website. After a couple of attempts I found an archived article headlined *Woman burnt to death in own back yard*. A woman 'with known drug and gang connections' had been found burnt to death behind her rented property in Manurewa. She had been doused with petrol and set alight after probably having been knocked unconscious. The inhuman brutality of the story made my skin crawl.

I sat there for half an hour, thinking of options and rejecting them all as being impossible, apart from one. There was nowhere I could hide, nobody who could shelter me without themselves being at risk. Whatever I told the Mercedes man or the police they probably wouldn't believe me. There was no way the police could protect me, at least not long-term and effectively. Just going to work would expose me to risk. And if they too suspected I had the money, would they even be prepared to protect me? The one remaining option was to involve nobody else and disappear leaving no trace for anyone to follow. Later on, I could let the police know why I had to do it and tell them of the threats I had received; let them work it out after I had gone.

The hours that followed were frantic. I took a sheet of paper out of the printer and stood at the kitchen counter making a list. Every now and then I dashed off and did something I had thought of, then I returned to my list and either crossed something off or added another item. There were moments when I wondered if I had lost my mind, if I was over-reacting and creating a hopeless and dangerous situation for myself.

At one stage I felt I was adding more things to my list than I was crossing off. I stopped and divided it into two lists: things I had to do before I left the flat and what I would do over the next few days from some other location. I felt a lot more in control once this was done and stopped to eat a sandwich before I continued my frantic preparations.

I knew that I was being watched more or less continuously and that they could grab me at any time and force me to let them into the flat. And what would happen after that? When they found that the money really was not there? It made me feel sick with fear to think that they might take me somewhere and set fire to me, either because they thought I had cheated them or simply to punish me for not having what they wanted.

I had to get away, and my hidden ace was that there was another way of exiting my apartment building and it was highly unlikely that they knew of it. Tucked away in the corner beside the lift in the ground floor lobby was a door leading to a small yard, surrounded by apartment buildings on all sides with a narrow lane connecting the yard to another street. When I first moved in, I had wondered if there was a way into that yard that I could see from some of my windows. I had found the door at the back of the lobby and followed the little lane out onto a side street a block away and behind my street.

My preparations went on for hours and into the night. Everything had to be gone through, carefully considered and taken care of in a way that would keep me safe from being found. It was nearly one in the morning, and I had been working and planning for twelve hours, fuelled by desperation and lack of time. To avoid raising the suspicions of anyone watching the building from the street I staged going to bed at half past ten. I turned off the lights in the rooms that could be seen from the street and closed the doors to the rest of the flat. When I needed to go into those rooms, I turned other lights off, so no light or activity could be seen by those watching from the street; at the time being over cautious seemed the best idea.

I packed my medium-sized wheeled suitcase and hung three supermarket bags full of ripped-up papers on the handle. My laptop and some smaller things went into my canvas carry-all. It was quite heavy, but with it slung over my shoulder I should be able to manage the suitcase. I had only one chance to leave safely and it must happen smoothly, without a hitch.

I walked through the hall, the kitchen and the living room in the diffused light from the street, surveyed each piece of furniture and every storage space, mentally checking off every drawer and shelf. I had done a thorough search to make sure that nothing too private or revealing was left. If someone broke in after I had gone there would be nothing that could lead intruders to my friends or family.

Instead of using the lift I went down the stairs, carrying the suitcase and trying to be very quiet. I opened the door in the corner beside the lift and closed it silently behind me. The short passage was completely dark, and I didn't turn on the light, just walked cautiously, pulling the suitcase behind me and trailing one hand along the wall until I got to the outer door. The little yard was like the bottom of a canyon: buildings rose up all around, only a few windows were still lit.

The gate to the lane was like a metal door with a spring that closed it when you let it go. Once I let it fall shut behind me, I wouldn't be able to turn back. The narrow lane ran right through the block and made a right-angle turn before it exited on the side street.

Carefully scanning the dark street in both directions, I stood for a moment in the shadow where the lane ended. I could see nobody, and the parked cars seemed empty. I had never done anything as frantic and important as this and there had been so little time to do it, with no time to reconsider things. I hoped the steps I had taken, and those I was about to take, would keep me safe. I had tried to think of all possible risks and now I must get away from here. I was intensely nervous now, terrified that something would go wrong in the last minutes, trying to think of strategies to use if I was accosted.

There had been a short moment of panic when the gate to the yard locked behind me, fear that there would be something I hadn't thought of; some loose end that would enable those trying to find me to follow the thread of my escape and eventually find me.

I took a deep breath, pulled myself together and stepped out into the blank space of my unknown future. Instantly my whole being was flooded with urgency, my mind screamed 'Run!' It took a huge effort to walk the three blocks to the car at a normal pace, just waiting for someone to step out and confront me. At the intersecting streets my nerves jangled with fear as I crossed. The last few meters were an exercise in self-control as I forced myself to walk at a normal speed. Quickly, I put the bags in the back and locked myself in before I fitted the key in the ignition with shaking fingers. As I drove away my eyes scanned the dark street and the rear mirror, but nobody followed me. The sparse traffic made it easy to check, but for fifteen minutes I meandered around the city, further and further away from my flat, to make absolutely certain I was not being followed. My rational self told me the Mercedes man wouldn't sit in his car all night or continually circle the block, but real fear isn't rational.

When I finally felt safe enough, I stopped briefly a couple of times to drop the supermarket bags of ripped up paper rubbish in public bins. I stopped at a cash machine and withdrew the maximum daily amount. A burly man on a bicycle raised a hand in greeting as he rode silently past, and I felt slightly cheered as I got back in the car. I drove to Lorraine and John's street and stopped just long enough to drop a big envelope in their letterbox. I thought of them sleeping inside and how wonderful it would be if I could ring the doorbell and ask them to let me hide there. But nobody could hide me and be safe themselves; anything I did that involved my friends or family would only expose them to danger too. The road forward had to be a lonely one. I returned to the car and drove out of the city.

By now I was exhausted. I had been awake for twenty hours and I had operated on adrenalin most of that time. Now I concentrated on driving safely, just under the speed limit, as I headed towards the southern suburbs looking for a motel. I found one in a commuter suburb I had never visited before, a small and old-fashioned motel with a sign advertising Wi-Fi access and Sky TV. It was too early to disturb them, so I drove past the place and parked outside a house, where a tall fence screened me from the eyes of the occupants. I undid my seatbelt, locked the doors and within a couple of minutes I was asleep.

4

Children's voices woke me from a sleep disturbed by disjointed dreams. Two little girls were peering in at me and giggling, and when they saw I was awake they ran off down the street, laughing and shouting. I sat up straight, checked myself in the rear-view mirror and started the car, light-headed with exhaustion.

The motel office was empty and tidy and the bellpush had a hand-written sign that said, 'Press Me!' but before I had time to press it a woman appeared from the back regions carrying a stack of folded towels. "Oh, goodness!" she said. "I didn't know anyone was here – I wasn't expecting anyone so early."

I tried to look friendly. "I've been driving nearly all night and I really need a sleep – have you got a unit available right away?"

"Goodness!" she said again and put the towels on the counter. "Where have you come from then?"

"I left Wellington late last night, but I had to stop a couple of times to eat and have a rest."

I saw her eyes on my bruised cheek and temple, and a

47

speculative look flickered across her face. "That looks sore," she said with an open invitation for me to explain the injury.

I tried to sound embarrassed and amused at the same time "Boxing, would you believe? You should see the bruise on my chest. Don't know why I took it up, but it keeps me fit."

Her look changed to interest and surprise. We had a brief conversation about why women took up boxing these days. "I never realised that girls do boxing till just recently", she said. "Imagine girls with those mashed ears or broken noses - not pretty."

But I was pleased, because I knew that if I had said that something more common, like netball, was responsible for my bruising she might have speculated that maybe I was making an excuse. That maybe someone had hit me, perhaps an abusive partner. But by saying boxing I had deflected her instinct to pry.

I filled in the form with a fictitious name and a made-up car registration number, hoping she wouldn't check it. She got a carton of milk from a fridge behind the counter and came to the door to point out unit 6. I thanked her, she handed me the milk and the key and went back to her stack of towels.

The unit was studio-style and spacious, with only essential furniture. The large bed in the overlarge room sagged in the middle and the bathroom needed a revamp, but there was a decent-sized table with two chairs, and an armchair of dubious cleanliness. I closed the door behind me and heaved a sigh of tired relief. Once I had made some decisions about what to do in the afternoon, I might be able to switch off my hectic thoughts and settle down to a proper sleep on a bed.

I put my lists and papers on the table and booted up the laptop. The first thing I needed to do was compose a generic draft email that I could adapt later and send to various people before I stopped using my email address.

The only message I must send straight off was to my employer to explain that I wouldn't come back, at least not for some time. The senior partner had been a supportive mentor for the last three years and I trusted and liked him. I wanted to give him a complete picture of my reason for leaving so suddenly both to avoid damaging my employment record and to inform him on a personal level. So, I explained the sequence of events that had started when Nick was killed and told him about the harassment, the threats and the beating. As an afterthought I included a link to the article about the woman who was burnt to death. He would understand why I had to flee, and I hoped he would respect my privacy. I ended by saying that I understood that my workmates would ask why I had left so suddenly and suggested that a mention of my parents might be sufficient explanation and that I would be grateful if he could keep the details to himself. Then I put my few food supplies in the fridge and went to bed.

It was early afternoon when I woke, rested and alert. I lay on the bed enjoying the quiet and thinking of my priorities. The sun was shining, and a brisk wind bent the treetops I could see through the window. The bright spring light made me feel better than I had since Nick died. I made a cup of tea and two slices of toast and sat down at the table with yesterday's lists. Some tasks had been crossed off. Now I ran a line through a few more; I had made progress.

I spent some time working out how much I must leave in my bank account to cover the various things that would continue to be paid by direct debit from my bank account whether I lived in the flat or not. I added up mortgage repayments, power bill, phone account and one or two other things and then multiplied the result by twelve, deliberately discounting the savings I could make by having phone and power turned off. Giving it a year initially seemed over the top, but the more I thought of it the more it seemed like a sensible precaution. Using my savings meant giving up my plans to visit my parents, but it was a small price to pay for safety.

By now Lorraine or John would have found the envelope in their letterbox. I pictured them reading the short note I had included with the keys to the apartment and my credit card, passport and insurance documents. No matter what happened now, at least I had the comfort of knowing that the things that were my ticket back to normal life, at some undefined date in the future, were safe.

I accessed my internet banking and transferred my total savings to my cheque account. Even taking into account the money that must be left I would be able to withdraw a surprising amount in cash before I stopped using the bank. Visions of bag snatchers and muggers rose in my mind; I would need some way to keep the cash safe. When I sold the car I would have even more money to worry about. But I had to do it. The only way I could exist safely was by becoming a cash-only person, leaving no electronic traces of my movements.

The messages to my parents, Lorraine and a couple of others took much longer and necessitated another cup of tea. The need to be careful and not give away any clues had to be balanced against the trust and the affection I felt for those I was writing to. In the end I wrote a very factual account of all that had happened, just as I had to my boss and ended up with what I felt was an acceptable message, with a paragraph or two that would change depending whom I was sending it to.

I have left town for a while. I can't tell you where because I don't know myself, but it's probably better that you don't know.

After Nick was murdered drug thugs came after me, convinced that Nick had left a very large amount of cash in my flat. They beat me up and promised more. One of them is very scary and referred me to a Herald article which made me realise that I must get out of the way – they could kill me if they thought I was holding out on them. The article was about a woman "with reputed connections to gangs and the drug trade" who was found dead in her garden, having been doused with petrol and set alight.

I will forward what I know to the police, but I cannot hang around – the police could never protect me from these people and there is no way I can prove I don't have the money. I also fear that the police might think that I am involved in whatever Nick was doing and that makes my situation even more hazardous. It's like being pursued from two directions at once and I cannot prove my innocence to either of them.

Lorraine, the key to the apartment is in your letterbox. Can you please go there (NOT alone, take John), empty my fridge, and turn it off and dispose of my rubbish. I found it very hard to figure out a way to leave the place safely. The drugs people were watching the building around the clock, and I didn't have much time, so some things got left undone. Please also call Sergeant Benson and tell him that you have the key to my place, so they can arrange for Nick's brother to pick up his belongings.

I will sell my car and leave bank accounts unused after withdrawing most of my savings. I will replace my SIM card with a prepaid one, but I will not call you from now on unless I absolutely have to. I am leaving enough money in my account for the mortgage payments, the power bill and my broadband rental etc, but I won't use the account directly after today. The whole idea is

I saved the message as a draft and went out. The next suburb had a decent-sized town centre with a side street full of car yards and I chose one with a row of second-hand cars lined up along the street frontage. A fat man with a beard approached as soon as I walked into the yard. He asked a few questions, gave the car a quick once-over and said 'six thousand max' without sounding particularly interested. His shrewd eyes watched me carefully to gauge how much I needed the money.

"No, I can't sell it for that little," I said. "I've had a look at TradeMe, and I think I should be able to get seven thousand and still leave you room to make a profit when you sell it."

But he wouldn't negotiate, so I left and continued to the next car yard. A pimply-faced youth offered me six thousand eight hundred. "That sounds good. I'm buying another car from someone on TradeMe, and they want cash. Can you pay me in cash?"

He looked uncertain now. "Hang on a moment", he said and disappeared into the little office, calling "Dad, are you there?" I could hear them talking and after a moment an older man appeared. "We can give you cash, but not till tomorrow or the next day. Don't know if the local branch has that much cash on hand."

"That's OK - I'm not picking up my new car until the day after tomorrow, so perhaps I could come back tomorrow?"

We shook hands on the deal, and I left. This would be the last place the police could easily track me to via the Vehicle Database, which was why I'd picked a different suburb from the one where I was staying.

The bag shop had a money belt of generous proportions made of cotton. I tried to imagine wearing it full of money, but I had no idea what the bulk would be, even if I asked for some large denomination notes. It was important that I could wear it under my clothes without attracting attention; being robbed would be a disaster. I bought the belt, continued to a supermarket and then I was finished for the day. Locking the motel unit door behind me was a retreat into the only safety that was available to me, and I realised that I must have been tense all the time I had been out in public. I put the food in the little fridge and tried on the money belt which was not very comfortable. I thought it might be best to wear it just above my waist and only wear shirts or T-shirts that didn't fit closely to make it less likely to be noticed.

I re-read the draft email message, made a few adjustments, and sent it to my parents, to Lorraine and three others, one at a time. The last email was to Benson, whose email address was on the card he had given me. I added a long paragraph explaining why I felt that the police could not protect me. I told him of the beating and gave him the details of the Mercedes and the men and their threats and I cursed myself for not having memorised their number plate. I checked my phone and told him that the calls from the drug man had not come up as a number on my phone, so I could not give it to him, but I told him the exact times he had rung in case Benson could check with my cell phone provider.

Then I took my old SIM card out of the phone and inserted the prepaid one I had bought in the supermarket that afternoon. Now I was anonymous, or very nearly; one more day and I hoped to be completely untraceable. With a frozen meal in the microwave oven, I poured a glass of wine and sat down with my pad and planned the next couple of days.

Some things must take priority. Over the next few days, I must achieve a lot, but doing them in the right order was as important as any individual task. My hair must be cut shorter and dyed another colour, but I couldn't do it until I had sold the car, been to the bank and booked out of the motel. There must be no link between my known identity and my new appearance, but once I had severed that link, I need have no worries about being caught on CCTV cameras in my new guise.

I would cease being a natural blonde with longish hair, and there would be a clean separation between what I looked like now and what I would look like when I board the bus to leave. Maybe the best plan would be to have my hair cut tomorrow, but staying the colour it was now. The motel staff wouldn't pay much attention to the length of my hair, and then I could get off the bus somewhere and have another colour put in and travel to a new place. With all my funds as cash I would leave no traces: no EFTPOS payments, no withdrawals from banks, no images on security cameras in banks and petrol stations.

Repetitive thoughts circled in my mind; the litany of tasks was my constant companion. Then the microwave oven beeped, and I ate my dinner while I continued working. The plan was now a mess of items crossed out, added, or moved to another place in the timeline, but it was taking definite shape.

It was like doing a three-dimensional jigsaw, so many

things that needed to fit with others. I must get a map book with plans of towns, so I could find my way to backpacker hostels without asking questions and drawing attention to myself. Probably the last place with CCTV I would visit was my bank, to withdraw my savings. What about a debit card? You can load them with cash, but do they have to be linked to a bank account anyway? But those present cards that you can load and give to someone else, they must be completely freestanding, I thought, but how much you can load on them at any one time, and can you replenish the balance? I would do some research on the internet tonight, so I was prepared tomorrow.

At ten o'clock I went to bed hoping for a good night's sleep, but in the back of my mind crouched the neurotic thought that I might have left a loose end that would set the drug people on my track before I could get clean away. I found myself repeatedly going back over all my precautions, mentally testing them, checking them for flaws. Not until I was a long way away and had cut all the links to the past there would be no peace of mind and untroubled sleep.

5

The next morning, I paid cash for another night's stay and set out early. I was determined to do as much as I possibly could in one day. I drove back to the next town, parked in a side street and set off to find a branch of my bank. The teller was bored and preoccupied and when I casually said that I wanted to withdraw a big amount of cash from my account because I was buying a car she just nodded and went out the back to get the money. She counted three thousand four hundred dollars and put it all in plastic moneybags. Now the only money left in the account was the balance I had decided to leave there. I walked out onto the busy street with a sense of relief. I had burned another bridge behind me.

The post office was busy, and I picked the desk the furthest away from the line of people waiting to be served. I put some more cash into my wallet and tucked the plastic bags with the rest of the money into the very bottom of my satchel, turning my back on the CCTV cameras. I bought an untraceable gift card, asked for it to be loaded to the maximum allowed and handed over five hundred dollars in cash. I planned to buy many more and minimise the bulk in my money-belt.

Three hours later I was in a café having lunch and ticking things off the list. The result was encouraging, now I had achieved constructive things rather than just being in flight mode. I had a map book with street maps of North Island towns in my bag, a local bus timetable and a book listing backpacker accommodation. The idea behind the paper-based versions of things was to avoid the internet as much as possible and leave no traces at all. Probably an overly cautious approach but at that stage, I would read booklets and make notes than risk even the slightest possibility of being tacked. I put the pen down and finished my lunch. My haircut appointment was at two and I wanted to buy a hat.

That evening I ate yet another frozen dinner and drank a couple of glasses of wine while I carefully copied every single file and photo from my laptop to a new USB memory stick. Once I was in some suitable place, I would toss the laptop into a lake or a river and buy a smaller one or a tablet. I had no idea if this was the only way to ensure I cut the link between my record of Google searches and my old email account, but I would rather sacrifice the laptop than be traced by using it. A tablet was all I needed to log on at Wi-Fi hotspots, read the newspapers and keep track of what was going on with the investigation. Later on, I might set up a new email account under a fictitious name and become a new person with no past.

. . .

The next day I returned to the motel late in the afternoon in a taxi, after successfully selling the car and acquiring even more cash. The motel owner was watering the flowerbed outside her office, and she looked up when the taxi pulled up.

"Hi there, hope you had a good day? Didn't you have a car when you came?"

"Yes, I do." I was an expert at lying now. "But there's something wrong with the wipers, so I left it in town, and I'll pick it up tomorrow morning when I leave."

She peered at my face under the brim of my new sunhat. "Your bruise is settling down nicely, I must say! It looked really ugly when you first came." She smiled, satisfied that I was now presentable, and went back to her watering.

Closing the door behind me I heaved a sigh of relief. These last two days had been busy, but I was beginning to feel that I might be able to cover my tracks. I had three additional cash cards from three different sources which I had bought wearing my new hat, but the bulkiness of the belt was still a problem, and I must continue to reduce the load and buy more cash cards.

There were email replies from my parents, from Lorraine and from my boss plus a very officially worded reply from Benson. They all advised me to return to the city, to trust the police to protect me or to tell them more of my plans. I composed a standard response with slight variations and sent them. In the message to my parents and to Lorraine, I assured them I would take great care and just stay out of harm's way. My kind boss replied, wished me well and told me that they would pay out my holiday entitlement along with my final pay. I responded and thanked him and promised to get in touch when things were safe once again.

Benson's reply contained phrases like 'inadvisable to leave during an ongoing criminal investigation'. Very much what I had expected him to say; I did not reply. I closed the email program for the last time.

I lay in bed that night and watched the late TV news with half an eye and thought how fortunate it was that my parents had spent most of the last nine years working in developing countries. At least they were safe from whoever might be thinking of putting pressure on my family to find out where I was.

Eleven days later, but only five hours travel by car from my starting point, I had covered many hundreds of kilometres, criss-crossing the North Island by bus, staying here and there and then taking off again. My zigzag journey had taken me from one side of the island to the other and back again. Each time I moved on I bought a ticket for a further destination than the one I intended to stop at, sometimes twice as far as where I really wanted to go. I had varied my appearance by sometimes wearing my floppy hat, sometimes a baseball cap I had bought in Rotorua and sometimes no hat at all. A hairdresser in Tauranga had completed the transformation of my hair, and now I had a short urchin cut in chestnut brown. I had spent a lot of time thinking of alternative names before I finally settled on Cara Williams as a permanent replacement for Karen Wilson. It seemed to be the only name that would enable me to quickly recover if I started saying that my real name by mistake. Lorraine had told me that Cara was Thomas's pet-name for Mia, he calls her Cara Mia. It felt nice to use a name that belonged to someone I knew, like a little link to my real life.

I had sat on hostel beds studying my map of the North Island, learning the names of the towns I would pass through on the way to my next destination, and now I was in what I hoped would be my last long-distance bus heading for Hastings. I knew how to find the backpackers' hostel where I would spend a couple of days at least and then either move or stay in Hawke's Bay. Everything I did these days was rehearsed to avoid looking as if I was unsure; the last thing I wanted was to draw attention to myself by asking questions. I left the bus station on foot and without hesitation. Walking long distances with my luggage had become a habit and I had not taken a taxi since I left the motel in South Auckland.

With my shoulder bag slung across my body it was easy to pull the suitcase behind me. In Tauranga I had bought a Surface tablet with a little paper-thin touch keyboard. It was light and made my satchel much easier to carry. My personal files and photos were saved on the memory stick in my money belt, where they would remain until I could return to my real life. After buying the tablet I had taken a quiet walk at dusk down by the Tauranga waterfront and at a secluded spot I crouched down as if looking into the water and let the old laptop slip into deep water without a splash. And there went, in one last effort at making me anonymous, my old email program and whatever else might have made me traceable, leaving only a little trail of rising bubbles. Now, several days later and walking towards the backpacker hostel in Hastings, I felt confident and self-contained. I knew where I was going and what I planned to accomplish in the next couple of days; my list was nearly finished.

. . .

Two days at the backpacker hostel in Hastings and a lot of research confirmed my idea that this was the region to settle down to my new life. Staying an extra day had given me enough time to make arrangements for the next step and provided an opportunity to familiarise myself with the area. I spent time in the library and the information centre, collected local maps and brochures. The supermarket had a useful noticeboard where locals put up items for sale and places to rent, which gave me a good picture of the general area. I noted down some phone numbers in case Hastings ended up being the place I chose to stay. In the library I read the local newspaper and made more notes. There were various small communities and three towns nearly in a cluster and distances were short. I was beginning to think that finding accommodation in the centre of the cluster would be perfect. I would have many more chances of finding work within commuting distance, either by bus or on a bike.

On my second afternoon at the hostel, I connected to the Wi-Fi system and created a new Gmail account under my assumed name. I didn't use it, but it made me feel that once again I had a tenuous connection to the important people in my life. I had no idea if someone who hacked into Lorraine's email account could check where emails sent to her had come from. Could someone who was really determined check each new address that turned up on her computer and find out where they had been sent from? I didn't know nearly enough to assess the risks involved.

Over a cup of coffee, I studied my maps and brochures, reading about district. It seemed that Clive might be the place best suited to my needs. It was on a main road and just about in the centre of the cluster, close enough to each of the three towns to commute by bicycle with bus services available for rainy days. It seemed big enough for me to be able to blend in without arousing much attention. In the evening a group of us sat outside at a BBQ table in the hostel garden, talking in the warm darkness. My new name was beginning to feel comfortable and rolled off my tongue without hesitation when someone asked what my name was. I had made up a story about my new name and when people commented on it, I said that I had been christened Caroline, but that everyone had always called me Cara. And over the many nights in hostels in different towns I had invented a life story and said my family had moved to New Zealand from England when I was ten, and I had always lived in the South Island but now I was taking the opportunity to see something of the North Island before starting a new job in Wellington.

In bed that night I tucked the money belt securely under my body and lay quietly ticking things off the list I knew by heart: take the local bus at 9.20, buy a ticket for Napier, get off halfway at Clive and find the Bed and Breakfast place I had booked. I'd found the address at the Information Centre and called to arrange a three-night stay. A quality B & B place was expensive compared to the backpacker's but being able to draw information from my hostess presented an irresistible opportunity. A local person's knowledge would be far more valuable than brochures and websites, particularly in a small community and I needed to know that I was making the right decision.

I went through the nightly routine that had become an obsession since I left Auckland. Lying quietly looking into the darkness I backtracked through the last couple of weeks and tried to pick holes in my own arrangements. Had I missed something, or had I left any clues? Would someone determined enough and with good resources be able to find me? I tried to examine every decision I had made and mentally evaluated my strategies. Satisfied at last that I was safe from anything but a chance discovery I could let go of my nightly ritual and sleep.

The next morning was still and very warm for so early in the season, a flawless day with near summer temperatures. The bus ride to Clive seemed impossibly short; fifteen minutes after leaving Hastings I got off the local bus beside a cluster of shops and waited till the bus disappeared down the road.

The village was a mixture of old and new, the streets were quiet and here and there a sign indicated that a small business operated out of a private residence: an accountant, a hairdresser, and a dressmaker. In less than ten minutes I arrived at the place I was looking for, a sprawling wooden villa from the 20's or 30's with a veranda at the front, a white picket fence and a Bed & Breakfast shingle on a post by the gate. My hostess seemed casual and friendly and introduced herself simply as Moira. She showed me to a spacious room overlooking the garden at the back of the house.

"The bathroom is not en-suite," she said, "but it's right next door to your room and you'll be the only one using it. It serves two rooms, as I said on the phone. I can provide dinner if you want it, just let me know in the morning."

"I'll only want breakfast, thank you. Would you like me to pay you now?"

"When you're ready - there's no hurry. You'll find me in the kitchen when you've settled in." She smiled and left me alone.

The window looked out on a garden with big trees and shrubs that hid the neighbouring houses. My room had a table and a couple of armchairs and a lovely old wardrobe with carved doors. After all the hostels I had stayed in, it was tempting to settle in for a week, but I had to find a tiny flat or something less expensive. The large kitchen was the kind nobody builds these days. Not a kitchen-cum-family room, but a large square room with glass-fronted cupboards above the benches and a big wooden table in the middle of the floor. Moira was emptying the dishwasher and listening to the radio.

When she heard me coming, she turned the radio off. "Just tell me if there's something you need that isn't in the room."

"Thank you, I will. I thought I might as well pay you for the three nights now."

"That's fine. I accept EFTPOS and credit cards."

"I'll pay cash, if you don't mind."

A brief look of surprise flitted across her face, but all she said was: "That's fine. I'll write you a receipt."

When she handed me the receipt she smiled. "Would you like a cup of coffee? I'm just about to have one, no charge, of course."

"Thank you, I'd love a coffee."

"If you go through the dining room, that door there, you'll find the terrace. I'll be with you in a moment."

We sat on a semi-circular paved terrace behind the house, under a pergola covered in jasmine. The garden was bigger than what I had seen from my room, deeper with a long stretch of lawn bordered by trees and bushes. "What a nice garden. Have you lived here long?"

'We moved here about fifteen years ago - the garden was well established with these lovely trees, but we changed practically everything else. And then we did the whole house up a couple of years ago and added an extra bathroom and the terrace." She cast a satisfied look up at the pergola. "This year the jasmine's going to provide enough shade to be useful in the heat of the day. Last year I had to use a sun umbrella over the table to get some shade. It's very hot and sheltered here behind the house, far too hot to sit out in the summer during the day."

I waited for her to ask me why I was in Clive, but she seemed to be quite content just talking about the garden and the weather. I looked at her pleasant, tanned face, with bright blue eyes and no-nonsense curly brown hair. A few carefully chosen facts strewn into the conversation might be better than waiting for the inevitable questions.

'If I like it here, I might look for a job and rent something small and stay for a while - at least for the summer."

I could tell that she was surprised. "Why would you choose Clive - it's such a small place? Wouldn't you rather be in Napier or Hastings where there's more choice of work?"

"At the moment I think a small place would suit me. I had a problem that I needed to get away from - I want to keep myself on the margin of things for a while." I looked down the length of the garden, concentrating on my rehearsed story. "I broke off with my boyfriend a while back and it didn't go well. He badgered me to meet and when I refused, he started following me around - I suppose you could say he was stalking me. I had been thinking of leaving my job anyway. So, I decided that the best thing I could do was to go and live somewhere else and just take time out."

Moira looked interested but said nothing. I accepted a biscuit from the plate she held out towards me, took a bite and continued. "And my family live overseas, so from that point of view it doesn't matter where I live. I've been taking my time – I've been all over the North Island for a while now trying to decide where I would like to live. I thought perhaps Taupo would be nice, but I like being close to the sea and this seems a nice area."

She glanced at me in a thoughtful way as if she was considering what I had told her. Then she smiled and said neutrally, "You're in a perfect spot here if you want a quiet life. There isn't much in the village for someone your age, no entertainment and no cinema. We have a pub and a couple of places to eat but not a nightclub or anything very smart. But it's easy to get to the bigger places all round us - a quarter of an hour in different directions and there is plenty going on in the evenings. You don't have a car?'

'No, I sold my car to give me a bit of extra money to travel and live on in case I don't find a job straight away."

'You'll find something easily here,' said Moira comfortably. 'There are lots of casual jobs during the fruit season. I mean in the immediate region, not just Clive. The picking season is just starting too, asparagus, then the early apricots and peaches, strawberries and cherries and then it just goes on and on for months – doesn't really finish till well into autumn. But of course, all those things are just simple manual jobs. What did you do before?"

I could have kicked myself. I knew the moment I said it that I was making a mistake telling her I had sold the car. If she had doubts about my story, she was not showing it, but I made a mental note to display some common-sense aspects over the next couple of days. I could imagine what she would be thinking: Why hadn't I kept the car until I needed funds and travel in comfort until then?

But she said nothing and did not betray by so much as a look if she found my story strange. If she found me trustworthy, she could be very useful. She looked like the sort of woman who knows everyone and everything about her community. I hoped she would take my story at face value for the time being.

I used the made-up job I had invented in advance to avoid saying I was an accountant which could be checked online quite easily. 'I worked for a big company doing data entry into the accounting programme, helping out with payroll and stuff like that – general admin type of work. But now I think I'd like to try something different. Perhaps I'll start with something casual and see how I like it here.'

'My God, I wish I had your experience!' Moira's exclamation was heart-felt. 'Now that I'm on my own I curse the fact that I always let my husband do the bookwork. Every time I have to do a GST return or anything to do with the Inland Revenue Department online my mind seems to stop working and I leave it until it's nearly too late. I'm sure it's bad for my mental health.'

'Your accountant should be able to do all that for you, if you don't like doing it.'

'I suppose it's stupid, but I don't want them doing everything for me. I want to feel I can do it myself, so I keep struggling on, thinking it will get easier each time.'

I had to laugh. 'I'll tell you what - if I stay here, I'll come and give you a hand next time you have to do it, if you like. It's not that hard, it's just that you have to click on the little question marks beside the questions to find out exactly what they want and what it means.'

Moira made a face. 'You make it sound so simple - I would love a bit of help from someone like you. I haven't wanted to ask anyone to help me, and being stubborn I don't want to give in. Not after telling the accountant that I can do it easily. What a liar I was – but he's such a condescending man and I can't stand being treated like an idiot just because I'm a woman without a career. Well, I am a nurse, though I haven't worked in nursing for years, but to him I was just someone's wife. And he has a really silly moustache.'

Now she was laughing at herself. "You know how sometimes you imagine that you could take an insult from someone who looks like George Clooney, but if they have a silly moustache, it becomes infuriating?"

I smiled at her indignation. "I couldn't agree more - obviously you can't ask him to do it for you now that you've said you can do it yourself."

"Quite -but it's not completely true that I don't know anyone who could help me. When James died a couple of his business friends turned up on the doorstep of an evening with a bottle of wine, offering all kinds of help – one at a time, not together. Which I turned down, of course. God knows what makes some men think that the minute a woman is on her own she'll suddenly jump into bed with anyone at all. These were men we'd known for years. As if I would ask them in to share a bottle of wine at night and then have a coffee with their wives a few days later as if nothing had happened - mad!"

We laughed together at the things people do and I reverted to the question of a place to live. "Have you any suggestions about a place to rent? I don't mean a house, but maybe a little flat or a sleep-out, just for the time being. I looked in the Hawke's Bay paper and in a real estate office, but apart from a family-sized house I didn't see anything to rent in Clive."

"Can't say that I can think of anything right off - it's not something I pay a lot of attention to," said Moira, her gaze on the garden and a thoughtful crease between her eyebrows. "But I might be able to find out if there is anything available locally. Probably the best thing would be for you to ask in the shops and maybe the pub. They'd be more likely to know. I think the pub has some sort of community noticeboard."

6

B ack in my room I unpacked some of my things and covered myself in sunscreen lotion before returning to ask Moira if I could have a key.

"I'll be here all day today - lots of work to do in the garden, but I'll show you where the spare key is, just in case. And there's a key in the door to your room, so you can lock that. Your window is on a safety stay and can be left open. I always keep the front door locked if I'm in the back garden - nobody can come in without me noticing.'

The residential area spread much further than I had anticipated. It stretched out along the main road and a considerable distance to one side. On the other side of the highway the houses had larger grounds with big trees and long driveways. I passed the place where I had got off the bus and continued to the bridge over the river and saw that here the village ended. Standing on the bridge I got a great view of the layout: on the far bank there was a large sports field and the road curved off into the distance. Upstream on one side there were houses with little jetties and boathouses; those must be the places with large grounds and long driveways I had seen from the road, and from the other side of the bridge I could look downstream, where there was some sort of launching ramp for boats and a walking path. I went down the slope and walked along the river towards the ocean. As I got closer to the sea, I saw that the river did not run straight out into the sea as I had expected but curved into a large area of water like a lagoon with a spit of land running between it and the ocean. I looked inland and realised that this was the meeting place of two rivers with a joint opening into the ocean through a gap in the shingle spit; a huge expanse of water protected from the ocean.

People were surfcasting on the seaward side of the spit and several vehicles were parked along the water's edge on the far side of the lagoon. The sun glittered on the water, and shags perched on poles. I took my sunhat off and let the sea breeze blow through my damp hair. There was a tangy hint of salt in the air and sea spray from breaking waves created glittering clouds of droplets. Further along the lagoon shore a white-faced heron stalked slowly through the shallows pushing one foot at a time forward along the bottom, stirring up little edible creatures. I stood there quietly revelling in the feeling of anonymity, relaxed and happy.

It was late afternoon when I approached the village centre again. I had walked round the outskirts in a huge semi-circle that had taken me through an area of large fields of vegetables, fruit orchards behind tall hedges and residential houses on big tracts of land, until I reached the main road the bus had taken that morning. It was hot in the sun now and I had walked for miles since I set out four hours earlier.

The flat money-belt strapped to my midriff under the T-shirt added to my discomfort. Under it my skin was damp, and the edges of the pockets were beginning to chafe. The belt was much slimmer now that I had converted more than half the cash to Post Office money cards, but it was still uncomfortable in the heat. If I found a safe place to live, I might be able to stop wearing it all the time and sleeping with it under me at night. I pushed my hand under the edge of the belt and held it away from my damp skin to allow the air to circulate, but as soon as I let go the damp fabric stuck to me again. Perhaps eighteen Post Office cash cards would make a small enough packet to keep in some sort of pouch that I could hang round my neck.

Heat, thirst and hunger had made me tired. I trudged along to a café I had seen earlier with tables and chairs outside under trees. I ordered coffee and a sandwich, helped myself to a glass of chilled water and went to sit in the shade outside. There was more traffic now than before lunch, a steady stream of cars and trucks in both directions. This might well be the ideal place, not too small and not too big, and between towns that were easy to get to.

A chartered coach from Northland went past with a load of tourists and a few minutes later a minivan advertising tractor rides to Cape Kidnappers pulled up in front of the pub and two middle-aged women with cameras got off. Someone raised the blinds in the restaurant, a window was flung open, and a man stood for a moment looking out at the road. Despite the temporary bustle it was a peaceful scene, very different from rush hour in a city or even normal city traffic; none of that competitive urgency you see on multi-lane roads.

I'll buy a bike so I can get to any of the towns round here,

I thought. It didn't take long to get here on the bus - I could probably bike from here to either town in twenty or thirty minutes, so I wouldn't be limited to working only in Clive. A bike is nice and anonymous, and it would keep me fit. But I must have a job that pays cash. I wondered if you could spend a whole life leaving no trace of what you do if you only earn cash and only spend cash. There must be people who live like that, and nobody would know how many there were or even where they were, and they'd never pay any tax. How odd that I'd never thought of it before and now I would be one of the invisible people.

I picked one of the three available shops at random, a general store, blissfully cool and quiet. A woman came out from the back and watched me as I picked out a few things and asked for directions to find what I wanted. While she was scanned my purchases, I said casually that I was looking for somewhere to rent, a flat or a room, adding that I had come for the seasonal work and would like to stay locally.

"Well, I don't really know, dear," she said. "That comes to $9.60. I'm only looking after the shop for a few of weeks while the owner is recovering from surgery, and I don't know the place like she would. But I think I remember someone mentioning a granny flat being empty somewhere around here - I can't recall who told me. I'd need to think a bit on that, bound to come back to me after you've gone. Ask me tomorrow."

She handed me the change and I said "Thanks, I'll ask you next time I come in."

When I walked back outside the main road was suddenly busier. It was quarter past five now, so I had spent an hour sitting outside the café watching the world go by, engrossed in my thoughts. Obviously, a lot of people commuted between the towns, and this was rush-hour in Clive. I set out for the walk back to the Bed and Breakfast place on legs that clearly didn't want to do any more work that day.

Moira opened the front door and looked at me with concern. "Good heavens – you have been walking for hours in the heat. You're quite sunburnt - look at your neck and shoulders!"

"Yes, I know, I can feel it now. It was so wonderful down by the river and the sea that I forgot the time and then I walked right round the village in all directions."

"It's so hot already this year – more like full summer than early spring. You look exhausted."

I smiled and pulled the sunhat off my sweaty forehead. "I can't wait to have a shower. I had a sandwich and a drink in a café by the main road and realised how tired I was, must have walked miles and miles. Once I sat down, I could hardly get up again. I hadn't planned to be out for this long."

In my room I threw the shopping on the bed, picked up my toilet-bag and my Samoan lava-lava and headed for the bathroom. Standing in the shower for several minutes relishing the cool water streaming over me was pure bliss. It washed the heat and tiredness away and gradually I cooled off. My thoughts returned to the conversation with the woman in the shop.

I would go back tomorrow afternoon and ask her again and enquire at the pub as well. Surely there couldn't be that many people with granny flats, or were they common? A single room sleep-out would do for a start, even a converted garage, it didn't really matter while the weather was warm and then I could find something else later on. Hopefully there would be jobs here that were paid in cash, but my only problem could be where to keep the money-belt because I didn't think I'd last long in a physical job in this heat if I had to wear it all the time.

I brushed my wet hair and smiled at my reflection. It had been an amazing discovery to find that now that my hair was very short it had a natural curl, slight but definitely a curl. After a lifetime of long or half-long straight hair I hadn't known I had curls waiting to make their debut. I leaned forward to check the roots. Being accepted as a natural brunette was part of the plan and while I was living here I had better learn to dye it myself so nobody would know what the real colour of my hair was.

I was well aware of my tendency to be too detail conscious, worried that if the very last T was not crossed something would go wrong. But in my present situation it was probably an advantage, making sure that nothing was left to chance. In the future, when things were safe, and life could revert to normal I would be able to laugh with my dad about what he used to call my 'pernickety streak' and until then I would regard it as a necessary talent.

I draped my dirty clothes over a chair, so they would dry and thought I might ask Moira if I could use her washing machine. The T-shirt I had worn was going to smell if I did not wash it soon and I might throw the money-belt in the wash too. I sat in the armchair by the open window and dined on crispbread and cold baked beans straight out of the tear-top can, using the plastic spoon I had taken from a café in Palmerston North. Now and then I looked out at my partial view of the garden while a medley of early evening sounds filtered in, and an exuberant thrush sang somewhere nearby. I felt relaxed and pleasantly tired and with the noise of a distant lawnmower as a backdrop I ate a banana and a tub of yoghurt for dessert, and tried to suppress the thought that a cup of coffee would make the evening perfect.

Nearly an hour later I was still sitting by the window when Moira knocked on the door and spoke through it. "Cara, would you like to join me on the terrace? I'm having a glass of wine to round the evening off."

"Thanks, I'd love to - I'll be out in a minute."

Moira was sitting in what was obviously her favourite chair on the terrace, angled to take in the view down the long lawn framed by trees. I sat down in the matching chair across from hers and accepted the glass she handed me, wondering whether I should offer to pay for the wine at the end of the evening.

If she was just being hospitable, she might take offence at the mention of money; maybe a bottle of wine on my last day would be a nice touch instead.

"This is lovely - thank you very much, a perfect end to the day. If I had a garden like this, I would probably never leave the place – more shades of green than I knew existed."

Moira turned her head properly this time and looked at me. "That's exactly what we intended - shades of green. A lot of people don't get this green-on-green thing. They think I need flowers to brighten it up and suggest colourful plants I could add. Some even insist on writing down names of plants for me." She laughed and shrugged. "But I like it just like this - restful and natural. Not just the many shades of green but all the various leaf-shapes too."

"Not that I know anything about gardens, but it's beautiful the way it is. It looks a bit like a painting. I like art – though I don't know very much about art either, now that I think about it." I had to laugh at myself. "And bright flowers are so obvious. What are those short palms down there at the end of lawn? They're a perfect focal point."

"They're lovely, aren't they? When they grow up you will

recognise them – young Nikau palms. I planted them there to add a new texture and to have something for the eye to be drawn to," said Moira. "When we bought this place, you could see the fence down there, and the roof of the neighbour's shed – which had seen better days. So, we took out the flowerbeds and the little concrete paths and dug a huge number of holes for more shrubs and trees. We had the idea of creating a sort of long view into the far end of the garden - and we liked the illusion that we have no neighbours. It's not that far to the end of the garden, of course, but these old half acre sections give you something to work with."

We sat companionably sipping our wine as the warm day cooled and the light changed, slanting through the trees in pale gold shafts. I told Moira about the woman in the shop and the mention of the granny flat. "I'll go back tomorrow and ask if she's remembered who it was. And I'll ask in the pub, as well. A granny flat would be perfect - all I need is a bedroom and a little kitchen or a bed-sit kind of room. Just so long as I can be self-sufficient and look after myself. Even a converted garage might do for now."

"I can't say it rings any bells. But a converted garage - are you sure?" Moira seemed a bit perturbed by the fact that I was prepared to live in something so basic. I realised how odd it must seem that I was staying here, in a top-quality B&B and at the same time I was prepared to live as if I was unable to earn a decent living. I was about to say something when Moira got up and reached for my glass. "Another wine, or a coffee?"

I was immediately self-conscious. Sitting here talking to Moira was very enjoyable, but I was embarrassed in case I seemed to be taking advantage. My unease must have been written on my face because Moira smiled and said, "Don't worry about it. I'm not fussed about charging for every single thing and it's really nice to have someone like you to talk to. Most of my guests are German and Dutch couples for some reason - and they mostly want to talk about what to see and do. Or they want to tell me every single thing they've seen and done."

We went to the kitchen together and returned to the terrace with a tray of coffee and biscuits. She was so easy to talk to and for a couple of hours I could nearly forgot what I was running away from and why I was here in a place I had never heard of a few days ago, far away from my own home and everyone I knew. We covered a wide range of subjects from our favourite Queen's hits to food we either loved or hated. Towards the end of the evening, we discovered that we shared an interest in reading and spent some time comparing notes on favourite books and authors. Moira had read hugely more than I had and from a much wider range of eras, thinking nothing of comparing a character in a novel by Thackeray to a person in an Ann Tyler story.

"I like the way Joy Cowley writes," I said. "Really flowing prose, but very clear. I read a great book by her a while ago about two sisters, who meet up at their father's funeral after years apart - I can't remember the name of the book but I loved it."

"Ah, that would be *Classical Music*," said Moira. "I've got it somewhere. I enjoyed it too, but I remember thinking wasn't it a bit much to spring so many unexpected revela-tions on the reader at the very end? Lifelong virginity, family drama and I can't remember what else."

"I know what you mean - it was a whole line-up of surprises one after the other in the very last chapter. But then the whole idea was that those two sisters hadn't lived in the same country or even communicated properly for decades - it wasn't till they realised that they could trust each other that they talked about personal things. Or that's my take on it, anyway."

"That's perfectly right – you've put your finger on it. How nice it is to find someone who loves reading. I know lots of people who say they love books, but they only read block-busters and things that bore me. You can't imagine the reac-tion I used to get a few years ago when everyone was raving about *The DaVinci Code* and I told people I only read three chapters before I threw it in the rubbish. Stunned disbelief – very funny! I think the only person who totally got the idea was a librarian in Hastings, she couldn't stand it either. You know, I'll really enjoy it if you stay in Clive - I haven't made a new friend for ages."

I was dying to ask about the husband, who had obvi-ously been around when the house was renovated not that long ago and who had died since, but I was hesitant about bringing it up. Nothing had been said about it apart from the mention of the evening Romeos who had turned up with bottles of wine and offers of help.

I looked cautiously at Moira, trying to judge if it might be all right to ask a question and decided to take the risk. "What happened to your husband, was he ill?"

"No, he was as fit as a fiddle. Forever on the go with projects and helping other people. But James did that 'well-off middle-aged male' thing. He decided now was the time to live out the teenage dream of owning a motorbike and feeling the wind through his hair – well, he had to wear a helmet of course, but that was the image in his mind. Bought a big shiny bike and all the gear and all his male friends were full of enthusiasm and envy. And like many other men of that age, he probably assumed that because he wasn't a risk-taking teenager, he'd be safe. But he had a terrible high-speed accident on a winding road and was killed outright."

"I'm sorry - that must have been awful."

Moira smiled. "It was, just horrible. For a long time, I kept waking up in the night thinking he'd gone to the bathroom when he wasn't there beside me. And I was completely unable to get going with even the smallest project. My initiative was paralysed somehow, nothing got done. But then it all came right about six months ago."

I was bewildered by this cryptic statement. What was it that had come right: another man or had she perhaps become religious? I said cautiously, "What happened six months ago?"

"I don't know," Moira said frankly and quite cheerfully. "I have no idea at all! It was like the proverbial bolt of lightning from a blue sky. I just woke up one morning and somehow or other my mind had processed things and I just accepted that my life was different now and got on with it. Very unexpected, I must say. People had told me of this two-year process and all the various stages you have to go through, but that's not the way it was for me."

She smiled. "Maybe I'm just a bit batty, but I'm fine, really fine. I enjoy life and though I miss him, of course I do, I loved him dearly and he was my best friend – but I have another reality now."

It was an amazing idea; that you could literally snap out of acute grief like that. I had never heard of anything like it. "My God, that's fantastic. Good on you - the strength of character!"

"Ah, but you don't know the half of it," Moira sounded exasperated and amused at the same time. "Seeing I'm telling you all this personal stuff I might as well continue. Some of my friends think I'm putting on an act and some are waiting for grief to come back and whack me - or perhaps depression. They even make me feel guilty that I'm not still prostrated with grief and sadness. I hesitate to laugh when

I'm with them, because they might feel it would be wrong - it's ridiculous! And of course, the result is that I have pulled back from some friends, because I know they find my recovery unacceptable – can you imagine how strange that is for me?"

"I believe you, just the sort of thing that would put people off – they have developed their role as 'the supportive friend' and they probably used to discuss your progress with each other over coffee. And then you took the wind out of their sails, so to speak, made their concern a bit redundant - so now they feel a bit miffed instead of being happy for you "

Now Moira laughed out loud. "I do hope you find a job and you stay here. My own sister is scandalised by the change in me - she says she's pleased, but I know she suspects me of being callous."

We stayed on the terrace late into the evening. It was only spring still but the air was warm and soft. Little lights had come on, shining up into the trees and dimly lighting the nightscape of the garden. Moira had long since closed the double doors to the dining room to keep the moths out and we stayed where we were until both the wine bottle and the coffee thermos were empty.

"I must let you go to bed," said Moira at last. "You walked for so long in the heat and you looked tired when you came back – you must be more than ready for bed."

I stood up and stretched. I was not tired, I just felt pleasantly sleepy now, despite the coffee. "I'll put some lotion on my sunburn and go to bed. Thank you so much for all this. It's the nicest time I've had for a while."

7

The early morning dream was vivid and terrifying, and I woke with an intense feeling of anxiety. It was as if the dream was still with me; forcing me to take notice of it and to remember it. I lay very still and tried to pull it together, thinking through it without moving or even opening my eyes. Disjointed images gradually emerged from the swirl of out-of-focus impressions in my mind, a sequence started taking shape. When I was satisfied that I could remember nothing more I replayed the dream in my head:

Darkness, a light rain falling, floating in dark water, running fast on wet grass, being wet and very cold. Standing at night among trees, clothes soaking wet, a chilly wind on my face. Being hunted, terrified, trying to be still and quiet, trying to see my pursuers.

Nightmares sometimes leave an impression after you wake up, but this one was different from any other I could remember. I opened my eyes.

The sky was lightly overcast, and a breeze was ruffling the trees, and today I must start finding somewhere to live and a job of some kind. I dressed in pants and a T-shirt, ruffled my hair up with damp fingers to get rid of the 'bed hair' look and went to the kitchen. Moira was standing by the open window holding a cup and looking out towards the road. She turned when she heard my footsteps. "Good morning, how is your sunburn today?"

"It's a bit tender in places. Just as well it's a cloudier day – maybe I can get around without any more damage."

Moira seemed to have had breakfast already and asked what I would like. "I'll just have cereal and yoghurt, thanks. And a cup of coffee if there is some made?"

"Of course, it's part of the deal. Would you like it in the dining room or on the terrace?"

I got a feeling that maybe Moira felt as uncertain about our situation as I did myself this morning. Somehow the roles of landlady and paying guest had become skewed during our chatty evening. What was our status now, were we friends? Or not quite?

After a moment I took the bull by the horns and said in the same way that I would, if I was staying at a friend's place. "Oh no, don't worry, I'll just have it here at the kitchen table – if I'm not in your way?"

Half an hour later we were still at the table, with a second cup of coffee each, talking about my job options. Moira had found Saturday's local paper and was looking through the job vacancies. "You'll have to check out the vacancies on TradeMe and that other job seeker website too, but I came across Saturday's paper so we might as well have a look."

She had the paper already folded open to the Situations Vacant page and pushed it into the middle of the table between us. "Here is one, look at this - sounds as if you'd be able to do it with one hand tied behind your back. And that company is quite big, well established."

As she pushed the paper across the table towards me, I

was gripped by acute anxiety. I read the ad carefully to give myself time to think of a good reason why the job was not suitable. I continued looking further down the page, completely stuck for something to say. Finally, I looked up and saw Moira's eyes locked on my face. Our eyes met and I said hesitantly: "I think I want a job which is a bit more…"

I hesitated, Moira said nothing, and I stumbled on. "Something less career-like, more casual perhaps." My voice died away as I realised how idiotic this sounded. I looked down at the coffee cup and tried to compose myself and quickly think of a way to make my stance sound more normal.

Moira cleared her throat. "Perhaps you'd like something simple and stress-free? If you want to switch off your brain and don't mind what you do, you could be a waitress for a while or take a cleaning job, perhaps?" Her gaze was steady and it was impossible to guess what she was thinking. I grasped the offered lifeline with a feeling of intense relief. "Yes, that's it, something hands-on and mindless, that's probably what I need right now. How do you think I should go about it?"

I had to keep this strand of conversation going smoothly now, or I might find myself struggling again. I couldn't afford to let anyone know the truth. It was imperative that I didn't confide in anyone, but at the same time I must retain my credibility.

Moira's eyes narrowed to thoughtful slits as she gazed out the window. Then she turned back to me and smiled. "I think I might be able to help, if you don't mind me interfering. I know lots of people who live in large houses and haven't done their own housework in years. Someone's sure to have lost their cleaner – it seems to happen regularly."

I smiled back, relieved that the tension had gone out of the conversation and hopeful that Moira was taking my statement at face value. "Thank you so much – and I wouldn't call that interfering, it's a great help. And if you know someone who wants to employ me it might make things easier because I have no references as a cleaner. But I don't mind what I do, gardening, cleaning, walking dogs – anything, so long as it is close enough to ride a bike there or take a bus if there is one."

Moira got up and picked our cups off the table. "I'll make a few phone calls when I've tidied up and checked my emails. I'm prepared to bet that if I spread the word you'll have a job within a week."

"I hope they won't discover that I have no cleaning experience."

"Goodness no, I wouldn't think so. If you can clean your own house or flat, then you aren't inexperienced - and I'll tell them I know you."

She smiled again, a smile of conspiratorial glee. "Which I feel that I do. Perhaps I won't tell them I've only just met you, maybe I'll hint that you are a friend of a friend, so they feel they have some kind of reference to your honesty."

I got up from the table, touched and surprised. "You're being so kind to me – I feel embarrassed. I don't know how you can be so trusting, because I can't prove to you that I am reliable."

Moira was putting the cups on the bench and spoke over her shoulder: "I think I know you well enough already. Personally, I'd trust you with my own house, so I feel fine about recommending you."

Her trust in me was very to touching. From the outset I had accepted that there would be times when I would feel isolated and lonely, that I would have to be strong. During many idle hours on buses I had tried to prepare myself for setbacks and problems. I had imagined myself in some tricky situation where an instant reaction might make the difference between danger and safety. With few escape routes I must always be alert and ready to use my wits; either lie quickly and well or flee. I had assumed that because I couldn' to tell anyone about my circumstances there would be nobody to provide any support. How I wished that I could confide in her, tell her the whole story and gain someone I could be totally open with. But the risk was too great; if the story of my interesting and dramatic situation became gossip, I would have to leave and continue my flight.

By acting on my instinct to go into hiding I had isolated myself from everyone I knew. I had methodically burnt each bridge behind me as I took myself into self-imposed exile. And it wasn't only for my own safety, but also to protect those who might try to help me. Maybe a time would come when I could tell Moira the story, but it was far too soon to relax my vigilance.

Moira turned around to look at me, perhaps puzzled by the long silence. I wanted to speak, but I felt tears about to spill over and said nothing, worried that my voice would sound wobbly.

She turned back and continued to load the dishwasher. "Well, you go and do your research at the shops and the pub, and I'll make a few calls later on. Perhaps you should go in and talk to Lauren who runs the café - that's the café beside the petrol station, Hastings side of the shops. She's lived here all her life, and she knows everyone."

I spent half an hour in my room reading the news on the internet and looking through TradeMe for rentals and bikes. There was nothing online about the investigation into Nick's death; there had been no mention of it for over a week. There were only two rentals available in Clive, both full-sized family homes, but there were three second-hand bikes locally at good prices.

I walked the few blocks to the main road and found the café Moira had mentioned. Lauren was just opening for the day, but she could think of nothing in the way of a rental that would suit me.

"No, I'm sorry love! I know of a couple of rental properties that are available or will be shortly, but they are houses. The only flats I know about are all occupied. Why don't you try the smaller of the shops up the road - they might know of something."

The lady in the store had remembered what she'd heard, and she was delighted to be able to help me. "I'm glad you came back before I had time to forget it again – I thought of it just after you left yesterday, it's down at Rusty Brown's place. Here, I'll draw you a map."

She grabbed a paper bag and drew a few lines on it. "Look here," she said leaning over the counter and using the pen as a pointer. "This is the main road, here's where we are now. You just go down the road, turn into the second street there, follow that street until you get to the tall green board fence on the left-hand corner and turn left there. Rusty's is a white house, it's about four or five along on your right, don't know the number. She's got a place in the back garden that she's done up. Her husband left her last year, and she wants to earn some extra money. Go and knock on her door and say I sent you."

I was delighted. "Thank you very much. Is she likely to be home during the day?"

"She's a home mum. She's got two little boys and she looks after Charlene's baby from next door - she'll be there."

. . .

Rusty was at home and clearly busy, trying to hang out washing with two small boys chasing each other around her legs and a baby in a stroller crying loudly.

The noise of the little boys laughing and talking, and the baby crying could be heard from the road. When nobody answered the door, I walked down the path beside the house, opened the little gate and closed it behind me without anybody noticing I was there.

"Hi, are you Rusty?"

The woman swung round. She had a round face covered in freckles, red hair in a long braid down her back and a generous mouth. Rusty was the perfect nickname.

"My name is Cara. The lady in the shop said you might have a granny flat for rent?"

"Hi! Yeah, I do. It's not really a flat, more like a room and a bathroom. I've only just finished doing it up, come and have a look." She gestured at the white building in the far corner of the garden. "It was a shed, a workshop my husband built. Come and see."

She dropped the pillowcase she was holding into the laundry basket and picked up the baby, who instantly stopped screaming and stuck a thumb in its mouth.

"Little bugger, isn't she? All she wants is to be up at this level - can't stand being low down. Never knew such a tricksy baby!" She smiled at the baby and walked towards the shed.

The room was the size of a single garage with a little kitchen bench at one end with a sink and some cupboards. A door led to a small bathroom with a toilet and a shower. Everything was painted white, the floor was covered with vinyl and it looked clean and tidy.

"See what I mean? I have some furniture to put in and I've nearly finished doing it up. I've got a mate who's a plumber and he got the shower in last weekend, so I've been painting the bathroom in the evenings since. I've got some ready-made curtains that I'm putting up as soon as I get the tracks up. And some shelves - and then it's more or less ready."

I walked around looking out the windows and inspecting the bathroom. "It looks fine to me. What's the furniture you are putting in? And how much do you want in rent?"

"I've got a small armchair, a single bed and a chest of drawers. And a little table and a floor rug. Oh, and an electric kettle. I'm afraid I don't have a fridge or a microwave oven. I've asked around and I think I'd ask $150 a week including the power, because it's on the meter for the house, so it can't be separated out. What do you think?"

"It's perfect. I don't know how long I'll be here, but I might stay for six months. I can get some things in a second-hand shop, and I can help you move the furniture in, if you like, and putting up the curtains."

"Cool!" said Rusty and bounced the baby up and down, then bent down to swat at one of the little boys who was trying to push his way through to the bathroom. "Stop that you little rascal! Once this lady lives here you two are going to *stay out*." She went out into the garden, and I followed.

"Don't you worry - I won't let the boys bother you. They seem out of control, but if I lay down the law they will obey. What's you name again? Cara, was it? Well, these two rascals are Pip and Squeak." She watched my face expectantly and grinned at my expression.

"Really? That's very funny."

"That was my ex - he made it up. We called the older one Phillip after my dad and that got shortened to Pip and then number two arrived and we called him Steven after my ex's dad, so guess what happened? He got nicknamed Squeak, so now I have Pip and Squeak, sons of Rusty Brown!"

She was clearly delighted with herself and her sons. She was a woman who liked her life and found pleasure in small things.

"Would you like me to pay for a couple of weeks in advance? I think that's the normal thing, isn't it?"

"That sounds nice. Come on inside and we'll have a cup of coffee before you leave."

"I'll hang the washing up, if you make the coffee."

"OK - thanks. I'll take this screaming monster inside with me."

We sat at a small table by the kitchen window and had coffee. The baby sat on Rusty's knee and turned a biscuit into a soggy mess. The boys got a biscuit each and disappeared outside again and Rusty made a plan.

"If you come back about half past three, we can fix those last things in the shed – I suppose I should stop calling it the shed now if you're going to live there. Charlene's back about quarter past three, so that's the baby gone - makes it much easier. I might send the boys round to Charlene's for a couple of hours too, so you and I can get on with it."

She looked out the window and grinned. "Pip said he was feeling sick this morning, so I kept him home from school, but look at him now, roaring around and feeling fine. It's his first year and I think he's ready to leave school already."

I gave Rusty two weeks rent in cash and left, feeling lucky to have a temporary home lined up and some human contact available instead of living in a sort of vacuum, which was what I had been prepared for.

. . .

Moira was out when I got back to her place, and she was still not back by the time I set out for Rusty's place again. She had a great set of tools in a big bucket and she worked at an incredible pace, never stopped until a task was finished.

"When my ex left me, I said he had to give me a complete set of useful tools out of his giant hoard – if you live on your own you have to be able to fix things now and then."

"I suppose you do," I said. "I've never done a lot of things like this, but I'm sure I can learn."

"You wait," she said. "Once you have kids you learn to take advantage of the time you have when they're off your hands - get things done while everything is nice and quiet."

We put up the curtain tracks and hung the curtains; not quite the right size, but they met in the middle which, as Rusty pointed out, was the main thing. We carried the few bits of furniture across from the house and sorted out an extension cord for the electric kettle and then it was ready. Rusty took a last look round and declared that it was finished.

We had worked well together and got far more done than I had thought we would manage. "Perfect," I said. "I didn't think we'd get it all done."

"Never doubt a determined woman," said Rusty. "Next time we'll do it in half the time, now that you've learnt to use the right tools."

She went off to pick up the boys and I returned to Moira's place, making a detour to the café to buy a ready-made sandwich to have instead of the lunch I had missed. I made a mental shopping list as I went: Bedding, a couple of towels, a few pieces of china, eating utensils, a microwave and a small fridge was all I needed to live a very simple but quite comfortable life.

By the end of the day the clouds had disappeared, and the air was warm and still. Moira knocked on my door. "Come out to the terrace and tell me what you've been doing. Have you had dinner?"

I opened the door, wrapped in my lava-lava and holding my damp towel. "I have had a snack, thanks. I'll be out in a moment."

I joined her with a bottle of sparkling wine in one hand and a jar of olives in the other. "We have to celebrate, so I bought this at the pub. And some olives they had in the shop – I hope they haven't been sitting there for years. I must get a bike so I can get around."

Moira smiled. "I'm sorry I was out all day. I hadn't planned to be, but everything I had to do in Napier seemed to take longer than usual. I went to see a friend before coming back and she had so much gossip to tell me that I only got back just now. I'm going to have some bread and cheese and ham instead of dinner. Do you want some?"

"I had a sandwich from the café after I left Rusty's place, but I'd love some bread and cheese." Ten minutes later we were back on the terrace with a simple meal and a celebration drink.

"Now, tell me who Rusty is, and what you've been doing."

I raised my glass. "I have achieved a lot today - I am renting a shed in Rusty's garden. She and I have spent a couple of hours moving some furniture in and hanging curtains. It's small, but nearly perfect."

"Good lord, that's fast work. I haven't even begun to ask

about jobs for you, but I will tomorrow. But living in a shed? It doesn't sound very nice. Is it clean, safe?"

"Oh, yes. You must come and visit. The final coat of paint in the bathroom should be dry by the day after tomorrow and then I'll move in. Rusty's husband built it and it's perfectly OK - very small but clean and safe enough." I tried to think of something in Moira's house to compare it to. "I think it's about the size of your hall and then add on the bathroom which is tiny. Rusty's mate partitioned off the end and put a door in and then another mate of hers installed the toilet and shower, so it's fully equipped. Rusty's husband left her, and the shed is going to provide some extra income."

I smiled at Moira's concerned face. "All I have to do now is find a second-hand shop so I can get some things to eat from and some bedding - just enough to make me comfortable."

"No, don't do that. I have most of what you need. Over the years you accumulate a lot of bits and pieces, so there's plenty for you to borrow from. We'll have a look at it tomorrow. And I have bedding for Africa, as they say. When we decided to run a Bed and Breakfast place, we bought a lot of new stuff, so a lot of the old things never get used."

"Marvellous, thank you! That saves me lugging things home on the bus, but at some stage soon I must get myself a little fridge and a microwave oven. I thought I might get one of those fridges people have in caravans, sort of half-size."

"Check on Trade Me and if you find one, we can go and pick it up together, or else we can get one from a second-hand shop – I'm sure it won't be a problem."

I slept an entire night without waking or having confused dreams and woke in broad daylight. It was half past eight and I got out of bed straight away, keen to get going now that I had a place to live and things to do. It was a revelation to find that having a fixed point of reference, being able to say 'this is where I live' could make such a difference, even if it was only a little rented shed turned into a studio flat. My feeling of dislocation and loneliness had not only been due to leaving my home and friends behind; it had also been because I didn't know where I was going to live.

Moira was on the phone in the kitchen when I came in for breakfast the next morning, so I helped myself to coffee and put bread in the toaster. The newspaper was on the table and I scanned the headlines while the bread toasted, then Moira finished her call and put the phone down.

"Well, I've got you a job, part time, but still, it's a start. Two days a week at the Benson's. One day a week doing housework and one day light gardening. They have a chap, who mows the lawns and does the garden already, but they need a bit more work done, and he doesn't have time to do any more."

My heart skipped a beat. Benson – God knows it is not a common name. What if they were related? Moira looked questioningly at me. She had picked up that something was wrong but couldn't understand it, so I had to put it right straight away. "Sorry, I didn't mean to react in a negative way. It's just that I know someone called Benson. It's not a very common name."

Moira put her own interpretation on this. "Ah, I see. Well, I think all the Benson's they are related to live locally." I thanked my lucky star I had told her the story about the stalking ex-boyfriend, for that was obviously what she had linked my reaction to.

I picked my toast up and started spreading butter on it.

"They must have a big place, then. Did you tell them I know nothing?"

"Of course, not - don't be silly. I said you know as much as most people about gardening and you're taking time out to have a break. I hinted at someone being a nuisance and that you had left 'the city', didn't specify which one, to get away from him. And it's very lucky for us that their cleaner left suddenly a couple of weeks ago - perfect for you."

"It's great, thank you. I'd rather they didn't know any details about me, but I suppose they might wonder why I'm doing this sort of work and in a place where nobody knows me."

"That's what I thought too, so I kind of vouched for you. I said you're the daughter of an old friend of mine from nursing school and that you came here because of me. You told me your dad is a nurse, so it's not so far-fetched."

"Oh, God, did you really say that? Did they ask where my parents are or anything?"

"No, I just said your parents work for a charity overseas, no details at all. Well, let's face it I don't know the details either, just what you've told me. But it's all right and you can start on Monday. Julia wants the gardening done on Mondays, so you're there when the gardener is, and he can direct you. She wants the housework done on Thursday or Friday, so the house is ok for the weekend. She said you can pick which day you do it."

"Well, I can do it any time, no problem. Do they have children?"

"Oh yes, four - two are university students, or maybe one is at a polytechnic, not around here anyway. And the two younger ones are at boarding school. But they entertain a lot and the boarding school kids come home at weekends, so they have a pretty full-on life."

8

So, there I was on a Sunday morning two weeks later. Sitting in bed in my shed drinking coffee and reading the previous day's paper. The window was open, and I could hear the boys playing outside and Rusty calling to them to come in and have breakfast. I lowered the paper and looked out at the plum tree outside my window and marvelled at relaxed I felt.

The past couple of weeks had flown past. I had dropped a thank-you gift on Moira's doorstep a few days after moving out; four bottles of a really good red wine and an extra big box of the chocolates that I knew she liked best. How lucky I had been to find such a useful person just by chance. I had not heard from her since; perhaps our short time together was not going to develop into a friendship after all, but I thought it was better not to push it.

During the week just gone I had managed to organise my life a bit more. I had taken my tablet with me on my cleaning day at the Benson's and asked if I could use their internet connection when I had finished cleaning. Julia was very relaxed about it and gave me the code for their Wi-Fi. "When I think of the untold gigabytes the boys use with their games and movies, so I can't imagine your emails will have any impact at all. You're very welcome to use it any time."

I used my new email account once from Moira's house to send brief messages to my parents and to Lorraine. The messages would arrive from 'Cara Williams' and they were signed Cara and very carefully worded because I wouldn't relax my caution even from my new account. They had replied with appropriately careful messages. My parents used conventional and polite expressions in their reply, just as they would to a not-very-close friend, saying that they were 'pleased to hear I was well' and that they were 'looking forward to seeing me next time they were home on leave'. I knew they would be concerned about me, but they had resisted putting that into words.

At the end of Lorraine's message was a cryptic little sentence 'Can't wait to have another cosy chat' which signalled that there was something she needed to speak to me about; it wasn't a phrase I had ever heard her use before. When I got home that day I curled up on my bed with a cup of tea and called her from my prepaid mobile number.

"Hi Lorraine, it's me, Cara." I was not prepared to discard my alias even for the duration of a phone call.

Lorraine picked up the clue immediately. "Cara - how nice to hear from you! I'm a bit busy just now. Can you call me on my other mobile in ten minutes? Here's the number."

I made a quick note on the flyleaf of the book I had on the table beside my bed wondering why she now had two mobile phones. A few minutes later I called on the new number, and she answered straight away.

"What on earth was that all about? Do you have two phones now?"

"Oh, I don't – but I got a prepaid SIM card so I can put it in my phone instead of the regular one and talk to you and text message you quite safely. I have no idea how dangerous it might be for you if I use my regular card. I've been hoping you'd call me some time – it felt so strange not being able to talk to you. But then it dawned on me that if we both have prepaid SIM cards ready to swop like this, we can talk as much as we want. I thought it was a really clever move but seeing I couldn't call you first I had to wait till you called me, so I could tell you about it."

I had to laugh. "Don't you laugh too!" said Lorraine. "John thinks I've seen too many spy movies, but I feel we can't afford to take any risks."

"Sorry, I wasn't laughing really. I think it's brilliant. I can text you some innocent kind of comment and you'll pop the prepaid card in and call me. That would work fine."

Lorraine was in full flight. "Just text me and say, 'let's talk soon' and I'll know it is you."

"The girl detective in person," I said.

"I prefer to think it's more like James Bond, if you don't mind." I could hear the smile in Lorraine's voice; and it was lovely to have a light-hearted chat to someone instead of being guarded and careful.

"But really, Lorraine, have you or John heard something worrying?"

Her voice changed, she was serious now. "Yesterday John told me he'd seen the chap who's in charge of Nick's case, Benson. They were in a meeting about something else, but afterwards John took the opportunity to ask how it was progressing."

"And?" I was on tenterhooks waiting to find out what she had heard.

"They know for sure that Nick was involved in the drugs trade, though he didn't say how or in what sort of role. And that article you told them about, the one about the woman someone set fire to? Well, they've never caught her killer but they know who ordered it done, a big-time drug syndicate boss. So, if they can link that person to Nick or the other way round it could all come together nicely."

I could hear a 'but' in her voice. "Yes? There's something else isn't there?"

"Well, they haven't found the cash yet, or the passports and whatever else Nick had stashed away somewhere safe. Benson wouldn't say if they suspect that you have run off with the money or if they think you know where it is. John said it was hard to figure out if the way you left town made your situation worse or better in that respect. But Benson also said that he understood why you had gone into hiding and John agrees – they both know that here is no way in the world they could have kept you completely safe unless they 'relocated' you. It sounds as if you came up against the worst possible person in the crime world - he's ruthless and brutal in the extreme."

"OK, so both sides still want to find me. I'm glad you don't know where I am, so you don't have to lie."

"Yes, and so am I - John couldn't keep that from Benson and I can't lie to John. I mean, John and I know you didn't take that money, but until Benson believes that too it has to be part of the investigation - so John has to act accordingly."

"I do understand – don't worry. Of course, you two have to do the right thing. I'm telling nobody at all where I am, but if I did it would be you. Even my parents don't know. I'm in the North Island, in a small community. I have moved into a tiny flat, well, it's a converted shed actually, but a nice shed - clean and tidy. I've got a two-days-per-week cleaning and gardening job for cash payment and I'm sure I will get more jobs of that kind."

Having managed to sound positive and cheerful I expected her to say how pleased she was, or perhaps how clever I was, but I certainly hadn't expected her to cry. Great sobs came through the phone and a strangled voice. "I can't bear it - you're all on your own and we don't know where you are. What if something happens to you? We wouldn't know and nobody there would know who you really are, it's awful!"

"Oh God, Lorraine, I'm sorry, I should never have involved you in this. I never meant for you to be so upset about it. I'm truly all right, I'm comfortable and I feel very safe here."

But she was already pulling herself together and she was not going to crack again. I know her so well; she was regretting making me feel guilty and now she would think of some way of fixing things.

"Sorry, I'm just being silly. But I know what you can do - just in case something happens you could write my name and phone number on a piece of paper and keep it in your wallet. And on the outside, you write 'emergencies contact'."

I was cautious. "OK, and what if my wallet gets stolen? What then?"

"It wouldn't matter. If a stray mugger got hold of it my name would mean nothing to them. And if the drugs people or the police got it then they already know my name, so it can't do any harm."

I was just about to say goodbye when a thought struck me. I said urgently: "Oh God - hang on, Lorraine! I've just remembered that damn key - how could I have forgotten it till now?"

"What key?"

"It was on the sidewalk next to Nick where he fell after he was shot. I just picked it up without thinking. I don't know why - it was a very strange situation. I'm trying to think what I did with it. Benson should have it, just in case it was Nick's - it might be really important. Wait a minute while I try and work it out."

I sat there, silently staring into space trying to picture myself putting that key somewhere, but no, nothing came to mind. "I think I've lost my mind – all I can remember is putting it on my bedside table. I was sitting on the bed the night it happened, just looking at it because it was such strange-looking key. I was wondering what if was for. But I can't remember seeing it since. I certainly haven't got it now."

"Perhaps it's still on your bedside table then?"

"No, I don't think so - I had it in my hand when I sat on the bed, and I can't recall ever seeing it again. Not even the night I left, when I went through everything and packed my bag. I took a book and my hand cream from the bedside table, so I would have noticed the key if it was still there. Can you please go to my place and check around my bedside table and under the bed? Just in case it fell off and I never noticed. I can't say that cleaning under the bed was a top priority in those last couple of days."

"OK, I will. And give it to Benson if I find it?"

"Yes, please. If it did belong to Nick, Benson will be furious that I didn't give it to him right away. What if it's the key to wherever that damn cash is? It could clear me, and I would be able to stop this life in exile. And don't go there alone – you've got to take John with you."

9

———

 ut now, on this sunny weekend morning a week later I felt cheerful and safe. I was planning to explore Ocean beach south of the Cape. It was a long bike ride over the hills, but the pictures in the brochures promised that it would be worth the effort. Rusty knocked on the door just as I'd finished getting dressed and handed me her portable phone.

"Hi Moira, how odd," I said. "I was just thinking of you this morning."

"Thank you for the present - completely unnecessary, but very kind of you! Do you want to come over for lunch and maybe we could do something, if you're not busy?"

"I'd love to. I have nothing to do - it only takes five minutes to do the housework here."

"OK, come over when you're ready and I'll think of something fun to do."

I found myself humming quietly as I got my things together and rode over to Moira's. I had really missed our conversations and the easy companionship we seemed to have developed, and now it seemed that it might continue.

Moira was in the kitchen when I arrived and met me at the door.

"I heard you have a bike now, very good idea. Come on in and we'll have a cup of coffee and decide what we're going to do."

I closed the door behind me and followed her to the kitchen. "Have you been busy? Lots of guests?"

"No, not many. It's a bit early yet, but I'm pretty booked up from the end of this month and just about fully booked from New Year for a couple of months. Enough to keep me busy. Now tell me how the job's going. I'm dying to know what you've been up to."

"Julia Benson's made lists of things she wants me to do weekly and other things to do at intervals, very helpful. And she's recommended me to a friend as well - someone called Helen who lives in Napier, so I'm going there tomorrow to see her. It's another cleaning job."

'Does she live somewhere on Bluff Hill?"

"Yes, that's it. Do you know her?"

"Not really, I think I might have met her long ago, but that's all. She's on some committee with Julia - I've heard her talk about a Helen. I think the husband's a lawyer or an accountant, something like that. Julia told me a long story a while ago about how they demolished an old villa and built a huge modern house in its place. Are they paying OK?"

"God, yes - it's nearly embarrassing. I was a bit cheeky when Julia asked what I charge. I thought I'd start high and if she protested, I'd come down a bit, but she said OK right away and now her friend has been told that's my rate, so I'll soon be quite rich."

"And how do you find it? Do you get bored? It's such routine stuff, housework - doesn't require a lot of thought and I thought you might get sick of it."

I leant back against the kitchen bench and watched her

potter around. It was so nice to talk to her again that I did not really care if we went anywhere or just stayed in the kitchen for the rest of the day.

"Well, it's not super stimulating, but it's sort of relaxing to do something that's just physical for a change. And one good thing is that the result is so obvious. You feel very productive when you can see the difference straight off. I could do this for a year, no trouble."

Moira didn't comment on the timeframe, but she wanted to know how The Shed was working out, using verbal capital letters as if it was the name of a grand house.

"It's fine, tiny and cosy. I've got everything I need, thanks to all the stuff you lent me. I bought the bike from a mate of Rusty's who was going to sell it on TradeMe. She knows a lot of useful people, our Rusty. Since her husband left her and she's been on her own I think a lot of local guys have been very happy to help her out."

She laughed. "I think I get the drift of that diplomatic comment. Sounds like one of life's survivors. I'll come for coffee one day and inspect The Shed and meet Rusty. Now - for today I thought it might be a good idea to show you around the district. We'll go for a drive, have lunch somewhere nice and so long as I'm back before four o'clock I'm fine. I've got a German couple coming for two nights and they want dinner tonight, but they aren't arriving until early evening."

Four hours later we returned to Moira's house after a comprehensive tour, and I offered to stay if she needed help with the preparations.

"Thanks, but I'm fine. Though it would be great if I could ask you next time I'm in a fix and running out of time. It does happen. But what I realised when I wanted to call you this morning is that I don't have your mobile number. I only just remembered Rusty's surname and which street you said it was. Give me your number and I'll text you about coming to see you once these visitors have left."

I gave her the number and went off on my bike. The day was clear and slightly windy, and it was a pleasure riding along the quiet streets. When I got back to The Shed the boys heard me coming and ran to meet me, clamouring to tell me things and pushing each other aside to be the one to open the gate. Rusty leaned out of the kitchen window and told them to stop blocking the way and to leave me alone. "Cara, could you babysit for a couple of hours tonight? I want to go to the pub and Charlene can't have them."

I parked the bike and went over to the back door. "Of course, what time are you going out?"

"I'd like to leave at quarter to eight. You can do what you like in the house. The kids will be in bed and they sleep like logs. Watch TV or whatever, have a friend in, anything you like."

"OK, give me a shout when you're ready to leave."

"I won't make a habit of asking you, but I thought we could have a deal? You do a couple of hours a week for me and I let you use the dryer when it's raining? And you'll be able to watch TV. I can't imagine what you do in the evenings with no TV."

I was pleased she had asked. It was another little piece of normal life, of being part of a family. Every little thing of that kind held a significance that I could never have imagined when I was surrounded by my normal life in Auckland. I mentally collected these little moments one at a time and felt as if they were like beads on a string.

· · ·

A couple of days later Moira came for a visit on a day when I wasn't working. Rusty was gardening when she arrived, the boys were roaring around playing jet planes and Charlene's baby was in her stroller bawling as usual. I had told Moira about the scene I had encountered on the day I went to see Rusty the first time and now she was laughing at the chaos as she came round the corner.

I introduced her to Rusty and the boys, and Rusty lifted the baby up, and she immediately stopped screaming. It was fifteen minutes before I could get Moira into The Shed. Rusty took an instant liking to her. Well, she seemed to like everyone, and once she started a conversation it always took a while before it was over. The boys and I sat on the garden seat and Pip asked me to tell them a story. I told them my version of 'Goldilocks and the three bears' which was the only thing I could think of at short notice.

Moira got the guided shed tour and seemed relieved at what she saw. "It's not too bad - I was worried it would be dark and depressing, but it's pretty good."

"I'm fine here. I don't need lots of space and I don't have a lot of belongings, so the lack of storage space isn't a problem. And you lent me so much bedding that I'll be OK even on a really cold night. Mind you, I'm not saying I could live through a winter here, because there's no insulation in the walls - it would be pretty hopeless trying to keep the place warm."

We had a cup of tea and talked about nothing in particular, and when she left Rusty came out of her back door to say goodbye. The boys, as usual, fought about who should open the gate. Little Squeak grabbed the edge of Moira's jacket to get her attention to tell her something. "Sorry!" said Moira and bent down to lift him up. "I was listening to your mum. What did you say?"

Squeak looked reproachfully at her. "I said - did you

know that Ca-cara used to have bears that ate her porringe and slept in her bed?"

"It's called porridge, stupid!" said Pip with great contempt.

"Yeah, that's what I said!" said Squeak, indignant and stubborn.

Moira gave Squeak a hug and put him down and as I walked her down to her car she said, "You have landed on your feet here." And I had to agree; living in Rusty's shed was perfect, providing a sense of inclusion in someone else's normal life.

Over the next couple of weeks my life settled into a new and comfortable routine. I got plenty of casual jobs via Helen, who seemed to have innumerable friends who needed a hand with spring cleaning, tidying up in the kitchen after parties, gardening or babysitting. I biked or took the bus to work and noticed how much fitter I was getting.

My spare time was divided between babysitting for Rusty, spending time with Moira and reading. It was too warm to wear the money-belt while I was working, but I had nowhere safe to hide the money. For the time being I continued to wear the belt every day. I got sore red patches where it rubbed my skin nearly raw. I thought of wrapping it in plastic and putting it in the toilet cistern, but on second thoughts I decided that if I knew that trick then so did everyone else. Another time I had a look at the little door in the foundation of Rusty's house and wondered if I could reach in and hide the belt under the house, but the thought of the neighbour seeing me put me off. My one remaining alternative would be to ask Moira, but this would mean having to explain why I had it in the first place. Then a brilliant opportunity presented itself one day at Moira's place and the problem solved itself.

"Just take whatever you like," Moira said, when I asked if I could borrow some books. "As you can see the place is full of books and you're welcome to regard it as a library. I seem to be completely unable to throw books away until they are so tatty they fall apart. I have this feeling that the moment I throw a book away I will get an urge to re-read it."

We went through the house talking about books and picking out one here and one there. The place was full of bookshelves and there seemed to be more books than anyone could have read in a lifetime. We were in Moira's bedroom looking over a great selection of classic novels, when the phone rang. Moira ran for the kitchen and I made an instant decision.

Quickly I undid the money belt, folded it and picking up a ballpoint pen from Moira's bedside table I wrote CARA on the belt. Listening intently for Moira's footsteps I scanned the shelves, looking for a place to hide it and trying to think of some section where Moira would be unlikely to pull books out on a regular basis. The second to top shelf was full of older classics, mostly nineteenth century English authors. I quickly pulled out four novels by Dickens, pushed the money belt in and replaced the books.

On the Saturday night that week I was babysitting at Rusty's. The boys were asleep, and I was immersed in a new book and enjoying a cup of tea and the piece of carrot cake that Rusty had left out for me. The doorbell rang and I went to the front door, wondering who came calling on a Saturday night. A tall dark man I had not seen before stood on the front porch.

"Hi, are you Rusty?"

"No, she's out and she won't be back till quite late. Do you want to leave a message for her?"

"She doesn't know me, but I heard she had a flat for rent?"

"She did, but it's been taken. I've lived there for a few weeks now."

He smiled and his dark, rather serious face was transformed. "Are you a newcomer too? I've just came here from Auckland, my name's Andy."

He seemed friendly and casual, but I tried to avoid being drawn into conversation. "You should try the shops on the main road and the pub – they always know what's going on and they might be able to suggest something."

"OK, I'll do that - nice to meet you." He smiled again and left. I closed the door and went into the bathroom where the window was always open just a crack.

I want to see where he goes and what his car looks like. I don't like the way he asked if I was a newcomer; why would he say that instead of presuming I'm local?

I watched him walk down the road and turn the corner three houses down. If he had a car he must have parked somewhere else and why would he have done that? A vague feeling of unease stayed with me for the rest of the evening. Rusty came home just after midnight with a friend in tow, full of noise and laughter and more than slightly drunk.

"Thanks honey! Hope the kids behaved?"

"Yes, they're fine, they went to bed soon after you left, and I haven't heard a peep since. Oh, and a chap called Andy came and asked if your flat was available."

"Andy? I don't know anyone called Andy." She turned to her male companion who was already sitting on the sofa watching the Sports channel on TV. "Hey, Steve! Do you know anyone called Andy?"

Steve grunted a 'no' without turning his head, and I said:

"He wasn't a local. He's moved down from Auckland, but he wants a place out here."

"Oh, well, he's out of luck. I'd rather have you in the shed than anyone else."

Rusty put her arm round my shoulders and gave me a slightly unsteady hug. "I mean it, you know - it's like have someone from the family living in the shed. But you're a lot quieter than any of my family would be."

She laughed and Steve laughed to. "True - and a lot better behaved too."

A day or two later I coasted down the steep part of Helen's street after a long and hot cleaning session, made a sharp left turn at the bottom and continued down the gentler slope towards the foreshore. Setting out south along the coastal walking and biking track I felt a sudden surge of happiness. How lucky I was after all to have somewhere safe to live, a job and a friend or two. I enjoyed this ride on a fine day: blue sky, glittering sea, gardens, parks and interesting things to look at. As I left the centre of town a wide belt of grass separated me from the main road. I watched the waves, gentle today, rolling up against the shingle beach. I was filled with a sense of freedom and hope; feelings to be treasured in this strange and rather restricted life I led.

When I stopped at the bridge with no cycle lane to press the button that turned on the digital "bike on bridge" sign someone spoke right behind me.

"Hi there, let's ride across together and hope two bikes are more noticeable than one."

I glanced behind me: a tall man in cycling gear, a wide smile below a bike helmet and closefitting sunglasses. "OK," I said and set out ahead of him. On the bridge at Clive, I stopped to admire the carved Maori canoe being paddled up the river and the same man came up beside me and stopped.

"I think we've met before – wasn't it you who answered the door in a place where I went to ask about a flat?"

He took his sunglasses off as he spoke, and I recognised him straight away. "Oh yes, I didn't recognise you before. Did you find somewhere to live?"

"I did - a nice little place where I can walk to a good fishing spot if I want to. I don't know many people yet, so I spend my free time doing outdoors things. Would you like to stop for a cold drink at the pub?"

I hesitated, unsure of his motives and acutely aware that I must be careful about getting friendly with too many people in this temporary life. But then I shoved the thought aside; it would be a nice to get to know one more person and so far Moira was my only social contact. Rusty and I had plenty of short conversations and the occasional cup of coffee together, but it was sporadic, and we had little in common apart from practical arrangements.

We parked our bikes outside the pub. I took off my helmet, ran my fingers through my hair and smiled at him. "I need that cold drink - it's been such a hot day. And my name's Cara, by the way."

He smiled back and I marvelled again at how that smile transformed him. "I'm Andy."

We walked together into the shady interior of the pub where the air was still and cool. There was nobody there apart from a girl behind the bar, slowly polishing glasses and watching a daytime soap on TV.

"What will you have? I'm having a beer."

"Juice and tonic, thanks."

I waited beside the door to the deck, watched him order and come across the floor carrying two glasses and a bottle. He was attractive in a calm and self-possessed way, and he had that lovely smile, aimed at me now as he handed me a glass. I reminded myself once again to be careful not to let down my guard. We sat in the shade, and I drank half the glass in slow sips to give myself time to think.

"I'm glad you found somewhere to rent. Did you go and ask in the shop?'"

"I did, but she said she didn't know of anything and then suddenly she remembered the place I'm in now. I think it must have been a garage in a former life, but it's been very nicely converted. I've got a good bathroom and my own entrance. Comfortable enough, but no kitchen - just a kettle and a little microwave oven. Eventually I'll find a proper flat somewhere around here."

"Well, mine was a shed that was converted into a tiny studio flat. It's perfectly fine though and I'm the first person to live there, so everything is new and clean. Do you catch a lot of fish?"

"I'm surf casting most days when I'm not working, but I only catch something now and then. I know it seems mad to most women, but just standing on the beach and watching the sea is a pleasure even if I don't catch anything. My land-lady has offered to cook any fish I catch, but I'd rather cook them myself."

He had the most amazingly blue eyes; at the moment they twinkled wickedly. "I like cooking and overcooked fish is worse than no fish at all. And she looks like the sort of woman who cooks things to extinction - I sense mushy, grey peas and limp asparagus. So I cook my fish in the microwave." I had to smile back; his pleasure in his fishing was very engaging.

He drank half his glass of beer in one go and sighed. "Brilliant - just what I needed. I've been out for a couple of hours. It's crazy how hot it is for this early in the season."

"Where do you work? I thought you might be on your way home from work?"

"No, I'm off today. I work in a restaurant in town, so I have a couple of days off each week, different days each week. What do you do?"

"I do all kinds of things, house cleaning and gardening and baby-sitting mostly. Sometimes I pick up the odd bit of office work. It's great - I take on more work when I need more money and when I feel like a break, I take on less or ditch one employer."

I tried to make it sound as if this was my normal way of life. If I could make him think I had always been a casual worker, I wouldn't have to invent any reason for a change of career or location. I took another sip and watched him over the rim of my glass. He looked relaxed and interested, not in the least suspicious.

"And I love my little shed at Rusty's, smaller than my previous place, but cheaper too. She and I swap a few favours, very handy. I do her baby-sitting and occasionally I help her in the garden, and she lets me use her washing machine and dryer."

I took another sip and waited for him to offer some further information or ask another question, but to my surprise he changed the subject.

"Would you like to come to the movies tonight? It's the only free night I have for five days and I want to go to that little private cinema." He looked at me as if he was unsure of how I would respond. "Apparently you can buy a glass of wine and it's like sitting in an armchair in your lounge - sounds good to me."

"I didn't know there was a private cinema. What's the film? Not that it matters, I haven't been to the movies for ages, and it would be nice to go out."

"It's called The Accidental Tourist, it's an old film from

the eighties or nineties, but I heard someone talk about it
and it sounds interesting. The combination of a small
cinema with comfortable seats and a good film can't be
bad."

"OK, let's try it then."

"Good - it's nearly five now and I need a shower and
something to eat. Remind me of the way to your place again
and I'll pick you up at seven."

The cinema was small and intimate, the seats comfortable
enough to fall asleep in. I had done four hours of spring
cleaning for Helen and my back told me that I had moved
too many heavy pieces of furniture. I uncrossed my legs and
moved a bit to lessen the tension in my lower back. My bare
arm brushed against Andy's on the armrest, and it was as if
an electrical current had zapped from his skin to mine. My
whole body stiffened, and I glanced sideways at him without
moving my head. He was watching the screen and seemed
not to have noticed. Slowly, slowly I moved my arm away
from his and tried to regain my composure. This was a new
experience for me, and it shook me to the core, the sort of
thing you read about in novels and dismiss as one of the
many myths of fiction. For the rest of the movie, I made sure
there was no possibility of any accidental contact.

Afterwards we went to a little bar around the corner, where
we started out at a table next to a group of six women with a
lot of jewellery and very loud voices. Andy made a face and
said, without either raising his voice or trying to lower it,
"Let's move to a table where we can hear ourselves talk."
Over a glass of wine and bar snacks we talked for an hour
without any need for me to dissemble. He seemed quite

incurious about the details of my life and I gradually relaxed and began to enjoy his company.

As we drove back towards Clive he asked, "Which one of your various jobs do you like best? Or do you just like the variety?"

"I don't mind housework, but I like gardening better. The babysitting I do for Rusty and her friend is just easy evening stuff – the kids are asleep and there's hardly anything that needs doing, so I read most of the time or occasionally watch something on TV."

He looked sideways at me, and there was something in that quick glance that I couldn't read. "Do you read a lot? What sort of books do you like?"

There was no need to pretend. "I like a lot of different things, novels, history, biographies – I'm an omnivore. I like reading about the Peninsular War. I don't read many thrillers, but I like Patricia Cornwell's books – the science is interesting."

"I read a great book she wrote about Jack the Ripper."

"Portrait of a Killer, yes, I read it too. She made a convincing case from the evidence she found - very clever."

"Well, it was very well received. The Metropolitan Police in London gave her top marks for the way she presented the evidence."

As we drove through the dark and quiet landscape, I realised that this was my first evening out since Auckland. It was nice to get to know somebody new; even just having a proper conversation with a new person was stimulating. He turned into Rusty's street and stopped opposite the gate I could just see his face in the dim light. "That was fun - thank you for asking me."

. . .

I was reaching for the door handle when I felt his hand on the back of my neck. That frizzle of electricity swept through me again and made my spine tingle. When I turned to look at him, he pulled me slightly towards him and bent his head to rest his forehead against mine. I sat completely still, his hand was still round the back of my neck and my whole body was aware of him. For what seemed like minutes neither of us spoke or moved and then I said, "I must go now, I've got to be at work really early tomorrow." It came out like a half whisper.

Instantly he let me go and I fumbled with the door and my shoulder bag and somehow got out of the car. Before I closed the door he said quietly, but without leaning over to look at me, "I'll see you around."

I lay awake for a long time that night, re-living that strange incident and wondering what on earth was happening to me. It was not like anything I had experienced before; everything about the evening was slightly out of kilter somehow. He had been nearly reserved at times, but very friendly. His questions were casual and without any obvious direction. But a couple of times I had felt that something I said had surprised him, though he had not probed, he had touched me but not tried to kiss me. The way he had held me had felt strangely intimate even though the only contact was his hand on the back of my neck and our foreheads touching. His complete stillness had made me feel as if we shared one breath, the way it affected me had caught me completely by surprise. I would have to be very careful with this man.

When I finally fell asleep, I dreamt once again the dream I thought of as the Danger Dream, the one I had first dreamt at Moira's place and had often thought of since. This time it went further and frightened me more.

Darkness; a light rain falling, floating in dark water, running on wet grass, wet and very cold. Standing among trees at night, clothes soaking, a chilly wind on my face. Being hunted, terrified, trying to be still and quiet. Strong arms grabbing me from behind, a hand clamped over my mouth, no chance to scream. Shivering with cold, clothes clinging to my skin, feeling the body heat of the person holding me.

I woke with a start, a lump of cold fear in my chest. Every nerve in my body jangled. After tossing and turning for half an hour I turned the light on and read for an hour till I was calm enough to go back to sleep.

10

My mobile sounded a text alert as I cycled towards the shop and I stopped in the shade of a tree to read the message "Pls call in or ring soon. Need to ask something. Moira"

Mystified I replied, "See you in 10" and continued to the shop.

"How is it at Rusty's? Are you comfortable?" The lady in the shop was always helpful, happy to chat away about something while I collected what I needed from the shelves.

"Yes, it's great. I'm very happy there – thank you for giving me the tip." We had this conversation every second time I went into the shop and she always beamed at me, pleased to have been useful.

"Oh, no problem, it was good I remembered whose place it was. Did I tell you that I could have got that flat rented out twice? Just after I told you about it, well about a week later maybe, a man asked for a flat and said he'd like something attached to someone's house, so he had some company. He sounded as if he wanted something just like Rusty's place. I told him he was unlucky, because it was only a week or so since I'd sent you there. But then I thought of the Johnson's little flat, so that's where I sent him. I should start charging a commission."

"Well, I'm glad I got in first." I put my selection on the counter. "It's perfect for me and Rusty and I get on just fine."

"Yes, that's what I said to this chap when he asked about you. I said Rusty had told me she and you got on really well together and it was all settled."

The hair on my arms stood on end but I tried to sound casual. "What did he ask about me? "

"Oh, I can't think precisely, just things like were you a local and whatever, nothing special. I just told him I didn't know what your name was, but I thought you'd come here to find work."

As I rode towards Moira's place I tries to decide if I should be suspicious or not. The man who asked the questions must have been Andy. But was it before he came knocking on Rusty's door or after? And did it make any difference? If it was before then he had been devious when I directed him to ask about rentals in the shop. And if it was after then he could have asked about me because he was interested in me. But somehow it did not feel quite right, it made me uneasy.

Moira opened the door as soon as I knocked as if she had been standing in the hall waiting for me to arrive. "I am sorry about this, Cara. I'm worried and I have to tell you, but I hope I'm not about to put my foot in it or make you upset."

I had never seen Moira look flustered before, but she was clearly uneasy. "Come and sit down in the kitchen," she said and walked ahead of me, even her back looked tense and worried.

She started talking as soon as we were seated opposite

each other at the kitchen table. "About an hour ago a man knocked on the door, quite polite and well spoken, about forty. He said he had lost contact with a friend who had recently moved to Hawke's Bay and he thought she might have spent time in Clive. I said I had a lot of visitors from all over New Zealand and abroad. He said his friend had longish blond hair, was about 'so high' and twenty-seven years old. Her name was Karen."

I sat as if stunned and fear crawled across my skin. I made an effort to sound calm. "Well, it can't have been me he was looking for then. Why are you so worried?"

Moira did not reply straight away, and I saw that she was choosing her words carefully, as if one badly chosen word could ruin this conversation. I was getting more nervous by the second. She cleared her throat before she continued. "I thought he might have been your ex who was stalking you - and I thought you might be using another name to keep safe from him."

She was looking intently at me now. "You could have done that, if you had decided to not leave any traces - you know, using a different name, getting rid of your car, taking jobs that are paid in cash and all that sort of thing. And for all I know you could have cut and dyed your hair too. But I didn't like him at all, so I said that the description didn't fit anyone who had stayed here."

She looked past me at the window with a frown. "No, it was worse than not liking him, much worse. I felt as if he had threatened me even though he hadn't said anything threatening. To tell you the truth, he scared me, and he had a sort of hard look to him - as if he was used to bullying people." She shook her head to dispel the feeling. "He had unusual eyes - very pale grey, nearly metallic."

She said nothing more, just looked at me across the

table, her hands clasped tightly in front of her. I was silent, weighing up the options; I had to make a decision and her description of those pale eyes made up my mind. The man who attacked me in the alleyway in Auckland had unusual, pale grey eyes, a light metallic grey like aluminium. I clearly remembered the chill that had gone through me when he looked into my eyes, just before he struck me the first time. I couldn't leave Moira in ignorance because now it was important that she knew the truth and could be prepared.

"Could we have a cup of coffee while we talk? This is going to take a few minutes – or hours." I tried to sound light-hearted, but I was tense, and my mouth was dry.

Moira nodded. "OK, let's do that."

While she made the coffee, I sat silent and worried, thinking hard about how to explain it as concisely as possible. I wanted to keep the story as simple as I possibly could. Neither of us spoke until she put the coffee mugs in front of us and sat down again.

"All right, this is the truth now Moira, about me and why I'm here." I twisted the coffee spoon in my fingers and looked steadily at her. "I'm from Auckland, and I *am* the person that man was looking for. But he's not an ex-boyfriend – I don't even know what his name is. I bought an apartment, and I was trying to save to go and visit my parents, so I got a boarder- his name was Nick. He was shot to death right in front of me in the street outside the flat, someone in a car drove past and shot him without even stopping. When I packed up his stuff for his family to collect, I found bank statements, lots of them in various names and different banks, and when I looked through them, I noticed something odd, so I looked more closely - it was money laundering, hiding huge amounts of cash. Nick must have been involved in something criminal, probably drugs. The police took all his papers and some other things from his room. He had spent very little time in my flat and I thought he was a sales rep who was out of town a lot, but that might have been a lie. He could easily have been part of some kind of drug enterprise."

I took a sip of coffee while I thought of how to proceed without making it too complicated. "A day or two later I was rung at work by someone who said that Nick had had a huge amount of cash and I had to give it to them. I said there was nothing like that among his things and I couldn't help them. And then they started following me around. They were watching my flat from a car parked outside, they followed me to work - wherever I went they were there, and they wanted me to know it. And then they beat me up and threatened me as I was coming home from work."

Moira stared at me with wide eyes. "Good God, that's terrifying. What did the police say?"

"I didn't tell them - I just didn't dare. You see the man who beat me up said he had an informer in the police and he would be told if I reported it. He knew so many things about the investigation that I believed him. And I didn't think the police could protect me. I mean, how could they have stopped him coming after me? And if the police offered me some sort of protection it would only be temporary. I didn't trust anyone but myself, I suppose."

I paused and thought for a moment. What had I left out? "Oh yes, the man who beat me up, he had very pale grey eyes, just like you described, like metal. Then he called me and told me to look up an article on the internet - about a woman who was set on fire and burnt alive by a drug gang. I was terrified."

"God, how awful! I would have died of fright. What did

you do? Did you just take off? Wasn't there someone who could shelter you?"

So, despite my intentions and not wanting to involve Moira any more than I had to, I found myself unable not to confide in her. The relief of sharing the story was instant. Despite the present fear that I might be found at any moment, I felt some of the lonely tension lessening. The story of my planning and escape took a long time to tell and several times I had to backtrack to get it all to make sense.

Moira sat spellbound. Every now and then she asked a question and then she continued just sitting there, her eyes never leaving my face. After an hour she got up and fetched a bottle of wine and glasses, and a packet of breadsticks. "That's the most incredible thing I've ever heard - it's like a film script. I don't know how you can be so calm about it all."

"Oh Moira, I wasn't calm at all - I'm not calm now. I was completely terrified most of the time and I've developed a compulsive habit of lying in my bed at night going back over what I'd done to cover my tracks – over and over again. I'm still scared that I will suddenly come across something that I've overlooked. I have never felt so alone ever."

I took a sip of wine and realised that I had broken a breadstick into tiny pieces while I was talking. I pushed the mess into a little pile: "See, I'm a nervous wreck. I just can't understand what brought that gangster here. How did he find out I'm in Clive? I just don't get it."

"Well, he hasn't found you, not yet. I don't think he thought you were still here, you know. I think he was on your trail, but I got the impression he didn't actually expect to find you in Clive. He might have been looking for you for a while because it seemed he was hoping to find out that you had been here, so he could continue from here."

A chill ran down my spine and I rubbed my upper arms, felt goosebumps forming. "That's all very well, but how did they pick up my trail in the first place? They simply can't have gone to every town in the North Island and every single hostel and B&B - they can't have!"

"No, of course not, that would take years. Did you use your mobile? Can they find out where emails come from? Or could it be chance?"

I shuddered. "What if they had someone shadowing me all the time? Oh, no, that's ridiculous - they would have jumped me straight off, not waited for weeks. I mean, it must have been something recent. I haven't used a bank card or my bank account, and I sold my car. I haven't done anything that would identify me."

I was trapped by something I couldn't see, something closing in that I was incapable to protect myself from. How could you protect yourself against the unknown?

But we agreed that none of it made sense; our speculation was useless because we did not know enough. "What will you do now? Are you going to stay at Rusty's? I mean, anyone who asked at the store would find you easily. We don't know how many people he asked saying he'd lost contact with a friend who'd come here."

We stared at each other, neither of us had any answers. Moira pushed her chair back. "I'm going up to the shop to pick up a loaf of bread. Not that I need one, but I want to tell my little tale to the shopkeeper and see if she's been asked about you. Provided you don't mind?"

"No, that's a good idea. At least we'll know a little more, perhaps." I tried to weigh up the risk against the benefit of possibly finding something out. "It will either give me peace of mind or force me to go on the run again - better to know right away."

"You stay here and don't open the door till I come back! Why don't you start making dinner and we'll eat together before you leave? There's smoked salmon in the fridge and things to make a salad with - and potatoes in the bag in the pantry. I'll be back as soon as I can."

Forty minutes later she returned. I had laid the table and made a salad, and the potatoes were simmering on the stove. When I heard her key in the door, I went to meet her in the hall. "Did you find anything out? Has he been asking about me?"

Moira looked a lot more relaxed than she had when she left. "I think it's good news, or do I mean that no news is good news? The drug baron had asked in the shop and she was the one who directed him to me, but not because of you, just because I let rooms to tourists. She sent him down the road to the motel as well and told him to ask at the pub."

"Did she wonder why you were asking?"

"No, not at all; I just said I'd popped in for a loaf of bread and then mentioned that someone had come and asked for a lost friend. You know, just causally gossiping. And she straight off said he'd been there first, and she'd sent him to me and the other places. Quite interesting really, because she knows that you stayed with me when you first came here and even so she didn't connect you with 'the lost friend' at all."

"Thank God! I hope the chap at the pub didn't make the connection either. The motel people wouldn't know me from Adam."

"Don't be so sure - around here everyone knows a lot about everybody else. But I invented an excuse to go to the café and he'd been there too, and their reaction was the same. There's no link at all in people's mind between you and his lost friend – must be because his description is so precise, and it doesn't fit how you look now." She put a paper bag on the bench and grinned, "Here's the excuse for me going to the café – they were just closing so I said I needed something for dessert and bought their last two chocolate brownies."

After dinner we stayed at the table and talked until late in the evening. I told Moira about hiding the money-belt in her bookshelf. "I feel like a reverse thief, planting money in your house. But it's all I have in the world and there is no way I can wear it while I work any longer, it makes me too hot, and it chafes. And I was worried about leaving it at my place in case it gets stolen."

"Of course, that's OK, leave it there. Probably safer there than anywhere else – nobody aside from me will be taking a Dickens novel off the shelf in my bedroom."

At half past ten I biked back to the shed. We had been unable to think of a single thing that might help us figure out why the man had turned up in Clive, but it seemed relatively safe to assume that nobody would connect me with the person he described as having longish blond hair. For the first time since I had come here, I looked over my shoulder each time I turned a corner. When I got to Rusty's gate, I looked both ways to make sure nobody was watching before I wheeled the bike through. Once inside my little house I locked the door and pulled the curtains before turning the lights on, feeling paranoid but unable to relax.

. . .

When Andy knocked on my door one rainy afternoon a few days later I was still undecided about the events of the last time I had seen him. I had failed to work out if something significant had happened or if I my imagination was playing tricks. The best option seemed to be friendly and careful and to avoid getting drawn into anything closer than a casual friendship. Moira's visit from the person we now called 'the drug baron' had unsettled me. What if Andy was linked to some faction of the underworld - how would I know? One side might use brutality and threats, the other might be prepared to patiently wait and find out if I had the money. And that unusual reserve of his; what did it mean? But when I opened the door and saw him on the doorstep, I once again felt that strange pull, as if my body wanted to gravitate towards him of its own accord. He, on the other hand, appeared unconcerned and there was no sign that he was interested in me at all. He smiled and apologised for coming unannounced.

"I couldn't call or text because I don't have your number. And there's nobody home in the house, sorry!"

Unsettled, I tried to sound as casual as I could. "It's nice to see you. Would you like a cup of tea? I was just about to make one."

He looked round the room, his eyes skimming over the interior seemingly without purpose, but to my overly alert mind it seemed like an interrogation. I turned to the bench and got two mugs down from the shelf and filled the kettle. When I turned back, he was taking a book out of his backpack.

"I thought you might like to read this if you haven't already. I really enjoyed it – it's funny and very cleverly put together."

I took the book out of his hand, being careful not to let our fingers touch. The book was called The Eyre Affair. I shook my head, "I've never heard of the author or the book. But a new book is always tempting - thank you. I've just started a book though, so I can't read it right away."

"No problem, you can keep it till you have time to read it. One good thing about this one is that the guy who wrote it has written a huge number of books. I Googled him and if you like this one you have a lot more to look forward to."

"I must admit that's a really good point. Sometimes it's frustrating how long some of my favourite authors take to write another book – like John Irving. I feel like sending him an email saying 'What are you doing? Get on with it!' It takes him years."

Andy smiled, "I know the feeling exactly." I put the book down on the table and went to make our tea. With my back to him I said, "I've been thinking about getting a library card. I don't know if living in Clive makes me eligible for the Hastings or the Napier library."

"I'm surprised you haven't got one already."

There was nothing suspicious in his tone of voice, but I cursed myself for my carelessness. Thinking quickly, I did my best to sound unconcerned. "Oh no, I'm a bit of a rolling stone, I've only been here a short time. I came to visit friends of my parents – well only her of course, because he died in an accident. And then I liked it and thought it would be fun to live here for a while."

His face was expressionless, politely interested but no more. "I thought you had always lived here. I had never lived anywhere but Auckland till I moved here. Where did you come from?"

Thoughts chased each other through my brain. More alert than ever to the dangers of being found out, I tried hard to sound as if I had nothing to conceal. "Well originally I come from Canterbury, but my last stop was Tauranga." It was at least partly true; I had spent a couple of nights there after I left Auckland, and it was what I had told Rusty too. I had been in Tauranga a few times in the past and knew I would be able to fudge it if I needed to provide credible details or a description of some kind. But he asked nothing else and there was a little pause. "But how about you - why did you come to Napier? It can't have been just for the fishing."

"No good reason really. I was getting fed up with the high rent I had to pay in Auckland and the commuting - you know, the usual metropolitan grumbles. We got a new barman at work, who had just left a job in Hawke's Bay, and he was always saying that he would never have moved away if his girlfriend hadn't made him. He talked about his favourite fishing spots and the great climate and where he used to go tramping."

He smiled, as if at himself and his strange reasoning. "So somehow or other it seemed to be the right time for a change – and here I am."

He left half an hour later. "I really came to ask if you wanted to go out for dinner tomorrow night. It's my night off and there's a restaurant I want to try in Napier, they have a great reputation and have won awards."

Perhaps the only way to figure out if he was friend or foe was to see more of him rather than avoid seeing him. I would be careful, make sure I didn't let him get too close, try to assess if he had an underlying motive in being here. "I'd love to go out for a meal."

"Cool, I'll book a table and come and pick you up about seven. And tomorrow night is on me. I think it's expensive, but I really want to eat there and going on my own would be no fun at all – you're doing me a favour."

I wasn't going to let him pay for me, but for now I let it go without protest. When he left, I stood in the window watching him, conflicting thoughts circling in my head.

Once again, he had confused me. He had seemed as friendly and casual as ever, but it was as if the strange little episode in the car had never happened. Had such an unusual and intimate gesture meant nothing to him after all? And though I wanted to keep my distance and retain my privacy, I felt confusingly disappointed, as if he had withdrawn an offer or broken a promise. I shook myself to dispel the feeling and turned away from the window.

11

Before Andy picked me up the next evening, I counted my money, which had accumulated to an amazing amount in just a few weeks. Each week my cash earnings paid for rent, food and various minor expenses and left a considerable balance. At first, I put the excess money into a plastic bag that I kept in the AllBran box, under the plastic bag of cereal. Over time the amount in the cereal box grew so I started another bag and taped the first one under the shelf in the cupboard under the sink. And now there was another full bag in the cupboard under the basin in the bathroom. This was the first time I'd taken all the money out and added up how much I had saved, and it was far more than I would have guessed, just over nine hundred dollars.

"Look at that," I said out loud to myself. "I'm an affluent member of the black economy." It made me smile to think that this simple lifestyle could sustain me indefinitely, so long as I could find casual work, without any need to dip into my hoard in Moira's bookshelf. I added two hundred dollars to the money in my wallet and put the rest back, making a mental note to take most of it next time I visited Moira.

. . .

The restaurant was quietly stylish; I looked at the understated décor and the other diners and gave Andy a wry smile.

"I should have dressed up a bit more; this is a really nice place."

His reply was quite serious. "You look lovely just as you are."

I was pleased with the compliment but disconcerted by the seemingly conflicting signals he gave me. I smiled without comment and picked up the menu. We spent three hours over the meal, discussing food and books and debating current issues, but exchanging very little personal information. It was hard to decide if this was due to my own reserve or if we were both unwilling to reveal too much.

Every now and then I would look up and catch him looking at me in a thoughtful way. Then he would relax, lift his glass of wine, or make a casual comment as if nothing in particular was on his mind. Over dessert he commented on a drug bust that had got a lot of news coverage the previous weekend.

"Isn't it amazing that so much of this stuff is coming across our borders. And they say this catch could be just a fraction of the total - there must be a huge market for hard drugs."

Instantly I was on my guard. Was this a test? I must respond as a normal person would.

"It's scary to think how many people use drugs. Out-of-control drivers causing accidents and parents spending the food budget on drugs. I think making a fortune from drugs is evil."

It was easy to sound genuinely disgusted, because that is what I really believe, there was no pretence involved. "It's all about money and their power over people. I bet they never think of the lives they ruin and the families they destroy."

"So, you aren't one of those who think we should make the drug laws a bit more lax - soften the impact for the users who get caught and all that sort of thing?"

"Maybe for users, yes, because the consequences of convictions impact on their lives. But dealers should get the maximum penalty, don't you think? What they do and the overall cost to society is huge, and it must be kept under control. Do *you* think it should be regarded as less serious than it is now?"

"No, I don't, but I've met a lot of people who do. I tried a couple of party drugs once when I was younger and decided right off that it wasn't worth it. I've never touched anything like it since - I just stick to alcohol for my legal highs. In the back of my mind, I have a vague suspicion that I might have an addictive personality, so the less chance for anything to take hold, the better I feel about it. How about you - did you ever try anything?"

"I keep well away from anything that might bend my mind – except as you say alcohol, but I'm not a great drinker either. I tried smoking pot once at a party at university, but it just made me feel nauseated, so I never did it again."

"What did you study?" His voice was casual, but I had seen that flicker of increased awareness.

"I started a commerce degree, but I quit after a year and a half. I quite liked the study part of it, but I was getting itchy feet. You know, feeling that there was a big world out there and that I should get out and experience life, not sit around for at least two more years. I regret it now."

I looked at my plate as I spoke and then raised my glass and looked directly at him. I half expected to catch him in one of those speculative looks, but he seemed unconcerned. "I suppose we all have our regrets about one thing or another. I always thought that one day I'd get myself an education and use my brain, but time rolls on and before you know it, you're turning thirty, and it seems like it's too late to start a whole new life."

I insisted on paying my share of the bill. "It's generous of you to offer to pay, but I can't let you. I earn so much cash and spend so little that I always have a reserve."

I got my wallet out and handed him six twenty-dollar bills. "I bet that's not enough though, so maybe I'm letting you pay a bit of my share. This is a very expensive place and I never even saw what the wine cost."

He gave in gracefully and took the money. As I stood by the bar watching him check the bill I noticed that he paid the full amount with cash. Another unusual thing about him, I thought, most men would have put the cash I had given him in their wallet and paid with a card.

In the car on the way back Andy reverted to an earlier topic. "You must have come across all sorts of people in your life as a rolling stone. I've heard that Tauranga is a hotbed for drugs and high living."

He sounded casual, but I was extra alert around him now, a vague sense of danger returned immediately. Was he suspicious and if he was, why? Was there an agenda behind his questions or was it just random conversation? I tried to sound only vaguely interested.

"Yes, I've heard that too, but I never came across it when I lived there. I tend to take casual jobs, mostly housework and gardening - I don't really get to know that many people. But it's a great life, no stress, a few belongings and no responsibilities."

"What is it that attracts you to this life as a rolling stone?

If it isn't finding new connections or love or whatever, what is it?"

He seemed genuinely interested and I replied with equal, but pretended, frankness. "I think it's a wish to see things, get to know places and to experience that 'what would it be like to live there' sort of feeling you get when you read about places. I'm thinking of doing the same thing in Australia next. Just work my way around and take cash-paid jobs, having a look at everything that interests me – local art, nature, markets – that sort of thing."

"Not a bad plan for someone as self-sufficient as you". He slowed down as we met a truck on the bridge and said nothing more until we parked outside Rusty's. I had already noticed that he was a good driver, fast but safe. It's one of the things I particularly like in men, along with a solid body and a sense of humour. But now I had to decide quickly if I should ask him in. What would he expect from me and would I be safe taking the friendship a step further? I knew I had nearly slipped up earlier in the evening; after a good meal and a few glasses of wine it would be easy to do it again. Until I could establish if he was a threat or not, I must continue to be careful.

"That was a wonderful meal. Thanks for asking me – I very rarely go out for a meal in a real restaurant. It's not much fun when you're on your own."

He looked searchingly at me in the near darkness in the car. "It was my pleasure, Cara. I just can't understand why you aren't being asked out all the time." I saw that trans-forming smile flash over his face in the gloom. "I mean, it's not as if you're dead ugly or deformed or anything."

I had to laugh at the backhanded compliment. "Oh, it's just me, a bit of a loner and not one for heavy drinking or sitting in noisy bars. I suppose most people find me too quiet."

I opened the door, ready to get out and then temptation overcame caution. "Would you like a final glass of wine or a coffee before you go?"

"That sounds nice. I think I can risk another wine - I haven't got far to drive or I could walk."

At the gate I put my finger across my lips. "Let's be very quiet till we're in the shed," I said softly. "Rusty's room is just around the corner, and I'll never hear the last of it if she sees us!"

I unlocked the shed and went in first to turn the light on and Andy followed, closing the door while I fumbled for the switch. Suddenly I felt his hands on my shoulders, lightly grasping me and then sliding down my arms until he was holding me around my body by my wrists. I stood very still and tried to breathe calmly, but my pulse was jumping, and my skin felt electrified where his arms rested across my body. He said nothing, but his breathing was faster than normal, and I knew he experienced the current between us just as I did. Neither of us spoke and the seconds ticked by. His body was warm and solid against my back, I felt his heart beating. After what seemed like half a lifetime, he bent his head forward and rested his cheek against my hair for a moment. Then he gave me a little squeeze and took his arms away and stepped away.

I nearly fell backwards; it was like coming out of a trance. I recovered my balance, switched the light on and walked across the room without looking behind me. I couldn't meet his eyes just then. I would give too much away, and I wasn't prepared to let him see the full effect he had on me. Picking a wine bottle from the cupboard under the bench I said lightly. "Well, I know you like a red. Let's open this one." I handed him the bottle and got two glasses from the shelf. I sat down on the bed, knowing that I might be letting myself in for something that I was not ready to deal with.

But Andy did not sit on the bed beside me, he sat on the only chair with the wine bottle open and ready to pour wine into the glasses I was holding. His expression was unreadable, and I couldn't tell if he was unconcerned or being reserved, or possibly secretive.

When he left after a quite intense discussion about a recent and very controversial article about a well-known radio host and his antics with under-age girls, he stopped at the door and got his phone out. "I must get your number before I forget."

There was no reasonable excuse not to tell him, and what harm could it do? I had a prepaid phone with no contract and there was no way to connect my number with my real identity, so I put my number in his phone.

Sleep evaded me as I tried to sort out what I felt about Andy and why. It was a strange situation; there was a strong physical attraction between us, but there was also something else. It was not physical lust or just recognising sexual attractiveness in someone. It felt like a deep emotional connection, and it was new to me. I had fallen in love before, but it had never come with this intense feeling of natural belonging. I was bewildered both by the feeling and by the fact that I was certain that he felt it too, but he was holding back from acting on it. I mentally re-lived those two episodes when he had touched me, in the car after the movies and tonight. Somehow the sexy tenderness of those touches, of being held like that, was more powerful than anything I had known before, as if his restraint made the contact more significant.

And then there was the added complication, the question of who Andy really was. At times I was certain that he was just what he appeared to be, normal and without deceit. On other occasions something he said or did, or even the way he would briefly look at me, sent alert signals like darts into my mind. Was he the mole, the one sent in to gain my confidence and find out where the money was? But the drug baron was himself trawling the neighbourhood asking questions about me. Andy could be some kind of freelance connection to the drug baron and on an independent quest to get the missing cash for himself. It was equally possible that he had been sent by the baron's competition to get to the money first.

That night my mind was chasing the same thoughts round and round and sleep was impossible; I got up to get a glass of water. Standing by the bench in the dark room I tried to recreate the feelings that had flooded through me when his hands slid down my arms and he pulled me up against him. The warmth of his chest against my back, the way his breath had quickened and how I felt his heart beats echo in my body. It was a supremely sexy moment, and I was sure he had been one short breath away from giving in and taking the next step. And then his arms dropped, and he stood back as if nothing had happened, and I had nearly fallen over. It was driving me crazy. I knew an involvement at this stage of my strange life was the last thing I needed, but I wanted more.

All I could do was keep my guard up and be very careful not to let anything slip. My brain told me to remove myself from Andy, send him packing and eliminate one potential threat to my safety, but my heart said 'no, no – take the risk, you might regret it forever if you don't'.

12

Rusty was hanging out of the kitchen window bellowing across the garden. "Hey Cara - would you like a coffee?"

I went to my open door. "Yes thanks, I'll be there in two minutes, just need to get dressed first." I discarded the lava-lava and pulled on clean shorts and a T-shirt and went across to the house. Squeak was sitting on a kitchen chair clutching his comfort rug and sucking his thumb. I patted the top of his head and then looked closer. "How are you, little man? You look a bit tired."

"I think he's getting something." Rusty was pouring coffee at the bench. "He's been a bit off-colour all day and he wouldn't eat his lunch. Pip is fine, he went to school OK, but I'm not letting Squeak go to play group while he's like this."

"Poor little chap! Come here Squeak and sit on my knee." I lifted him up and put my arm around him and he leant into my shoulder and closed his eyes. "That's definitely not like Squeak. Poor little boy."

Rusty studied the face of her son from across the kitchen table. "Mm, we'll see. Half the time when I think there's something going on the little buggers wake up the next morning as fit as fiddles and screaming for breakfast. You never know with kids."

She took a sip of her coffee and gestured to the packet of biscuits. "Have one - they're those new ones they advertise on TV, very nice."

The little body on my lap sagged a bit more and I looked down; Squeak's eyes were closed. "Look at him, he's gone to sleep. Do you want me to put him on his bed?"

"I'll take him, back in a moment."

There were footsteps outside and Rusty's friend Steve came in, banging his work-boots against the doorstep to knock them clean. "Where's Rusty then? Is she out?"

Rusty's voice came through the door from the hall ahead of her. "No, here I am. Just put Squeak to bed, he's not very well today. Want a cup of coffee?"

"Nice, just what I need. I've been at work since half past six trying to get my dad's old Holden fixed so he can go away on holiday with mum without breaking down halfway. Wish he'd get a new car; it's not that he can't afford one – that car is more than half replacement parts by now."

He sat down at the table beside me, large and friendly and smelling vaguely of oil and grease. "Hey, Cara – I just remembered something. You're not a secret blonde, are you?"

I was taken completely by surprise, struggling not to look alarmed. "Blonde? I wish! Did you ever hear of a blonde dying her hair brown? Why do you ask?"

He laughed. "I had this guy turn up at the garage a couple of days ago, well recently anyway. He was after some chick he'd lost track of, short girl with blond hair. He had some idea that she could've come here. The only newcomer I could think of was you."

I tried to look only mildly interested. "Well, it's not me. Maybe there's someone new you haven't heard of?"

Rusty grinned. "Yeah, right! If some new blonde moved in round here Steve would know within minutes."

"'Course I would! But I told him 'no'. I didn't like the look of him at all, wouldn't have told him even if I had known who it was. He was some kind of hard act from the city, ready to throw his weight around."

I went back to the shed pondering this new information. It was disturbing to hear how extensively the drug baron had been asking around, but if he only got negative answers, perhaps he would give up.

Some days later I was returning from a hot day gardening at a friend of Julia's, dusty and tired. I came around the corner of the house wheeling my bike, thinking of a shower and stopped in my tracks. The shed door was wide open, but there was nobody in sight. I stood there for a moment listening before I went up to the door and looked around, hoping that whoever had been there was gone. The little kitchen cupboard was open, the bedclothes were on the floor and the mattress was half off the bed.

The bathroom window above the hand basin had been broken and the window was wide open. The toothpaste tube was on the floor, trampled on with toothpaste streaked out in a long smudge. I took a deep breath and looked out over Rusty's back fence to the property next door, but there was nobody out there. Leaning out I saw scuffmarks on the painted weatherboards on the wall under the window.

I was going through things, to see what was missing, when Andy called. "Hi, would you like to go to the movies again? I've got a free night and the tide's wrong for fishing."

"What a flattering offer! But I can't, I've just come home from work to find I've been burgled, and a window is broken, so I need to get it fixed right away."

"What did they take?"

"I don't know. I've only just started checking, and I must carry on and see what I can do about the window. Call me later!"

But nothing had been taken. Whoever had broken in had made a very thorough search, even the plates and groceries in the cupboard had been moved around. The back of my neck prickled; someone had been looking for something hidden. A regular burglar would surely have taken anything portable that could be sold for cash. I tidied and sorted the kitchen cupboard, put the mattress back on the bed and put the sheets and towels in Rusty's washing machine. I had just cleaned up the toothpaste and the broken glass in the bathroom when there was a knock on the open door; Andy stood on the step with a plastic carrier bag in each hand.

"I thought I could be of more use here than sitting around at my place." He came into the room and looked around. "Did they break the window-frame or the glass?"

"The glass in the bathroom window, the frame is OK. I'm just waiting for Rusty to come home so I can find out who I should get to put new glass in. She's sure to have a friend who will come and fix it if she whistles."

He had a look in the bathroom and returned to put the bags on the table. "What did they take?"

"Nothing that I've discovered so far, not even my tablet. They turned it on and then they left it - maybe because it's got a logon password so it's no use to anyone else. And they didn't find my hidden funds, but they had been through absolutely everything - taken things out of the cupboards, even stripped the bed."

As soon as the words were out of my mouth, I knew I had told him too much.

"Very unusual, are you sure they haven't taken anything? Jewellery or something small, the sort of stuff they can sell easily."

"No, honestly, nothing at all - I have so few possessions it's easy to check."

"Have the cops been?"

"What? Oh – no, I didn't call them." I could hear how stupid this sounded so I added an explanation. "It's not as if I'm insured and have to make a claim, and once I started cleaning up I forgot about it. It's probably a bit late now."

He shook his head at my casual approach, and I tried to put it right. "If Rusty wants me to, I'll do it when she gets back."

He emptied the bags and started sorting things into piles. "I hope I got the number of windows right. I've got four proper window locks with keys, and a chain for the door – for when you're at home, so you can feel safe. And I got a deadlock for the door, so it can't be opened with a credit card. I noticed that stupid lock the first time I came. But I need to borrow a drill and some tools from Rusty or one of her mates. We'll just have to wait till she gets home. How about a coffee?"

I had not said a word since he emptied the bags out, stunned by the way he had assumed responsibility and organised everything. I put a hand on his arm, something I had never done before. "Thank you! That's the most perfect thing you could have done - I was thinking while I was tidying that I might never feel safe here again, but it will be like Fort Knox with all this hardware installed."

He laughed and punched me lightly in the shoulder. "Ah, but you don't know what I'll demand in return - just wait, I'll think of something." I was uncertain of how to take this, so instead of responding I filled the kettle and busied myself making coffee.

"So, what are these hidden funds you were talking about - do you have cash hidden around the place?" He was looking down at the pieces of hardware on the table, but I could tell that he was curious.

"Just whatever is left over each week - because I get paid in cash. I have a few hundred hidden in three places at the moment, but it's still there, I've checked. Nobody has any idea I have it, so that can't have been what they were after. Well, I didn't check the AllBran packet, but if they didn't find the other places, I don't think they would have found that lot either."

"Why don't you put it in the bank each week?" He was looking at me now. "Wouldn't that be safer when you're living in this place on your own?"

I did my best to sound unconcerned and smiled at him. "Don't worry, I will do that from now on. It's just that I usually head home straight after each job to get cleaned up and then after a while I discover that I've got an ever increasing amount of cash that I haven't used. And I hide it till I get around to going to the bank." In my mind's eye I pictured the money belt in Moira's bookshelf and thought 'that's my bank and I will use it from now on'.

When Rusty got home, I went over and told her what had happened and she reacted much as expected, friendly and concerned, but very casual about reporting it. "God, I'm sorry Cara! I feel awful that you got burgled. Thank good-ness they were disturbed or whatever happened, so they didn't have time to take any of your stuff. Not much point reporting it when nothing was taken, the cops have enough real trouble to worry about."

I deliberately did not tell her what a thorough search the intruder had made, I just said that nothing had been taken. The last thing I wanted was for Rusty to start telling people that she wondered what they could have been looking for, seeing that nothing was stolen. Just the sort of thing she loved speculating about.

Now she patted my arm and said comfortingly, "I'll go and ring Brendan to come and fix that lock in the morning. He's the guy who built your bathroom. He has every useful tool you can think of - in more ways than one, ha,ha! And I'll ring the glass people too; they're just up the road."

I gave Rusty's tool kit in a bucket to Andy and he started on his mission to make the shed secure.

Two hours later the shed was transformed: window locks installed, bathroom window fixed, and the security chain screwed to the door frame. I returned Rusty's tools and when I came back across the garden Andy was on the path, ready to leave. "I'll be off and leave you to settle down again."

"Oh no don't go - I owe you a meal. Not to mention paying you back for all those things you bought to make the place secure. Why don't we go and have dinner at that place on the main road and I can use up some of that damned cash instead of hiding it all over the shed?"

We spent a couple of hours over mediocre food and good wine, debating everything and anything apart from the break-in, but as we walked back to Rusty's place Andy brought the subject up again. "I just don't get it, Cara. Why would they spend all that time taking the place apart and then not take anything? Even if they didn't find any valuables, you'd think they would have taken something."

"I know, it's weird - I don't understand it either." I tried to sound as if the puzzle was of no particular concern to me.

"It's nearly as if they were looking for something specific. Not the hidden cash obviously, because how could they have known that was there, but something else?"

I tried to deflect his train of thought. "Maybe they were disturbed and had to go before they were finished?"

He sounded as if he was idly speculating, but my alarm lights were flashing red. Was there something behind his interest other than concern? He could have introduced the thought that 'they were looking for something' to draw me into a conversation where I might reveal what he wanted to know. I felt very unsettled by the thought and for the hundredth time I wished there was some way I could find out more about him. Being attracted to someone, who might be using you for his own gain, was like walking on an emotional quagmire.

As we rounded the corner to Rusty's street, I was still debating with myself if I should ask him in, but the decision was taken out of my hands. Andy stopped beside his car and got his keys out. "Thanks for dinner - I'll see you soon." He kissed my cheek, got into the car and drove off, leaving me feeling more frustrated than ever.

It was still only half past nine, so I rang Moira to tell her that my shed had been broken into. "Good grief, that's awful. Do you want me to come over?"

"No, I'm fine, but I've been wondering if it's linked to the drug baron. Because he was back, a few days ago - I hadn't told you yet, but he went to that little garage down the road and asked Rusty's mate if there was anyone new in the village, same description as before. He's not stopped looking."

"So, he's still here – unless that was about the same time he came here? He is very thorough – he must have some reason to suspect you have been here, or that you are somewhere in the district. I wonder what it was that alerted him?"

"I've been thinking about that too. The only thing I've thought of is CCTV cameras. They're everywhere these days. But it would have to be the most incredible coincidence if some video clip on TV had me in it, it just can't be that."

"No, that's too far-fetched – surely nobody would recognise you from a chance video clip. Not when you've changed your appearance completely. I do wish I had checked what kind of car that man had when he came to me, at least we could keep an eye out."

"Perhaps Steve at the garage noticed, but then I wouldn't dare ask him," I said. "It would seem odd, and he would wonder why I asked. I don't want anyone getting suspicious and start gossiping about me. In Auckland he followed me around in a silver Mercedes with dark windows."

"But listen, Cara, if you start feeling uneasy you can tell Rusty that you're leaving, moving on. I could pick you up and pretend I'm taking you to the airport or the bus station, but instead I take you back here to stay with me - you would be safe here."

"You are a star, thank you! But I hope it won't come to that. I'll come over and see you tomorrow after work."

The next afternoon I cycled round to Moira's to drop off a couple of things for safe keeping. "Hope you don't mind - I've brought my tablet and some more cash. It doesn't feel safe to leave anything remotely important in the shed, so I thought maybe I could leave it here and use the tablet when I visit you."

"Of course," she said. "I'll give you a key to the house so you can get in if I'm not here when you come - the key fits both the front door and the terrace door. I'll leave the alarm system off until this is all cleared up, so you can come in any time."

As I put the key in my pocket, I had an idea. "And I'll give you my parents' and Lorraine's numbers, just as a precaution in case you need to find someone who knows me."

Moira's face registered horror, but I did not understand why. "What is it? You look as if I have said something awful."

"Oh God, I'm sorry Cara! When you mentioned giving me your friend's phone number, I instantly thought that I would only need that number if you were injured - or something."

She looked so guilty I nearly laughed. "For goodness sakes, Moira – don't think of the worst possible situation right away. You'll probably never have to use it."

But there was a twinge of cold fear in my chest at the thought of Moira calling my parents and Lorraine to tell them I was injured or 'something'.

The afternoon became evening and still we discussed and speculated. I told Moira about my indecision about Andy and whether I could trust him. Moira tried to understand what I was talking about.

"Well, what sort of things is it that makes you say you can't trust him? Does he ask you things that don't seem like normal questions for people who are getting to know each other?"

"Oh no, he's not asked anything specific, but sometimes I get a feeling he reacts in an unusual way to something I have said." It was hard to describe the feeling. "Sometimes when I say something, I catch this alert reaction from him, nearly speculating. And then I realise that I've said something that might sound as if I'm faking it, lying about my background. It's just a flash of something, a look in his eyes or a slight change of tone."

Moira emptied her cup and stood up. "I think you're overly aware of everyone's reactions because you're scared that someone will find you. And let's face it, you're right - that horrible man who came here is trying to find you. Why don't you stay for dinner? I've got a chicken breast and some fresh pasta, plenty for both of us."

Later that evening I leant back in my chair and looked at Moira across the kitchen table. "I would like you to meet Andy, Moira. You would look at him from a different angle and tell me if you think I'm paranoid."

"Am I right to think it worries you because you want to continue to see him and get to know him better?"

Her eyes were twinkling with mischief and I felt that blush, the curse of the true blonde, rising on my face. I might be a fake brunette, but I still blushed like a blonde. "Oh well, maybe. I do like him a lot. And that's part of the puzzle too. I know he likes me, he's attracted, but he holds back. It's as if he is tempted to maybe take a step forward, but he restrains himself. I can feel it happening when he does it, like a physical stepping back."

"Aha," said Moira in a pretend serious way. "It's a troubled romance."

"Don't be silly! But you have to admit it's not what usually happens. I mean, I've fended off enough guys in my life to know that a lot of them will take the slightest sign of encouragement as an invitation to push you backward onto the nearest bed."

"You're right, I didn't mean to be flippant - but it's quite nice, isn't it? You deserve some fun."

"Yeah, and if it goes on like this much longer, I'll probably take the next step myself and find myself turned down."

We laughed and changed the subject, but when I left late that evening Moira said, "Why don't you bring him here for a drink some time? Or ask me to meet you somewhere, so I can have a look at him?"

"OK, next time he asks me out I'll text you and then you can call me and ask me over for coffee or a drink- and I can pretend it's all just a spur of the moment thing."

I hugged Moira and cycled off into the warm dark night, trying not to think of someone following or watching, waiting to pounce.

13

———

A week later Moira called and asked if I would do a one-off job for a friend of hers who lived out in the country. She was giving a big party for her husband's fiftieth birthday and needed some extra help.

A change from my usual house cleaning and gardening seemed like a good idea. "That sounds OK. Are you going to be there?"

"No, I had to say no -I am going to a concert with a bunch of friends and we've bought the tickets. You'd better take my car because they live miles out of town. I'll get a ride to the theatre."

She gave me the phone number. "Call her soon - she needs to know if you can do it or if she has to find someone else really fast. Don't hesitate to say no if you don't feel like it. I only said I would ask if you were free."

So, I called Jean, who was brisk and cheerful. "It's going to be a marquee event - seated dinner, manned bar, tables cleared between courses. Nothing fancy but reasonably formal. We're expecting about a hundred and twenty people and my usual helper has gone off to be with her daughter

153

who's had a premature baby. I'd like to meet you for a chat, where do you live?"

"Why don't we have a coffee in town, and you can tell me exactly what it is you want me to do?"

I knew she wanted to have a look at me before she gave me the job and I was fine with that, but I wasn't going to invite her to the shed. A meeting on neutral ground seemed like a better idea in case either of us decided not to go ahead. We agreed on a café in Napier when she was going into town two days later and that was that.

The day before our meeting I was biking to Napier to do the cleaning at Helen's place, when a grey Mercedes with tinted windows passed me. It was where the bike path runs right alongside the highway and seeing that car so close startled me. For the first time in my life I realised what 'a heart-stopping moment' means. My heart literally missed a beat as the car continued on ahead of me and disappeared from view. There was no sign of it as I rode through town and up the hill to Helen's. I did half a day's work, ate my lunchtime sandwiches in the tranquillity of the Waterfall Garden and set out for Clive.

When I passed the Information Centre, I saw the Mercedes again. parked in the angled parking area and the driver's door was open. A rather busty blonde got out and looked around as if deciding which way to go. I heaved a sigh of relief and continued on my way - obviously just another silver Mercedes with tinted windows.

Jean turned out to be a little sliver of a woman. She was so tiny and skinny that she looked like a ten-year-old from behind, but she seemed to have enough energy and logistical skills to run a small army. Within minutes of seating ourselves at an outdoor table she had given me a complete run-down of the arrangements, ticking them off on her fingers as she talked.

"It's all organised really - marquee, glass and china hire, BBQ, portable toilets all booked, plus food and wine of course. I don't need wait staff - the kids are going to do that. They do all the grunt work when we have parties, the simple stuff like clearing tables and doing dishes."

She shrugged. "What I mean is, anyone can do those things, and it needs no judgment at all. Moira tells me you're exactly what I need, someone who can keep a constant over-view and order the kids around. When my regular helper said she couldn't do it I thought I would do it myself, but I've had second thoughts. I'd rather enjoy the party and have you there. Will you do it?"

"Yes, of course. Not that I've ever done anything like it before, but it sounds as if you just need a sensible adult to direct operations."

She beamed at me. "Exactly! Just to keep the kids on track and make sure they don't slope off behind the marquee with a bottle of wine. Moira says you are amaz-ingly organised and competent."

I tried to appear suitably modest and repeated that I would be pleased to help her out. Just as we were parting, she remembered something. "Oh, yes - I nearly forgot. One of the people from the vineyard was going to come to super-vise wine and drinks, we've had him before, but he rang this morning and said he's broken his wrist. You haven't got a mate who could fill in, do you? I really don't trust the kids with running the bar."

"I know someone who might be able to, but I don't know if he's available - I'll have to check. Can I call you later today?"

When I got home, I called Andy and he answered directly, so I knew he was not at work. "Hi Andy, its Cara. Would you be free on Friday night to do a job with me?"

"Of course, tell me what you need." There were no questions, no hesitation. It seemed as if he was expecting to be able to do whatever was needed. After the last little while I was beginning to think that maybe he could do just about anything.

"Sorry, it's not doing something for me, it's a paid job. I know this is short notice, but a friend of Moira's needs help at a big party she's giving out in the country. I'm going to supervise a bunch of teenagers who are working as wait staff, but the guy who normally looks after the bar and the wine has broken his arm. I told her I only know one person who might be able to do it, so she's not expecting miracles. If you can't, she will just have to find someone herself."

"She's lucky - it's the first weekend in weeks that I'm not working. Of course, I'll do it. What time do you want me to pick you up?"

"Cool. I'll call Jean and tell her and find out what time she wants us."

On Friday afternoon Andy picked me up and we drove inland for twenty-five minutes along a minor road through hilly countryside, constantly climbing higher towards the western mountain ranges. Jean's place turned out to be a lifestyle block with a long tree-lined driveway, a mowed field for parking and a big sprawling house. We parked beside a small fleet of vans and walked towards two big marquees erected on the lawn on the far side of the house. Jean spotted us and came to meet us. "I'm so glad you are here - the place is like a madhouse, but we're making progress."

I introduced Andy and Jean gave him an appreciative look, glanced at me and winked. I thought 'ah yes, I'm not the only one who finds him attractive'. She rounded up a team of nearly identical teenagers of both sexes. They were all tall and sporty looking with reddish-blond hair and freckles. Jean rattled off their names; three were her children and the other four their cousins. Anything less like their mother was hard to imagine, but when we were introduced to the birthday boy there was no mistaking where the look came from – same mould, different generation.

There was a lot of activity, but no chaos. Jean's skinny little paws had a firm grip on the event and things were well under way. She took us on a tour: kitchen marquee here, dining marquee there, huge rotisserie BBQ manned by an expert, trolleys for dishes and glasses all lined up and tables just about to be set by the teenagers.

"Very impressive," said Andy and smiled his wonderful smile. "I can see a born organiser has masterminded this."

She smiled up at him, flattered and flirty. "Thank you! I'm used to having big parties here, so a lot of it is routine."

During the next three hours we worked hard and by half past six, when guests started arriving, the place was perfect. Music was playing, drinks lined up, car parking attendants at the gate and nothing left to chance. I kept forgetting which teenager was which, but I had the rebel in the bunch identified within half an hour and warned Andy; a charming young chap who listened and then wandered off and did something completely different. "Don't worry," said Andy. "I've got my eye on him already. We'll keep him so busy he won't have time to get up to any mischief."

The crowd milled around on the lawn having drinks until Jean banged on the large brass gong on the terrace and announced that dinner would be served in ten minutes. In a sort of miraculous mass movement, they all settled in groups of eight at round tables and I had to start paying real attention.

Halfway through the evening I was walking discretely along the inside wall of the marquee, checking that tables were being cleared properly before dessert, when an older man seated at a table stopped me. I thought he wanted me to get something and stepped closer, but he got up and put his hand on my arm. "You have to excuse me, my dear, but I've been watching you for a while. I'm sure we have met, but I can't place you."

I had never seen him before and said so as politely as I could, but he was insistent and a bit drunk. "I must have seen you somewhere but in a different context. Where are you from?"

I moved to one side, just enough so he had to take his hand off me. "I'm from Christchurch - I'm just here on a working holiday."

He hesitated, noticed that his wife was glaring at him. "Well, never mind. But I never forget a pretty face. I thought I might have seen you in court."

And with that he sat down again, and I continued my round, but I was taken aback by that last comment. Why had he said such a strange thing?

An hour later I was standing by the house giving Jean a run-down of how things were going in the kitchen marquee, when a group of men walked past. "Who is the older one in that group of three that just went past? The grey-haired one, with the big nose."

Jean turned and looked after the loud trio. "That's Big Boss Sullivan; he plays golf with my husband. He's a retired lawyer. Why, do you recognise him or was he annoying you?"

"So, he has a bit of reputation, has he? Yes, he was a bit overly friendly. Pretended that he thought he recognised me, but I've never seen him before."

Jean grinned and made a dismissive gesture. "He thinks he's bit of a lad and he gets frisky after a few drinks. But tell me - was his wife around when he talked to you?"

I grinned back. "Oh yes, she was, and if looks could kill he'd be dead by now – and probably I would too. Listen, how long do you want us to stay? I think the kids have the rest of the tidying up under control now and I'm running out of things to do."

"I know. I was just saying to Andy that you can leave any time you're ready. I'll just go inside and get your pay." She disappeared inside and I went to find Andy. By the time we got back to the house Jean was waiting. She gave us an envelope each, shook hands with Andy and hugged me. "Thank you both so much! You've saved me. This would have been really hard work for me without you two. Drive carefully now – it's a windy road."

She picked up a bag from beside her feet and handed it to me. "Here's a nice bottle of bubbly for you to have when you get home - I wrapped it in damp newspaper so it'll keep cold."

Once we had extricated the car from the cars that had arrived after us and were heading down the drive, I opened my envelope. "Wow!"

"What's wrong?" Andy was keeping his eyes on the narrow road. "Has she paid us fifteen dollars an hour?"

I smiled in the dark. "No, I got paid four hundred for roughly seven hours work - completely mad! Do you want me to open yours?"

"No thanks, I couldn't bear it if you found out I was paid

less than you. No, just kidding, do open it." And as expected there was another four hundred.

"Well, I'm not complaining. Perhaps the guy she normally gets to be the wine maestro charges a lot or she's not aware what the average wage is? Wonder what her husband does?"

"I don't know, but I can ask Moira."

We continued on a downward slant over hilly country. The road crested a rise and suddenly in front of us was a panoramic view with a necklace of lights where Napier and the smaller coastal communities sat along the curve of the Bay. Andy slowed to a stop and we sat for a couple of minutes just looking out into the velvety darkness. We were approaching Clive when he suddenly said, "Was that old guy bothering you? I saw him calling you over and grabbing hold of you."

I was surprised that he had noticed. "Oh no, he was a bit drunk already and just wanted a chat, pretended he thought we'd met before. His wife got irritated, and I got away."

"I was just about to come over and check him out when you walked away." His voice had an edge to it, and I thought his reaction was out of proportion to what had happened.

"Oh God no, it's not worth thinking about. I shook him off easily. Jean said he's a retired lawyer with a reputation for getting flirty after a drink or two."

When Andy replied, his voice had lost its edge. "I didn't like to see you bothered by the old goat."

We were silent until we stopped in Rusty's street. I held up the shopping bag with the bottle. "Shall we share this now or do you want me to save it for another time?" I tried to make it sound as if whatever he replied would be fine with me.

"Well, we probably deserve a drink after all that work - and watching everyone else drinking. Even those kids were sneaking glasses of wine. What is it?"

I unwrapped some of the newspaper and peered at the label in the bad light. "It's Moët et Chandon. It looks expensive."

"That settles it!" Andy turned the ignition off. "I can't leave you with that – you might drink it on your own."

Neither of us had had a meal apart from bits and pieces snatched in the kitchen marquee while we worked, so we opened the champagne and sat down with a bowl of almonds and some crackers on the table between us. As before I sat on the bed and Andy sat on the chair. We were both tired, content to sit quietly, just talking and enjoying the wine. Andy told me of 'the freckled cousin who drank the dregs out of the bottles all evening and then disappeared'.

"What do you mean 'the freckled cousin' - they were all freckled. Was it the rebel?"

"No, he was too busy - this was one of the others, a cousin, I think. When I hadn't seen him for a while, I sent one of the girls to find him and was told he was asleep and snoring behind the marquee. He deserves a damn good headache in the morning."

I got up to get the bottle from the little fridge to refill our glasses one last time. As I passed Andy's chair he reached out and grasped my wrist. I paused and looked down at him and he sighed and spoke without looking up. "I just can't figure you out." He sounded sad.

"What is it you can't figure out? I'm a simple person."

For a moment he said nothing, I could tell he was hesitating, then he let go of my wrist. I fetched the bottle and came back to sit down on the bed again. I emptied the bottle evenly between our glasses and now he smiled. "Perhaps I've got it wrong, but there are things about you that just don't make sense. It's as if you are hiding the real you and I don't know how to find you."

He shook his head and made a wry face. "Sounds like a lot of new age rubbish, I know. But it's true. Sometimes I feel that you are acting out a role you have created for yourself - the rolling stone, the casual worker, the girl who dropped out of university." He stopped, sat up straighter. "God, I'm sorry! I apologise, that was uncalled for. I'm not trying to pry - but one day I would like to know the real Cara."

I was getting flustered now, not sure of what to say. I could admit I wasn't completely the person I pretended to be and tell him that I had a good reason to do this. And then what? He would want to know more, of course, and I couldn't tell him. Or I could deny his theory and try and laugh it off. But I had a feeling he wouldn't believe me, he would know that I did not completely trust him. There was no easy solution.

He never took his eyes off me and the longer I stayed silent the harder it became to say anything at all. I just continued to look back at him, mute and helpless. And then the whole complex and frustrating situation became too much, not improved by champagne at the end of a long day without a proper meal. Suddenly tears were flooding my eyes and I knew I had lost it. I covered my face with both hands and bent forward until my head nearly rested on my knees. Tears seeped between my fingers and dripped down my legs and the more I tried to stop, the harder I cried.

He said nothing. I heard him rise and knew he was leaving, but then I felt the mattress sink beside me and he put his arm across my back. "Please don't cry. I'm sorry I've upset you. But don't cry - I can't cope with it."

But I couldn't stop, the dam of held-back emotion had burst. My confusion about him, my loneliness and my fears for my safety combined into an overwhelming sadness.

Andy reached around me, took a firm hold of my upper body and swung me around, then bent across and lifted my feet onto the bed. He held me sideways against his chest and I felt his hand on the back of my neck, pressing my head against his shoulder until I was completely supported and resting against him. Still, I cried and cried. After what seemed like a long time the tears slowed, and only occasional sobs escaped. He said nothing at all, just held me firmly against his body and rested his cheek on the top of my head. It was just like the two previous times he had touched me; complete physical trust. I knew without a doubt that nobody had ever given me such a feeling of connection before.

Gradually I calmed and relaxed against him. He kissed the top of my head, and I sat up, but he got up and pushed me down on the bed. "Stay there, don't move."

He crossed the room, and I heard the tap being turned on. I lay there exhausted with my eyes shut and felt I could neither move nor speak. He came back and crouched on the floor beside the bed and wiped my eyes and cheeks with something cold and wet. It felt wonderful. "Andy, I ..."

But he put his fingers over my lips. "Shush, lie still." He sat down on the floor and put one arm firmly across my body, pinning me to the bed. "Just lie here for a little while. We'll talk later."

14

I woke to the sound of Pip and Squeak sitting on my step singing 'The wheels of the bus go round and round' over and over with great energy. I felt disorientated and it took a moment to realise that I was lying with my head at the foot end of the bed. I was still dressed in yesterday's clothes, the pillow was under my head and the spare blanket that usually hung over the back of the armchair had been tucked around me. From the way the light fell into my room it must be halfway through the morning. I felt as if I was calmly suspended in space. I lay there for a few minutes listening to the boys until there was a knock on the door.

"Ca-cara, can we come in? Are you awake?" and Pip chiming in, "It's not early, can we come in and see you? What are you doing Cara?"

I got off the bed and opened the door and the two little boys rushed in, both taking at once. I poured us a glass of juice each and got the biscuits out, and then we sat on the garden seat and talked for a while before I said I must get myself tidied up and went back inside.

. . .

There was a note on the table that I had missed, written on the back of a petrol station docket. "Sorry, can't cope with crying. Don't be so worried - we will talk about it later. A."

I tried to reason my way to a decision while I showered and tidied up. But the combination of my feelings for Andy and the risks I had to weigh up didn't gel into anything satisfactory. On and off during the day I went through the options again, but there was only one thing I could do if I wanted to continue seeing him. I had to tell him half the truth and take the risks associated with lying, even if it was lying by omission.

If he was who he said he was, just someone who had moved here for a change of lifestyle, then his occasional flashes of scrutiny could be explained by something about me not ringing true in his mind. But what if he was involved with drugs despite the opinions he had voiced? He might be a really great liar. Like me, I had to admit; I had turned out to be good at lying too. Or was he after the money everyone thought I had hidden somewhere? That would mean he was connected to criminal activities. Could I continue to be with him or would I have to walk away? Could love make you change your moral stance and do something you knew was wrong and still be happy?

In the end I made my mind up. I wanted to be with him. I had never known anyone like him before and having a relationship with him for a short time would be worth the pain if he left in disgust when he found out I had lied. And if he was not what he appeared to be, then I would leave him.

He called in the afternoon and suggested a walk along the river path. He made no mention of the previous evening either then or when we met at the corner. We walked in silence through the village and across the bridge. I had nothing to say until he started the conversation, and he said nothing. Despite the silence I felt comfortable and happy to be walking beside him. My future happiness was possibly in the balance, but I felt no tension. It was as if we had suspended judgement and existed in a quiet space where nothing needed to be said. I wanted to spend forever with this extraordinary man.

As we left the road and set out along the path he reached out and took my hand. Without looking at me he started talking very quietly. I knew better than to interrupt; I sensed that he had thought it all out and needed to tell me in his own time and in his own way.

"I'm sorry I got you upset last night. But sooner or later I had to bring it up. I'm certain you aren't the person you seem to be. I thought I needed to get to the bottom of it and either have you trust me and tell me the truth or else just stop this now."

He fell silent as we met a family with a dog, but as soon as they had passed, he continued. "But I have changed my mind."

Now he stopped and turned to look at me. He let go of my hand and my heart missed a beat, I knew he was about to say that this was the end for us.

"I don't care who you are or why you are living this charade. I don't even care if you don't trust me. I want to be with you, and I'm prepared to take it one day at a time and face the music later."

I let my breath out. "I thought you were going to say you would stop seeing me."

I turned and continued walking and he followed. I was going to be more comfortable talking about this without looking directly at him. Lying to him, even by omission, would be a lot harder than lying to anyone else.

"I spent the morning trying to decide what to do, too." I

was not going to go into details, but I wanted to be as honest as I could. "You are right about me - I've fled from my normal life, and I'm trying to live here, very quietly and without attracting attention."

I felt him looking sideways at me, but I kept my eyes on the path ahead. "I can't tell you the details, but it's imperative that I do this for a while if I am to be safe. I mean physically safe."

"Is someone trying to find you?"

"Yes. I got into a situation that I had no control over, and I've had to leave my normal life behind, probably for a longish time."

"Just one question then and I'll not ask anything until you are ready to tell me. Are you married or were you in some sort of relationship?"

"No, there is nothing like that. I've never been married, and I was not in a relationship."

We continued walking along the pale limestone path across the meadows by the sea and eventually back towards the road.

"I am not going to ask you anything either." I glanced sideways. "But I would like to tell you one thing, so you know where we both stand in this. I have felt right from the start that you're hiding something from me. But it might be that you find me puzzling and that I picked up on that. But now I've come to much the same conclusion as you - I'll take my chances for the time being."

There was no immediate reply. I looked up at his profile and knew that he was considering what to say and how to phrase it, he was not finding it easy.

"OK then, let me put it like this. I have wondered about you, who you really are since I first met you. Maybe, as you say, that's what you have sensed. But I can assure you there is nobody else in my life. I did have a partner for a few years, but she left a couple of years ago and it's not a problem to me or to us. Can we leave it like that?"

"Of course." I noted that he had concentrated on the 'attachment' aspect of his background and not told me anything else I didn't already know. But considering my own evasiveness and lack of trust I could hardly blame him.

When we turned to retrace our steps, I noticed that he was looking out to sea. "Is this a good fishing day?"

"Not right now, but a bit later it might be good, the tide's right for it. But I'd rather spend the evening with you."

"Well, there's no reason we can't do both, is there? You can fish and I'll sit somewhere and read a book - and then we can have dinner."

After walking back and picking up Andy's car and his fishing gear, we were on the beach not far from the river-mouth. The sky was covered in light cloud and a chilly breeze was coming from the south. I sat in Andy's car and read, grateful to be out of the wind that had chilled me within a few minutes on the beach.

"Sorry I'm not much good as company for a fisherman," I had said as I headed back to the car. "It's much colder here than it was in the village – I should have brought a jacket."

"Never mind, it's good to have you waiting in the car. I'll give it an hour and then we'll go back."

I texted Moira and asked her to call and invite me for a drink in an hour. I knew she would understand what I meant.

When he returned, without a fish, I had fallen asleep. "Wake up sleepy head, what are we going to do about dinner? It's not going to be fish, not today."

I yawned and considered our options. "I know what we

could do, we could go and get fish and chips and then we'd still be able to say we went fishing and had fish for dinner."

"You have a very devious mind, but let's do that."

We were waiting to turn on to the main road when my phone rang.

"Hi Moira," I said. She sounded amused at the other end, acting out her part. "Would you like to come round for a drink? Fairly soon?"

"That would be lovely, thanks, but I have a friend with me. Is it OK if I bring him?"

At the end of the short conversation, I turned to Andy. "That was my friend Moira. She's asked us for a drink, and I said yes. OK?"

"Fine, but I've got to change. I couldn't go in my stinky fishing shoes."

I waited in the car while he went in to change his shoes and he came out looking smart in a dark crewneck jersey instead of the sweatshirt he had worn on the beach. "Now you've made me look scruffy."

He knew I was joking, but he said quite seriously. "You never look scruffy, you look lovely whatever you do with yourself." There was a slight pause and then he added, "Even when you've been crying your eyes out for quarter of an hour." He reached out and briefly gripped my hand.

Moira greeted us in a faded T-shirt and jeans, looking relaxed and friendly. I introduced them to each other, and we followed her to the kitchen. A delicious smell came from the oven and the room was cosy with light and warmth. I shivered and Moira looked at me. "Are you cold?"

"No, not now, but it's funny how you shiver when you come into a warm room sometimes."

Andy smiled. "It's a comfort shiver."

I could see that Moira took to him right away, but I knew she would keep in mind all the things we had discussed the other day. She would not be swayed by charm alone and her judgement would be as sharp as ever. The breeze had grown into a stiff wind, and it was too cold to sit on the terrace. For the first time since I had known Moira, we sat in the living room, and it felt strangely formal sitting in the chintz-covered armchairs. Moira lit lamps on little tables, organised wine and glasses and chatted to us while she pottered around.

It was interesting to think that three people in this civilised room were concealing things, but nobody was going to risk a topic that might make it obvious. Moira wasn't about to ask Andy where he was from or what he did. Andy wouldn't ask Moira how long she had known me, and I would not ask anybody anything.

Instead, we talked about the previous evening's party and how it had gone. Andy told Moira about the older man who had, as he put it, 'tried to make a move on Cara'. I laughed it off and said it was nothing, just an old guy showing off after a couple of drinks too many.

"Who was it?" Moira was clearly interested, and I realised she might well know him. "Oh, some chap Jean called Big Boss, a retired lawyer."

Now Moira burst into a peel of laughter. "Oh my God! He's just hopeless, that one. I think he nearly made a career out of philandering when he was younger. His poor wife, God knows why she didn't leave him. Do you remember how I told you that after James died some of his friends turned up on the doorstep with a bottle of wine offering to keep me company in the evenings? All of them married!"

"Aha, so he was one of those guys? I can't say I'm surprised."

Andy was fascinated. "Are you kidding? Did these guys just come along expecting you to welcome them in for a bit of whatever when you were just widowed? What idiots!"

Moira smiled at his indignation. "Thinking with their willies instead of their brains, I suspect. There were one or two that I would have expected it from, like Sullivan, but others really surprised me. Gosh, how boastful that sounds - as if hordes of them turned up! It is only three or four who have tried it on in the year since James died, that's all."

At half past seven I checked my watch and looked at Andy. "We should go and pick up our dinner." Turning to Moira I added, "Andy failed to catch our dinner, so we have to buy fish and chips, or we starve."

"Oh, no – don't do that. Stay here and share the casserole I made. It's just sitting in the oven slowly cooling off. I made a lot so I could freeze a couple of portions, lamb casserole with ginger."

So, we stayed for dinner in that comfortable kitchen that really was beginning to feel like home, had a lovely meal and enjoyed each other's company. Something I said made Moira think about Pip and little Squeak and we laughed and agreed that maybe it would be best if Squeak's pet-name was changed before he became an adolescent. Andy invented a string of really bad puns that Squeak's teenage friends might use against him and we had barely stopped laughing when Moira abruptly changed the subject.

"I had a daughter once. She died when she was one."

I didn't know how to react at first. I was shocked that I hadn't known, worried that we had caused Moira pain by talking so much about little Squeak and confused as to why she told us just now.

Andy saved the situation. "That must have been awful – such a young child. Was it long ago?"

It was the perfect opening for Moira to tell us more if she felt like it or simply tell us how long ago it was and put the subject to bed. "It was terrible – it broke my heart. It will be sixteen years ago in December. She got meningitis and died in just a few days. James never got over it. Sometimes I can nearly feel her weight in my arms. Thinking of Squeak brought it back." Then she smiled and added, "It was such a treat to have a warm little body to hold after such a long time. All our friends' children are growing up so fast."

I wasn't going to ask anything more. Somehow it was enough to know the basic fact and sometime in the future she might show me a photo. But the story was not over. Moira looked at me with a slightly wary expression as if she was going to say something shocking. "Cara, do you remember how we sat on the terrace your first night here? Did you ever think it was strange the way we became such good friends so quickly?"

"Not really - I just thought of it as luck. You know, sometimes you meet someone and for some reason you feel you've known them all your life. And you trust them without any real proof that they are trustworthy? It's only happened to me once before, but that was the feeling I had."

Andy was looking from one to the other, saying nothing, just waiting to hear what would come next.

Moira said, quite seriously and very surprisingly, given her down-to-earth character: "I think it was meant that you and I would meet each other and become friends. I felt it the moment you arrived on the doorstep. Don't get me wrong, you know I don't believe in navel gazing or the supernatural." She smiled as if to reassure me that nothing had changed. "Our daughter was conceived when we were on holiday in Italy. We had been told that we could never have a child and we were over the moon when we discovered I was pregnant. Because of the Italian connection James insisted that we call the baby something Italian and we christened her Cara – a word instead of a name."

I was staring at Moira, fascinated and slightly shocked, Andy was looking at me, and Moira lifted the wine bottle and said calmly, "Anyone want a top-up?"

Both Moira and I knew that Cara was not my given name, but the coincidence still had an emotional impact. When I found my voice I said, for some reason I couldn't explain even to myself. "What did she look like? Like me?"

"No, not at all. James was part Maori and had dark eyes and curly black hair and my little Cara looked just like him, curls and all. She had skin that looked lightly tanned and the biggest brown eyes; very pretty."

And then we talked of other things and no further mention was made of my namesake, but I tucked the thought of her away in my heart and marvelled for the hundredth time at the kind fate that had led me to Moira's house.

At eleven we said goodbye and drove back to Rusty's house. We both got out and stood for a moment by Andy's car, neither of us quite sure of what to say. In the end I took the lead. "Oh, for goodness sakes - two consenting adults, and we seem to have turned into shy teenagers. Funny! Are you coming in?"

But once inside, the same awkwardness gripped us again. I thought I knew what it was. Despite having shared moments of intense intimacy and emotional upheaval we had never even kissed. It was as if we didn't know where to go from here, and neither of us wanted to take the first step. Possibly Andy was thinking of the evening before, still somewhat uncertain of my emotional state. I stood close to him without touching and looked up at him, wanting to remove any doubts.

"Last night's chaos was *not* your fault. It wasn't what you said that upset me. It was the whole situation suddenly coming to a head - my strange life, the things I can't do, the people I no longer have around me, the fear of being found."

I stopped, but he said nothing, now he was the one who was stuck in silence, so I continued. "I've had to meticulously cover my tracks, always looking over my shoulder, not trust anyone. So, when you seemed to care in real terms about who I am and why I'm here, it all crashed down around me, because you are important to me now."

He reached out and pulled me to him, tilted my chin up with one hand and kissed me. Of all the many kissers I had known nobody had ever kissed me like that. A searching kiss; slow and lingering. It went on for a long time and I could have stood there forever, but he broke away. "I'm sorry I couldn't do anything, last night I mean. I'm useless when women cry, no idea what to do."

I nearly laughed; he was so wrong. "What do you mean, you couldn't do anything? What you did was to comfort and calm me and give me the space to recover. It was perfect - I don't know how you knew to do that thing, to kind of pin me to the bed and hold me still until I went to sleep. It made me feel safe - nobody could have done anything better for me just then."

He looked awkward, but I could tell that he was pleased. "Well, I was desperate to try to comfort you. I could see that you were completely tormented and all I wanted to do was make you calm again."

He bent to kiss me again, but I put a hand against his

chest and held him off. "I have never met a man as gentle as you."

For the first time I caught a glimpse of the man behind the man, so to speak. He took a firm grip of my shoulders and looked at me with an expression of pent-up energy that I had never seen in him before. His dark face was not only serious now; it was intense. "Gentle! I'll show you what I really want to do."

This time his kiss was hard and probing and his hands left me in no doubt about the passion behind his self-control. I knew something special was about to start for both of us. And in the back of my mind, I also knew that whatever started now would probably not end well.

At dawn Andy left and I went back to sleep, and once again I dreamt the Danger Dream: *Darkness; a light rain falling, floating in dark water, running on wet grass, being wet and very cold. Standing among trees at night, clothes soaking wet, a chilly wind on my face. Being hunted, terrified, trying to be still and quiet. Strong arms grab me from behind, a hand clamps tight over my mouth, no chance to scream. Shivering with cold, clothes clinging to my skin. I feel the body heat of the person holding me. Listening for sounds of movement. Warm breath brushes the side of my head, a quiet whisper more felt than heard "No noise, don't move."*

<h1 style="text-align:center">15</h1>

The day was cool and gray and I was riding my bike to Napier to do Helen's weekly cleaning, thinking that I should have brought a jacket in case it rained on the way back. There were cars stopped on the curve ahead and as I got closer, I saw that there had been an accident on the bridge a short distance further on. A few cars were stopped with their emergency lights flashing and I heard sirens in the distance. As soon as I got there, I realised it was serious. Halfway across the bridge a van had crashed nose first into the concrete bridge railing and a small car was on its side with the roof hard up against the barrier on the other side. I wheeled my bike a bit closer. On the far side of the crash was a police car with roof lights flashing and an ambulance approaching. Nobody could get past, not even on foot; the crash completely blocked the width of the bridge. There was a strong smell of petrol, and someone was screaming inside the van.

I leaned my bike against the railing and took my helmet off. Glancing out over the river upstream from the bridge I saw something like a bag or a bundle of clothes in the reeds on the far side. And then, just as I was turning away, a movement caught my eye, a little leg kicking. There was a very small child in the water among the reeds. I stared in disbelief for a moment and spun around to alert others, but everyone was busy trying to get the occupants out of the vehicles. It was a chaotic scene; shouted instructions across the wrecks, screams of pain or panic and sirens approaching. There was no way I could get over the bridge to the far side. I would have to try from my side, and I didn't have much time.

I ran back to the end of the bridge, climbed over the road barrier and leapt down the slope to the wide boggy edge of the river. My heart was pounding as I jumped over waterlogged tufts of tall grass, then into the deep muddy water where reeds hindered my progress. I was gripped by a sensation of being completely powerful and able to do anything. I felt no fear and never thought of hesitating when the muddy river bottom sucked my feet down and dragged at my legs as I waded forward. Adrenalin surged though my system like a drug; all I felt was a frantic need to get there before that child disappeared under the water. I abandoned the attempt to wade as far as possible and flung myself forward doing breaststroke across the channel of open water until I could once again wade through the reeds.

When I was at the spot where I thought I had seen the child; there was nothing there and my heart sank. I spun around, measuring with my eyes the angle from where my bike was. I was at least ten meters too close to the bridge, so I set out again. And then I saw her, one little arm flailing, her body half submerged now. The dense reed stalks had prevented her from sinking faster. I launched myself from a standing start and felt as it I literally flew through the air. I reached out and grabbed the arm and pulled. She came up like a little fish, covered in mud and river gunk. I nearly fell sideways as I pulled her closer to me, water splashed into my eyes, but I somehow righted myself. Her tiny hand grasped my top and clung on; the other hand was still holding a small stuffed dog.

I clutched her to my chest. She was very young, perhaps only a year old, and weighed very little. Realising how easily the action of grabbing and lifting her had unbalanced me I held her tight against me with one arm and started slowly turning to face the bank. It was as if I had become disassociated from the crash scene on the bridge, there were only the child and I and that muddy river trying to stop us from getting out.

And then, like an angel appearing from nowhere, a man's voice spoke just behind me. "Reach out with your free hand so I can grab you." I stretched my left arm sideways, and he grabbed my wrist and held me steady while I turned around. He was large and slightly overweight, and he was standing on what was obviously a firm patch on higher ground. "Hand me the baby."

"No, just pull me out, will you? I've got a good grip on her."

But I wouldn't hand her to anyone until we were out of the river. What if he dropped her and I could not find her again in the muddy water?

"OK, hang on tight!" he said and the next moment he had lifted me and the child vertically by my left arm, straight up in the air and onto firm ground. By now two more men had reached us and together we made our way toward the road, not a great distance but heavy going. I looked up the slope and saw that the crash scene was a hive of activity. There were now two ambulances and several police cars, and a long line of cars backed up along the road. A St John's ambulance man was at the top of the slope by the road barrier waiting for us. By forming a chain, we passed the child up from one pair of hands to the next until the ambulance man took her. I was soaking wet and covered in filth, and now it was over, I trembled from head to foot.

The others started clambering up the slope, but I changed my mind and decided not to go with them. My bike, helmet and the little backpack with my phone were on the far side of the crash. If I came up this side, I wouldn't be able to get to them for ages, people would insist on talking to me and I wouldn't be able to simply leave on my bike and go home, which suddenly seemed more important than anything else.

I turned and moved as fast as I could across the marshy grass and pools of muddy water, waded through the reeds to the open water. A dozen strokes took me across and then I had a longer struggle to get back on firm ground. By the time I was trying to get back up the slope to the road I was exhausted. No adrenalin fuelled my body now, and I nearly didn't make it to the top. I kept slipping and tripping, but in the end I got there. On this side nobody paid any attention or even realised what had gone on in the river. They were trying to force open the door of the van to get to the woman who was still screaming inside it. The smell of petrol was stronger now, and I hoped there would not be an explosion.

The clasp on my helmet nearly defeated my cold wet fingers. I was filthy and uncomfortable and cold; all I could think of was to get home. I cast a last glance at the crash scene, turned the bike around and set out back towards Clive. As I coasted down the slope to the bike path, I saw a fire truck coming towards me from the Hastings direction with red lights flashing and sirens blaring. I felt a huge relief at the thought that the woman in the van would at least not burn in the wreck.

As soon as I got home, I called Helen and told her I would not be able to make it because the bridge was blocked by a crash. My phone rang before I had time to put it down. Andy sounded so normal and casual it made me smile despite the smelly mess I was in. "Would you like to go for coffee when you get back from Helen's?"

"I'm at home now, but I'm filthy. I have to get into the shower. Sorry, I'll call you later."

"You've not had an accident on the bike, have you?"

"No, not exactly, but I'm sopping wet, and covered in mud. I'll call you!"

I closed the call without saying goodbye, frantic to get into the shower. The smell of the river mud told me that something had decomposed in it quite recently. My cold, damp clothes clung to me, and I tore and struggled to get them off, my shoes were half full of muddy water. Everything was flung aside on the bathroom floor; a shower had rarely been so welcome. I scrubbed and shampooed and scrubbed again. I was standing in the shower with my eyes shut when I heard a voice.

"Shall I come in and join you or are you planning to come out sometime soon?"

Dimly through the steamed-up shower glass I saw Andy. "God, you gave me a fright! How long have you been standing there?"

"Come out and we'll talk."

I turned the water off and opened the door and grabbed my towel to dry the worst off before I stepped out. My damp skin did nothing to put him off. He gave me a hug and took the towel out my hand. "Hold your arms out." He dried my arms and sides and then continued down my body and legs until I was dry. I reached for my cotton robe and noticed that my filthy shoes and clothes were no longer scattered over the floor.

I had to laugh. "You're like some kind of good fairy who turns up and takes care of things every time I'm in trouble - I can't believe it. What did you do with my clothes?"

"A bit less of the fairy stuff, if you don't mind. I never saw such filthy gear – and smelly. I threw them outside on the grass and wiped the floor – what a mess."

We sat on the bed side by side with cups of tea and chocolate biscuits while I told him what had happened. He listened without comment until the story was finished.

"My God, your life is one long drama, isn't it? I could tell something traumatic had happened, you sounded desperate. So, I thought I'd better come and check for myself. I found the door wide open and a trail of smelly mud leading to the bathroom - and by the way, that door was open too, filthy clothes flung all over the place and you in the shower trying to scrub your skin off. But the smell told me why you had sounded desperate." He grinned. "But it was such a pleasure watching you out of the corner of my eye I didn't mind cleaning up the mess."

I put my hand on his thigh and gave him a squeeze. "I really was desperate - if I hadn't been able to shower that muck off me in the next few seconds, I would have been sick."

A little voice said, "Are you going to be sick Ca-cara?"

"Hi, Squeak. No, don't worry, I'm not going to be sick, I was just kidding. Come in and have a biscuit and meet Andy."

Squeak sat on my knee and ate his biscuits and then

wriggled off to leave. "What do you say Squeak?" And Squeak obediently said, "Thank you Ca-cara" and went outside again.

Andy was amused. "Why does he call you Ca-cara?"

"I think he got it wrong right at the start, and he hates being corrected - Pip is always telling him off. I don't think he ever stutters apart from when he says my name - it's just another of life's many mysteries."

Moira called about half past six, just as I was thinking of making something to eat. "Have you seen the news on TV?" She sounded as if she was worried about something again. "No? Then can you come round here right away, and we can watch the repeat of the news at seven. There's something you've got to see."

I ran over to Rusty's laundry and hauled my washing out, hung it to dry, then I rode to Moira's and arrived panting just before seven.

"Here!" she said and put a glass into my hand. "You might need this."

She led the way into the living room. The TV was on and the repeat screening of the six o'clock news was just about the start. "Sit down." She put a bowl of salted almonds on the little table and sat down in the chair on the other side. I took a sip of my wine and watched the news, mystified. The third item was about the crash on the bridge.

"Oh, no!" I hoped against hope that there would be nothing about me.

"Keep watching."

And there it was: someone on the Napier side of the crash had a perfect shot of me bounding down the slope, crossing the river and hauling the little girl out of the water. You could hear the voices of those closest to the phone quite clearly, despite the racket going on behind them. A man's voice: "What's she doing, oh my God - that's a baby, she's just pulled a baby out of the water."

A girl's voice, nearly shouting: "She must have seen it from the other side. And look at that!" She was commenting on the big man pulling me up onto the riverbank. The video must have been edited, the next shot was of me throwing myself into the water and crossing back to the side I had come from. The final image was a long view of the child being carried towards an ambulance.

The news reader was talking now. "According to the hospital in Hastings the little girl is unharmed but being kept in for observation. Her mother, who was trapped in the van, has two broken limbs and bruising. It seems that everyone was very lucky to get out of this alive. The driver of the other car is in a serious condition in hospital. Napier police say that nobody knows who the young woman is who rescued the baby. She was last seen riding her bike away from the crash scene."

Moira turned to me. "I have recorded it this time around. I'm sure your Andy would like to see it. And here you are looking as if the only dirt you had come across today was when you cleaned someone's house. I have never seen anyone as filthy as that last shot of you getting out of the river."

She looked across the little table at me and I could see that she was shaken by the whole thing. "You know you're a heroine, don't you? And this will attract a lot of attention, especially locally. Thank God that guy with the phone wasn't right up close and your filthy face was a pretty good disguise."

"You can't imagine the smell, the most sickening ever - like something rotting. I'm never going near that river again. But seriously, Moira, I feel really worried now. Being on TV is the last thing I need. I know I was filthy, and my hair is different now, of course - but still."

We looked at the recording twice and agreed that probably nobody, who hadn't expected to see me there, would recognise me. But I knew there were no certainties.

"There's still the drug baron. Wonder if he could recognise me? He's not seen me since I changed my hair. Or at least I don't think he has."

Moira shook her head. "I don't think there's much chance you'll be recognised. You were a girl with long blond hair, and this is a not very close-up video of a girl with short dark hair and a face splattered with mud. It would be a fantastic coincidence if anyone recognised you."

"But remember that somebody burgled the shed. And they were not after easily sold stuff - they were searching for something specific. They thought they'd find something to indicate where the money is, or who I am. They might even have thought that I had the money right there, in the shed."

Moira frowned and thought for a moment. "That could be it, but it doesn't mean that they still think you are the person they are after. Say that they found out that you are a new resident here, and they broke in to see if they could find out if you are who you say you are. And they found nothing to indicate that you are the one they are looking for so they might well be looking somewhere else by now."

I had to accept that her logic made sense. The people who burgled the shed would have found nothing to indicate they had found the right person. The only thing that might have aroused doubt would be that there was nothing that confirmed my identity one way or the other. But why would they expect to find anything like that anyway? People take their driver's licence and credit card with them when they go out. By the time I biked home I had begun to relax about it. Moira was probably right and the risk of anyone making the connection was remote.

I went to bed feeling exhausted again and fell asleep as soon as my head hit the pillow. I was woken by a light tapping on the door. Instantly alert I went to the door, touching the new security chain to make sure it was fastened. "Who is it?"

It was Andy who replied, so I unlocked the door and turned on the light once he was inside. "Sorry, I didn't mean to scare you, but I had to see you - we had the TV on in the kitchen for the news and I saw that video clip of you. I hadn't realised how incredible it was what you did."

He held me by my upper arms and gave me a little shake as if to emphasise what he was saying. "You didn't do yourself justice when you told me about it. Without you that kid would have sunk without a trace. Obviously, the people on the far side of the crash didn't see her?"

"No, I don't think they could, the reeds would have been in the way. I could only just see her from my end because I was sort of looking sideways into the reed bed. And when I first got across to the other side, I couldn't see her either. Not till I looked round, and by that stage she had sunk a lot more - there wasn't much of her above the surface."

"Yes, I saw you looking back towards your end of the bridge to get a bearing and then you went nearly straight to her. But the person holding the camera didn't see her at all until you lifted her right out of the water. Awesome!"

"I've been thinking about how she might have sunk there in the reeds, and would they ever have found her? It gives me the shivers. But the really incredible thing was the way she wasn't frightened once I pulled her out, no crying or anything."

I thought back to the moment when I got a good grip on her and held her tight, the way she had simply accepted me and seemed so calm. "It's a marvel that she didn't hit anything - she can't have been strapped in and then she got catapulted through an open window, don't you think? And did you see how she was still clutching that soft toy?"

He chuckled. "What a little survivor! Well, she's very lucky you came along and saw her. I bet her mother wants to thank you."

I shook my head. "No way, she'll have to wait. I don't want any attention beamed at me. It would turn into one of those sickening soppy things the papers and TV love."

He was looking at me with a slight frown. At first, I thought he was going to let it go, but he decided to bring it into the open. "Are you worried that whoever is trying to find you will see it and recognise you?"

I had to be honest. This was a real worry now and he had to accept that there was no way I could allow any publicity about me. "Yes, very worried, I can think of nothing more disastrous. It makes my skin crawl to think of it. Moira called and asked me to come over and watch it on TV. She thinks nobody would recognise me."

Andy's face changed just a fraction and he put his arms round me, but his voice was calm. "Well, that's OK then. I imagine once the first excitement is over, they won't show that clip again."

I wasn't as certain as he was, but then I had spent some time thinking about it. "So long as it doesn't end up on social media and YouTube because then people could look at it as many times as they wanted."

I shivered, even though his arms were around me, and he tightened his grip. "Back to bed - you've had too much happen in one day. I think you need a distraction."

. . .

In the morning I lay contentedly in the narrow bed with my head on Andy's shoulder watching the light slowly creeping around the corner and into the room. The curtains glowed with the increased light and the whole room took on a golden tone. I was waiting for Andy to wake up, but in the end, nature caught up with me and I had to go to the bathroom. When I got back, he was lying with his hands behind his head, looking thoughtful. I sat down on the edge of the bed and put a fingertip between his eyebrows. "You're frowning. What are you thinking about?"

"I really worry about this man who's trying to find you. I know you don't want to talk about it, but I'll be better equipped to deal with things, if I knew exactly what it is you fear he will do."

"It's not your problem - it's something I have to face alone. I can't let others take risks for me. Not that I don't think you can handle it, but it's so dangerous that I refuse to drag anyone else into it."

"But Moira knows something about it? You said she thought you wouldn't be recognised from that video clip."

Now I understood that look that had flitted across his face the previous evening and I had to decide how to phrase what I was about to say. The last thing I wanted was to insult him, but on the other hand I couldn't tell him the whole story either. It was hard to believe he was not straight up-and-down honest, but love can muddle your judgement, and he had turned up in a strange way. He might be connected to the criminal world and that he might have sought me out on purpose, so the situation we were now in had me teetering on a thin edge between suspicion and trust. I believed that he loved me, but I could not discount the possibility that he was also prepared to use me. So, in the end I compromised with another evasive lie. "Moira had someone come and ask for me. A man arrived on her doorstep and described someone he was looking for, he said he thought she might have stayed at Moira's a short time ago. He described me as I used to look."

"Yes? Was that it?"

"No, because I had already explained to her that I was trying to avoid being found, so she told this guy that nobody of that description had stayed at her place, and he went away."

The irony of this statement made me smile despite my problems. "And I must admit she was telling the truth, she had not had a guest who fitted his description, because I look different now. But she knew he was looking for me and he scared her."

I thought of how badly his visit had affected her and how upset she had been when she told me about it. I must make Andy understand this and the responsibility I felt. "I would do anything to undo the fear she felt when he came. If it hadn't been for me, she wouldn't be in that situation. I know that fear well - I have stood in front of him and felt sick with apprehension, knowing that violence was a second away. But I can't undo what's happened."

I was glad that I had avoided having to lie and say that Moira didn't know the details, because of course she did. Andy looked thoughtful and serious, but he let it go. His hand gripped mine and all he said was, "Just remember that I'm ready to help you in any way I can. You're not alone, even if you won't share the risk. There are things that I can do to protect you that you probably can't or won't do yourself. I know how to fight, and it might put him off if he realises that you are not on your own."

16

When I was setting out for Helen's the next morning Rusty came running out of her back door just as I reached the gate. "Hey, Cara - wait!"

She took hold of the handlebar as if she thought I would ride off right in front of her. "Cara, I saw it on the news last night, but when I got home from Charlene's you were in bed and I didn't want to wake you up. I can't believe I know someone who's famous."

"Oh, for heaven's sake Rusty, of course I'm not famous. All this will be forgotten in a week. It was just something that happened, and I was there and saw it, that's all."

"Of course, it won't, you're a hero. Charlene and I nearly had a fight about which one of us was going to call Bernie and tell him we know who you are. It's so exciting, I can't believe it happened right here."

They say that in extreme situations your blood 'runs cold' and at that moment I could vouch for the truth of that. It felt as if icy water was coursing through my veins instead or warm blood. Of course, I should have known that in a small community, things are different and news travels fast between households.

"Who is Bernie?"

"He's the dad of that little girl you saved from drowning. His wife was in the van and that little tot got thrown out and over the bridge rail and into the water without hitting anything. They say it's a miracle."

I had to think fast. Very likely a few others in the village recognised me, but they would not necessarily know where I lived or what name I went under. Perhaps it would blow over. I would have to endure being thanked and hugged, but it might pass without adding to the risk of discovery.

"Sorry Rusty, I have to dash, I'm due at a cleaning job in Napier. Do you think you could ask Bernie not to make too much fuss about this? I don't mean it isn't important that his little girl is all right, but I don't want it to be about me, I really don't."

Rusty looked at me as if I'd lost my mind. Not to grab my fifteen minutes of fame? To pass up a chance of instant glory? But she said kindly, as if she was humouring me, "OK, I'll tell him. If you get asked for too many TV interviews, I can go instead of you."

She was so excited and happy that it seemed a shame to dampen her enthusiasm, but I couldn't explain my reasons. I could tell that she was disappointed with my reaction, but there was nothing more I could say.

The bridge showed clear signs of damage. There was orange plastic mesh filling a gap in the barrier where the van had hit and skid marks and fluorescent paint on the road. Little pieces of glass and plastic glittered along the edges.

I slowed and looked down at the riverbank and the thick edging of tall reeds where I had seen what I thought was a bundle of clothes. A shudder went down my spine. If she had sunk and drowned yesterday, then I might have crossed the bridge today not knowing that she was down there, hidden in the reeds under the murky water. The thought of that little body slowly sinking into the cold mud was heartbreaking. God knows how long it would have taken to find her or if they ever would have.

Helen was full of questions about the rescue of the child and why I had left like I did. I stalled her by saying that I had been so cold and dirty that my total focus had been getting home and into a hot shower. I added that with my bike and bag on the far side of the crash I had worried that someone would steal my bag, so I had made my way back by the only means available. Eventually she let me get on with the cleaning, but later in the morning I heard her talking about it on the phone, the story was that day's hot topic.

When I started out on the ride home, I was intensely worried. There must be dozens of people who had recognised me as Cara and who were, even as I rode home, busy telling others that they knew me. I could not stop this from spreading because it was just the sort of thing people love to talk about: a dramatic rescue, a small child and a rescuer who rides off into the sunset. The more attention given to the story, the more likely that the press would follow up and search me out.

By the time I reached Clive I was in a muddle of indecision. My instincts told me to flee and just vanish again, but my common sense told me I might not get away with it. Now that my disguise was recognised by so many, I would have to start the process all over again, but could I change my appearance enough? I went straight to Moira's place, leaned the bike against the fence and walked around to the back of the house.

She was sitting at the dining table cleaning silver with the French doors open to the terrace, listening to the radio. Seeing her there so quiet and content made me stop and consider the risk to her, if I involved her in any way. Simply by being at her place I was dragging her into my tangled life and exposing her to danger. I turned around to slip away before she noticed me, to disappear out of her life for the time being and leave the district somehow. But just at that moment she looked up, saw me standing on the lawn and came out with a smile of welcome. "Hi Cara, have you recovered?"

"I don't know - I'm so worried and I don't want to drag you into it, but I don't know what to do." For a dreadful moment I thought I was going to cry, but I managed to pull myself together.

Moira studied my face for a moment and said calmly, "Come in and we'll make a cold drink. You look hot and frazzled." She led the way to the kitchen, and I sat at the table in that familiar and comforting space watching her make a jug of lemon and water with mint and ice. She put it on the table in front of me. "Why don't you get some glasses - and the biscuits? I'll be back in a moment."

She went out and I heard her checking the lock on the front door and then closing the doors to the terrace.

She came back and poured us each a glass of lemon drink. "Now then - it's clear that your sudden fame is back-firing in some way. You look shattered, but whatever it is, remember what I said before - if you need to disappear you can come here. We can do it so nobody finds out."

"We can't, Moira! It's everywhere - they're all talking about it. Any moment now someone will turn up at the shed with a camera and a microphone. And being on TV in close-up and with a clean face would be the last straw. But I can't think of how to get away, I've been thinking about it all day at Helen's, and I don't think it can be done. I can't disguise myself very much now – my hair is already short and ..."

She held her hand up and I fell silent. "Stop, Cara - slow down. I'm sure we can figure something out. I've been thinking about this ever since you told me your story, about what to do, if things went wrong. I think it's a pretty good plan - if we talk through it together, we'll find the weak spots."

"Have you? God, Moira – you're amazing. But I don't see how I can disappear without someone catching on. I feel as if there's a searchlight trained on me wherever I go. I'm really worried someone will turn up with a camera and want to interview me."

"Never mind, just listen to this and tell me what you think." She poured more drink into my glass and leaned forward with her elbows on the table.

"What we need to do is to make it seem that you've simply done a runner – that's the crux of it. Not to have you being seen at the bus station or the airport, but just vanish. If people think that you've simply taken off there is no need for me or anyone to explain how that could have been achieved. You disappear tonight, leaving your bike and most of your stuff behind in the shed. Just take a few clothes and whatever you would take if you left in a hurry without a suit-case. Make it seem as if you grabbed the most vital things and ran - hitchhiked maybe. So, you can't take your suitcase or anything you bought for the shed. And if I'm asked, I'll say that I didn't know you were planning to leave and I am baffled."

I sat mesmerised, holding a biscuit in one hand and the glass in the other; both forgotten, while she explained the plan.

"This is how you do it - you leave very quietly in the dark, just walk away from Rusty's and I pick you up."

"Someone will see me, or you - they're bound to."

"No, I don't think so. You will walk to the next street corner from Rusty's as if you are going towards the river. Turn right at the corner and cross that street and there is the path that leads to the green. You know where this is, just a little lane that runs between the houses?"

I nodded. I had gone for a run there a couple of times when I was newly settled at Rusty's. It was a path just wide enough for two people to meet and it went through the block and opened out into the green.

"Well, that path goes past the side of my friend Pat's place and she's overseas for another week or two. There's a gate in her fence along the path, so you can go into her garden either from that side or from the street. I went and tried the gate after you told me your story. I thought it might be locked while they're away, but it's not. So, within a couple of minutes of leaving Rusty's, you can be in Pat's garden and nobody will have seen you in that lane in the dark. I'll come past and pick you up from her street gate."

I tried to think of what it looked like, but I hadn't even noticed that there was a gate into one of the properties along the path. "Good lord, did you really think of this back then, that I might need an escape route?"

"Yes, I had a horrid feeling that this might develop into something worse. And I can't fight or shoot people, so I thought the best I could do was to have a plan for how to spirit you away. With that path and Pat's place being empty it was just perfect."

She drew a little map for me to make sure that I knew exactly where the place was. The relief was huge; a much better solution than any I had been able to think of.

"That sounds as if it would work, I think. And then you

can drive me to a bus station somewhere a bit further away, perhaps Dannevirke or Taupo, and I can move on from there. Would you mind doing that?"

She shook her head. "What? Are you mad? As you said yourself, you can't even change your appearance again now that you've already cut your hair short. And if the drug baron sees you again on TV, he might recognise you. But isn't the safest thing to stay here, invisible in my house and let everyone think you've left Clive?"

She was right and in the back of my mind I knew it. "But I must get as far away from him as I can – he thinks I can lead him to the money. Or he thinks he can force me to tell him where it is - which I can't, but it's impossible to prove. If I stay here, you're as much in danger as I am."

It made me shudder to think of what he could do to me and how he might punish Moira for hiding me. I had no way of proving that I knew nothing about the money. He was brutal and ruthless, and he did not like being crossed.

"Listen, with all this publicity and if you seemingly disappear, he will assume that you've left the district. I don't think trying to really leave is a good idea. For a start, where would you go? Who would you stay with? I'm sorry to add to your worries, but I saw him again in Napier. I don't think he would expect you to be still in Clive, if you just vanish from your place and leave a note for Rusty saying you're hitch-hiking north. Word would spread and if he asks people, they'll say you've done a runner."

"When did you see him, and where?"

"The day before yesterday. He didn't recognise me, but I knew him straight away. He was at an outside café table in the main street with a chubby blonde."

"I saw her one day! She was driving a Mercedes like the one that followed me around in Auckland and I had a look, but when I saw it was a woman driving, I thought it was just another car like it."

That settled it in my mind. I had to disappear out of sight and my best chance was to go along with Moira's plan however much I did not want her caught up in this. We went through the plan again and then one more time. We rehearsed the route and the way I would get into her car practically while it was still moving and how I would be unloaded in her garage and get into the house unnoticed. As far as Moira was concerned nothing was going to be left to chance.

"We've got to get this absolutely right - no improvising. And what about Andy? He's going to go crazy when he can't find you – it's quite obvious he's in love with you. I saw the way he looked at you when you came over that night. I don't want him coming round here banging on the door in full view of the neighbours. We must have a sort of separation between him and this place, so nobody thinks there is a connection."

She was right again. Andy and I had been to her house together just that one time and it was unlikely that anybody had noticed our visit. We had never been seen anywhere together, all three of us. But we could not keep Andy out of the escape plan. I knew he wouldn't sit still and wait to see what developed if he could not find me. He would take matters into his own hands; his determination and energy would drive him to take action and heaven only knew where that might lead. The last thing I wanted was for him to draw attention and danger to himself by starting some sort of search for me.

Moira was studying me across the kitchen table, waiting for me to come to grips with this. She knew without that in regard to Andy I had to make my own decision. I went to the bathroom, washed my hands and stood for a long time looking at my refection in the mirror and thinking, but there could only be one answer.

I returned to the kitchen. "OK, you're right. I think Andy would do something, but I haven't a clue what that might be. He's very proactive and not one to simply sit back and wait, so we have to tell him. But at the same time, we must keep him from being seen coming here – what do you think we should do?"

She thought about it while she tidied things off the table. I tried to reason through it. "Is there a way for him to come into the back garden without using the gate or the garage? Or should we ban him from your house. and I just talk to him on the phone? Or maybe I could meet him somewhere at night?"

"I think one thing has to be clear, Cara, if this is going to work. You must stay in the house *all the time*, and you can't go out even in the middle of the night and you can't be in the garden. You've got to stay inside and out of sight. If I have guests staying you have to stay in my bedroom and use my bathroom and not move around in the house at all. Thank God I never hired a cleaner. I haven't got any guests coming for a few days, so we're OK for a little while."

"But what about Andy?"

"I'm sure he can come here if we are really careful about how we arrange it. He comes back from work so late and nobody would find it odd to see him around long after dark. He could even go home, turn his lights on and walk here. But we can't risk that anybody sees him coming to this house."

. . .

And that's how we left it. I went home and I was no sooner inside than Rusty was on my doorstep, full of exciting plans.

"Oh, there you are - I've been waiting and waiting. Bernie's family would like you to go to see them so they can thank you and show you the little girl - tomorrow morning about eleven if you can. I hope you will, they're so keen to see you and they wouldn't have known where to find you if I hadn't told them."

She was pleased with herself and sure that I would agree, and I did. I smiled and tried to sound as if I had thought better of it during the day. "You're right. Better to let them thank me and feel they've done the right thing, and then we can all get on with our lives."

She beamed at me, said she would call them right away and went back to the house. It was cruel to deceive her; she was a lovely cheerful girl and she had been a good friend to me, but I couldn't take her into my confidence. I closed the door and started my preparations.

Into my big canvas satchel went toiletries, makeup and Andy's book followed by as many clothes as I could cram in, then I tied my jacket and a pair of trainers to the strap and that was that. My tablet and memory stick were already safe at Moira's place. I filled the wheeled suitcase with the rest of my clothes and books to be retrieved at some later date, and then I took the last money bag out of the cereal box. Cash had continued to accumulate and now there was just over four hundred dollars in the bag again. I put the money bag on the table with a short note to Rusty.

"Dear Rusty

I'm sorry to have to trick you and leave like this, but I don't want any more publicity. Sometime in the future I might be able to explain why I have to do this. I will hitchhike north tonight. The money in the bag is for you. I have packed my clothes and things I want to keep in the suitcase and perhaps you could keep that for me until I can get someone to pick it up. You can have the bike and the other things - they might come in useful for your next tenant. Thank you for being so kind to me, I have been very happy here. Please give the boys a hug from Ca-cara."

I tidied up a bit, stripped the bed and left the sheets folded. There was little else I could do apart from wait for time to pass. I pulled the curtains across the windows, turned the light on and tried to read but my attention wandered. I wondered if I should warn Andy by text, but I suspected that a message now might prompt him to come straight back and upset all our plans, so I left it for later.

At half past ten I turned the light off and sat in the dark, nervous and tense, trying to keep my mind busy. At twenty-five to eleven Moira texted that she would be cruising past Pat's gate in exactly ten minutes. She would turn her headlights off as she came around the corner and she would indicate a left turn as she approached Pat's driveway.

I put the key on the table, picked up my bag and walked through the dark garden for the last time, leaving the shed door unlocked. The lights in Rusty's house were off and her bedroom curtain was pulled across. I stood for a moment by her gate looking left and right before I ventured out onto the street. It was completely quiet, and I could see nobody in either direction. After walking rapidly to the corner and crossing the street, I found the start of the path to the green and turned in. The whole process only took a couple of minutes.

I found the gate to Pat's garden, pulled it quietly closed behind me and walked carefully around the dark house. The unfamiliar dark garden was full of hazards; Pat was obviously fond of large planters and pots. I bumped into a one or two, but without falling or making noises that might alarm the neighbours. Where the driveway ended a medium-sized tree cast a dense shadow, perfect for me to stand and wait. A few minutes later a car came quietly down the street with only parking lights on. It indicated a left turn, I stepped out and Moira slowed to a stop. I got into the car with my bag in one fast move and she drove away after a pause of only a few seconds.

"Did it go all right?"

"Yes, fine – there was nobody around at all."

She turned her headlights on as we rounded the next corner and accelerated away. At her house the door to the garage was open, she drove straight in and closed the roller door from the outside. I stood waiting in the dark garage and after a couple of minutes she unlocked the door that opened into the back garden. I let out a huge sigh of relief when we were inside the house. Some lights were on, and the curtains pulled across.

"I left the house the way I always do if I'm out at night - I didn't want anything to look different." She laughed a bit at her own cunning. "I even took the car out of the garage just before it got dark and parked it a couple of blocks away - left the garage open like I do when I go out for the evening, but I sneaked back to wait until it was time to pick you up. So, the neighbours haven't heard me go out at half past ten at night and then come back nearly straight away."

When she first told me about her plan she had said 'we only have once chance to get this right'. I was very lucky to have a friend like her.

"Did you eat anything after you left here? No?" She got a can of soup out of the pantry. "Toast?"

"Yes, please. I'm going to text Andy, so he doesn't go to the shed on his way home."

He was due to finish at midnight, but there was always a chance they would close earlier. I sent him a message and said that I had left the shed and would be in touch in the morning. On second thoughts I added that I had left a note for Rusty telling her I had left town, but I was at Moira's place.

17

Moira was determined that no chance carelessness would reveal that I was in the house. "If I'm out you mustn't go too close to any of the windows on the street side of the house. I think the kitchen window is OK unless the light is on – we put tinted glass there when we double-glazed that side. I'll check it, but I'm fairly sure people can't see in unless the light is on." Moira looked a bit embarrassed when she continued. "I hope we'll never need to resort to hiding, but it's best to be prepared. It seems a bit dramatic, but you should know just in case. We have a 'safe room' – otherwise known as the attic."

She took me to the passage leading to her bedroom and stopped by the linen cupboard and pointed up and there in the ceiling was a large trapdoor that I had never noticed before.

"James and I never thought of it as a safe space of course, but now it's perfect. I'll show you how to do it."

She took what looked like a broom handle from the corner by her bedroom door and showed me the hook at one end. "You use this stick - just hook it through the loop on the trapdoor. All you have to do it pull a tiny bit and then the spring mechanism takes over and lets the stair down. And it's very quiet. Listen!"

She put the hook through the loop on the door and pulled. Nearly instantly the trapdoor opened downwards by itself and a wooden stepladder in two telescoped sections slid silently down until it rested at an angle to the floor. "Isn't it great? James put it in when we renovated so we could store things and get up there without having to balance on ladders. Look, it's even got a kind of low handrail."

She pointed upwards with the stick. "Do you see that orange bit of rope on the left? If you are up there and want to close it you only have to pull on that rope, just a tug. And then the springs do the rest, and it closes itself. And it's very quiet."

Moira gave the ladder a little upwards push, let go and the whole thing closed up again like magic. She turned around pointing the stick at me: "If you are here on your own and someone breaks in you will hear them. We'll leave the stick right here and all you have to do is get up there, take the stick with you and then pull on that cord. It would only take a minute and because it's so quiet I don't think an intruder would hear it and come running from the other end of the house to see what's going on. Provided they don't break in at this end, of course. And we'll keep all your clothes and toiletries in my bedroom and bathroom. That way there's nothing in any other room to show that you're staying here."

We were heading back to the kitchen when the phone rang, we both jumped. All the talk about intruders and hiding in the attic had made us nervous. Moira picked up the phone and listened for a moment. "Hi Andy – yes, here she is."

She handed the phone me and left the kitchen and I sat down at table. "Andy, where are you?"

He sounded tired. "I'm at my place. What happened? Something must have gone wrong, are you OK?"

"Yes, I'm fine, don't worry. I'll tell you all about it when I see you. Moira has really saved me - she had a whole emergency plan that I didn't even know about - I'm perfectly safe for now. You sound as if you need some sleep. We'll catch up tomorrow – call me in the morning. But you can't come here until we work out a plan."

"OK, take care of yourself."

I should have known. His tendency to take charge and sort things out made it impossible for him to not to do what he felt had to be done. Moira and I were still sitting in the kitchen, talking and drinking more wine than was good for us, when there was a tapping sound from somewhere. Moira leapt to her feet. "God, what was that? Did you hear it?"

Then it came again, slightly more insistent and Moira said firmly, "Stay here!" and left the kitchen. I heard her open the terrace door and the next moment she appeared in the kitchen with Andy behind her.

"It's as they say - you can't keep a good man down. He did exactly what we worked out might be a good way to get here - he walked, sneaked round the side of the garage and into the back garden."

"And please note the dark clothing, the baseball cap, every care taken to make me anonymous and invisible." Andy was trying to be light-hearted, but his eyes were serious. And there was no joking when I told him why I had left the shed. I had to tell him enough to make him understand my reasons for leaving, but I wasn't ready to be completely frank.

"Moira saw the man who's trying to find me - in Napier a couple of days ago. And with me on TV it seemed too risky to stay in the shed. Though I look different now he might have recognised me and if he did, he would only need to ask around. By now everyone in the village must know where I live - and Rusty had organised a meeting with the parents of that little girl. I'm sure they will have the press there, so I had to get away. A photo in the paper or on TV would be the last straw."

"OK – and what did you tell Rusty? Will she suspect that you're here at Moira's?"

He was satisfied when I told him what I had put in the note for Rusty. "That sounds OK. And I can say I'm stunned you've disappeared if they ask me why you left."

He stayed with me in Moira's private guest room and left at dawn to go back to his own place before it got light.

Over the next few days, we led a strange life. Andy would turn up after work, having made his way through the neighbourhood like a thief in the night. He let us know when he was coming and varied his routes, even crossed people's back gardens in the dark of the night. Moira gave him a key to the terrace door so he could come in without waiting outside. He left very early, before it was light, and went back to his flat.

"How do you cope? I can't imagine how you do it." Moira was expecting signs of exhaustion, but he just laughed. "It's like shift work, you get used to it."

On days when Moira had guests I stayed in her bedroom, keeping very quiet and only talked to Andy on the phone while Moira carried on her normal life. A couple of times the three of us played Scrabble, Moira and I watched movies and talked about our lives both past and present.

She heard bits of gossip in the village and reported back that Rusty was devastated that I had left so suddenly. Bernie and his family had been waiting for us to arrive, with a reporter and a photographer from the local paper and a TV news crew in the house. Poor Rusty had to call and tell them that I had vanished during the night and gone back to Auckland.

Gradually Andy found out more about why I was on the run. It was inevitable that I became less guarded when we all spent so much time together. But I never forgot that perhaps I just confirmed what he already knew. I still did not know if he was what he seemed or something else altogether.

One evening, when we were having a cup of tea in the kitchen, Moira referred to the 'drug baron'. Andy's reaction was instant. He looked hard at me across the table without saying a word and there was silence for a minute. Moira realised straight away what she had done, and I was thinking fast about what I would say, but in the end, there was only one way of dealing with it.

"All right, I will tell you," I said and looked straight into Andy's unflinching blue eyes that had never left my face while I was thinking; now I had to be honest.

"I know you thought that I was running from a dangerous ex-lover or a stalker or something of that kind. But it was really nothing at all to do with me personally. I had a boarder who was murdered - he was gunned down in front of me in the street where I live. It seems certain that he was involved in some kind of drug racket. I'm not sure what it was, but it involved huge amounts of money. I think he was killed because he had cheated some very nasty people and stolen money from them. Or maybe he had tricked them in some way – whatever it was they killed him for it."

Andy asked nothing, just continued to look at me silently. I had no idea what he was thinking; his face told me nothing. "There is so much I don't know. I can't figure out why they killed him before they found where he had hidden the money - if that's what he had done. Maybe they thought he had left it in my flat and they killed him before he could hide it or take off with it. The head guy is a very dangerous man – he's the one Moira and I call the drug baron. He is the one who came looking for me here."

Now Andy interrupted. "I remember the shooting on the TV news. But why are they after you?"

"I'm sure they thought Nick had the money hidden in my flat. You see, they knew something that I had never understood - Nick really lived somewhere else. He just used my flat as his secret place - when I thought he was on the road as salesman, he was elsewhere doing God knows what."

"OK, but why are they chasing you, if the money was not kept at your place?"

"They thought I was lying when I said it wasn't there. There is no way of proving a negative. There's someone in the police force who tells them things - so they knew the police hadn't found any money at my place. They thought I had hidden it somewhere. Or maybe they thought I knew where it was and that I was waiting to be able to get to it."

I paused for a moment, quickly assessing how much to tell him. "They harassed me and followed me wherever I went and when I couldn't give them what they wanted they beat me up. And the drug baron told me that the police thought I might have that money too - everyone was after me."

Moira said urgently, "It was even worse than that, Andy.

The scariest thing is that the drug baron told Cara to find an article from a couple of years ago about a woman they had doused with petrol and burnt alive. Apparently for some offence or other that she had committed against them. They are ruthless and brutal."

She paused for a moment and glanced at me. "Cara couldn't ask her friends to hide her. It would have been too risky, and it would put them in danger too. She's had to do incredible things to protect herself and to prevent anyone from being able to trace her. What we can't understand is how he got on her trail and came to look for her here."

Andy frowned. "It seems nearly impossible. The chance of being found, when you are living like this, hidden in the black economy, not driving a car – I don't get it. Maybe someone who knows you saw you in town and recognised you - even before you were on TV after that bridge incident?"

Moira interrupted him. "But what are the chances of that? And how would it have got to the drug baron? We thought of it, but it would have to be the most incredible coincidence."

"I agree - it seems impossible. And they obviously can't have found you because of the video clip on TV about the bridge crash, because the burglary happened before that. And that must have been them; it can't just be coincidence that you get burgled while they're trying to find out where that money is. And it fits with the way that they took nothing, just searched the place."

I watched and listened carefully; some nuance might tell me if he already knew it all or if he was hearing the story for the first time. I was beginning to think he was genuine, but my paranoia would not let me totally believe it. And I never really stopped thinking about how I had been tracked to

Clive. It had that enervating quality of having happened despite seeming impossible.

The next evening, when we were sitting in the kitchen talking after Moira had gone to bed, I brought up our discussion from the river path. "Andy, do you remember when I said there was something about you that I just had to take at face value, because I couldn't figure out what it was that seemed odd?"

"Yes, I do. Do you still feel that way?"

"I know there's something and I still don't know what it is, but at least now I don't think it is because you're involved with the drug baron."

I didn't say that I still wondered if he knew about the money and was playing a confidence trickster's waiting game. He stared at me for a long moment and when he responded he sounded incredulous.

"Do you mean to tell me that you thought I might be someone the drug baron had sent, some criminal trying to find out what you had done with that money? And you let me make love to you?"

I shrugged and nodded. "Yep - I decided that if you turned out to be a criminal, I would leave you, but it would still have been worth it. I mean the experience of having been with you would be worth it. But I would walk away."

"Really?"

"Yes, really! Of course, I would. It would be very hard to do, but at least I would have something to remember."

He got up and pulled me to my feet and held me close, speaking into my hair. "Incredible - nobody has ever felt that way about me before. But I promise you that I'm not one of the drug baron's men."

Now was the moment to spring the big question. "So why do you have a gun?"

His whole body stiffened, and he pushed me away so he

could look at me. He had the strangest look on his face. "You think I carry a gun?"

"I saw it - yesterday morning when you were getting dressed to go back to your place. You took it out from under your baseball cap on the chair and put it in your jacket pocket,."

His mind must have been replaying the scene in his head. The room had been nearly dark, and he had thought I was asleep, and now I had told him that I had known about the gun for more than twenty-four hours. The issue lay like a hand grenade on the floor between us and he did not know if the pin was still in it or not. I knew it was a harsh way of dealing with it, but I had to see his reaction.

"I don't normally carry it. I have a licence for a handgun because I belong to a gun club in Auckland. I do a lot of target practice. Until you left Rusty's place and came here, I kept it in a locked case in my flat. But I think being armed could be useful right now."

"Would you really use it?"

He looked surprised and smiled briefly. "Of course, I would. If someone threatened you, I would certainly use it. Waving a gun around, if you can't bring yourself to use it, would just add to the danger. And I have no idea what we are up against here, so now I carry it. It is under my baseball cap on that chair when we're in bed so I can reach it fast if something happens."

I sensed an attitude that I had occasionally glimpsed in him before, some kind of internal focus. It reminded me of something that I could not put my finger on.

He reached behind him and put his hand up under his sweatshirt and pulled the gun out. "I have it with me all the time - when we're up and dressed, I tuck it in at the back of my jeans - hoping you won't feel it. No point in having it if I can't get it out fast." He handed me the gun, butt end first. "Here it is. Do you know how to use a gun?"

I took it and was surprised at how light it was. "It feels like a toy!"

"It's a Glock, a semi-automatic pistol, sometimes called the plastic gun."

"I once shot with an air rifle at a target when I was a teenager. What would happen if I picked this up and fired it at the drug baron? Do you think I could hit him?"

He smiled in genuine amusement, for the first time for what seemed like ages. "If you hit him it would either be because he was standing no more than a couple of meters away and stood really still - or possibly because you aimed at something else and hit him by accident. Mind you, it's got eight bullets in the magazine so you could always try again."

Now I smiled too. "I think I'd better leave the shooting to you then."

He shook his head in a baffled way and put the gun away. "And you are going to taking this in your stride? Along with everything else, like me possibly being a criminal? I can't believe it – no scenes, no panic?"

I liked the way he put it. "Yep - I'm a bit surprised myself that I am so philosophical about it. But what else can I do? My life is so strange now – I come up against things that make me feel I am living someone else's life. I have to take things as they come and deal with them the best way I can. I can't change much of what's happening to me. All I can do is to think forward and plan well and be prepared for the worst."

18

The day was cool with light drizzle, I felt restless and unmotivated. Moira had gone to comfort a friend, who had run over her own dog on her driveway and Andy was at work. The house was very quiet. I was in Moira's bathroom cleaning my teeth after lunch when the doorbell rang. I went down the passage from the bedroom, taking care to stay out of sight of the windows, and stopped just clear of the door to the kitchen. I stood still and listened for a minute and heard nothing. Then the handle of the terrace door rattled. My heart was in my mouth and for a moment I was frozen to the spot. The idea of running out the front door flashed through my mind. Then he shook the terrace door hard. I had one moment to act, while he was still on the terrace.

I ran down the passage, past the open doors of the guest rooms and grabbed the stick leaning into the corner by the linen cupboard. My hands shook, I missed the loop, the hook slid along the ceiling, and I had to take aim again. This time it engaged, I gave a tug on the stick and the trapdoor did its spring-loaded thing; the steps slid down and I went up them like a scalded cat. I threw the stick on the attic floor and yanked on the orange rope. The springs once again did their job, the steps telescoped its sections together, the trap-door shut, and I was left in nearly total darkness.

My heart was pounding. I listened intently, but there was no sound apart from my pulse echoing in my ears. Very slowly I knelt on the board floor and bent forward to listen for sounds from below. Still nothing, but I stayed in that position, too tense to move. And then a sharp cracking noise somewhere not too far away, not a sound I could identify. Silence for a couple of minutes and then he opened the door to the linen cupboard directly below me, no more than a couple of meters away. The door shut again, and I heard nothing for a few minutes until the distant sound of a door slamming made me jump.

Dreadful images of Moira having come back and being confronted by the drug baron instantly popped into my head. But the silence continued and after a few minutes I decided that the sound of the door could have been the intruder leaving through the front door, slamming it behind him. I cursed the fact that I never carried my mobile phone around in the house, but there was nothing I could do, I couldn't warn Moira. I failed to open the trapdoor, I pushed it but nothing happened. I had to stay in the attic until Moira returned an hour later.

Poor Moira got a terrible fright when she walked down the passage toward her bedroom, and I called out from the attic. But her fright turned to laughter when she realised I was up there in the dark and did not know how to open the door from the attic end. "You poor thing – I hope you haven't been there very long! Just feel along the edge of the door where you stepped off the ladder. Slide your hand along towards the centre of the hatch and find the little toggle thing. Push it hard."

The ladder opened up and I came down the steps blinking in the light. "It's dark up there and I didn't have my phone."

"There is a light switch on the vertical beam next to the trapdoor – I forgot to tell you. It's quite low down so you can turn it on and off while you're on the steps. Were you practising?"

But when I told her that this had been the real thing her face went pale.

"Good lord!" She set off toward the kitchen and I heard her check that the front door was locked and then the terrace door. I went around checking windows and found the answer in Moira's bathroom.

"Moira, come and have a look at this!"

The bathroom had a full-sized window with opaque glass and it had been left open that morning, held by one of those safety catches that you can only open fully from inside. But the catch was undone and dangling from the window frame. "Look," said Moira and pointed. "He's wrenched off the piece that was screwed to the window frame."

"That would be the crack I heard from the attic - and then getting in was as easy as walking through a door."

I closed the window and hooked up the ordinary little catches and Moira said suddenly, "I bet he looked in all the rooms. Is your bed made?"

A chill went down my back and I knew I had slipped up. "Yes, but my book and my phone are on the bedside table. Oh God - now he knows you're not living here alone."

. . .

My chest tightened and once again I experienced that awful feeling that my only option was to set out alone into the unknown; this time with my pursuer very close behind me. Moira got the drift right away. "Oh no!" she said forcefully. "No way! It wouldn't work. We'll wait until Andy gets here and make a plan."

We left the attic steps down and put the stick on the attic floor so we could get up there with no delays and just pull the steps up and spent the rest of the day in the kitchen with the door to the bedroom passage open. We were apprehensive and it was hard to keep up a normal conversation. Neither of us wanted to call Andy and tell him, because we knew he would leave work and come straight away. Every so often one of us would say something and then add, "I wish Andy was here".

When dusk approached, I could wait no longer. "I'm going to call Andy - we have to warn him, so he doesn't run into the drug baron on his way. I'll call him now and tell him what happened. And I'll say that we'll have the attic steps down and ready so we can get up there really quickly if we have to."

Moira nodded. "OK – why don't you tell him to approach from the street behind us? The house he's looking for is the one with no front fence and no trees on the front lawn. It backs on to my garden and he'll be able to come down the side of that house and get over the fence - just in case someone's watching from our street."

I knew what she was thinking. The drug baron would have thought the house was empty when he broke in. If he was watching he would have seen Moira return and now he would be waiting for me to turn up too. If he never saw Andy come in, it was all for the better.

I got a 'not available' message from Andy's phone and left him a long message, then sent a text as well.

"Did you get him?"

"No, his phone is off. I've left a message and sent a text. I hope he hasn't got a flat battery and comes along without having got my messages."

"He probably has the phone turned off for some reason – remember the other day, when you thought something was wrong, and he had turned it off by mistake. Let's take our books and go up in the attic now. We can sit on the old packing crates. I put a couple of those small torches up there so we don't have to have the big light on – I don't know if it would show around the edges of the trapdoor."

We made ourselves comfortable in the attic, but neither of us could concentrate on reading. Intermittently we talked quietly, but most of the time we just listened for anything happening in the house. After a while I began to worry about not having heard back from Andy and then I realised that I had left my phone on the kitchen table.

"How stupid! I've left the phone in the kitchen. If Andy's called back, he'll worry about why I'm not answering. I'll run down and get it."

Moira lowered the steps, and I ran to the kitchen, and picked up the phone. I had one missed call and a text.

At exactly the moment when I walked through the door from the kitchen to the hall, still looking down at the phone, there was a crash of broken glass from the dining room.

I yelled, "Pull the steps up, quick!" and headed for the front door. Footsteps pounded through the dining room. As I turned the knob to open the front door someone was so close that I imagined I could feel the air moving round the approaching body. Right behind me a man's voice shouted, 'I'll get her'.

I went out that door so fast that it felt like flying, down the path and out onto the street, turned right and went for it. Thoughts flew through my mind like scattered birds taking off in different directions. *Thank God I've got shoes on, I hope Moira got the trapdoor shut, does she have her phone so she can warn Andy, I hope those men didn't hear what I called out to Moira, don't think they would have got the words, they were making so much noise, wish I didn't have this pale sweatshirt on, do I dare run up to a house and knock on the door, no, stupid idea.*

It seemed as if I was running at the speed of light through the dark evening; a blur of fences and hedges whizzing past, sort of out of focus. It was fully dark now and a light rain was falling. I knew I had made the right decision, running out instead of trying to get up the attic steps. They would have caught me or grabbed the steps and stopped them folding up.

I was much further ahead of him now, still running at top speed, but he was losing ground. He's not used to running, I thought, he'll soon be tired out, those stomping footsteps sound as if he's flat footed.

I turned corners without thinking, went down a narrow lane between two properties, slowed and realised I could no longer hear him. I ran the length of another block, turned into a gateway without slowing and came to a stop behind a shrub at the side of a garage. I leaned against the wall, trying to control my panting breaths. My lungs were sucking in air, desperate for oxygen and my heart was pounding. There was no sound from the street, all I heard was my own rasping breaths.

. . .

I gave it a few minutes to make sure, peeled off my pale blue sweatshirt and dropped it on the ground. Now my clothes were all dark; black tights and dark blue T-shirt; only my shoes a lighter colour. I waited until my heart rate slowed and I felt I could run really fast again if I had to. I left my hiding place and walked cautiously down the short drive-way. There was nobody to be seen in either direction. I walked along at a normal pace, but with all senses on high alert. To the end of the block, around one corner and then another and suddenly I knew where I was. This was the road out to Cape Kidnappers, and I was way outside the village boundary. I trudged through the dark, into the coun-tryside, no streetlights here. My aim was to make my way in a big slow semi-circle towards a point where I could safely start heading back.

An hour later I was walking on the wide grass belt beside the main road, keeping to the extreme outer side and hoping to blend in with hedges and trees. Every so often a car came along and each time I pushed my way into what-ever vegetation was available and stood like a statue. I was slowly approaching the village, getting colder with each step, trying to keep my focus and alertness fine-tuned. A litany of worries ran through my mind.

Is Moira safe, wonder where Andy is, hope he's OK, what happened to my phone, did I drop it when I ran out the door, what if the drug baron goes to Rusty's and frightens her and the boys, God, I'm so cold, here's another car.

The drug baron caught up with me when I was a couple of hundred meters from the village boundary. It must have been pure chance; he must have been cruising around in the car. Perhaps the other man, the one who had chased me, was looking around the village on foot. Hearing a car behind me I did my 'blend with the trees' act, but he spotted me. The brake lights glowed bright red, the car slowed and did a U-turn. This time he was driving a dark car, smaller and less noticeable than the Mercedes, but I knew it had to be him. I started running again, really fast straight forwards and we passed at speed; he was heading back towards where I had been, driving on the wrong side of the road and I was running full tilt towards the village.

The village represented safety and I had to get there fast. It must have taken him by surprise to see me running towards him and continue on, probably the last thing he had expected me to do. I was way past him by the time he stopped and turned round again and came after me.

But soon I heard the car stop just behind me and then he was after me on foot. Glancing back over my shoulder I could just see him against the parking lights on his car, then I tripped and stumbled. I lost pace and focus and in a second, he had grabbed my arm and yanked me around to face him.

"You fucking bitch - you're in for it now. Don't you bloody mess with me!"

He did not raise his voice, but even in that dim light his face had a look of contained fury, which was somehow more frightening than if he had been shouting at me. Then a knife appeared in his other hand. I caught my breath and tried to step back from him, but he kept his grip on my arm.

"You're coming with me. We're going to have a serious talk, you and I."

I had one second to make a move and then it would be too late. I spun around, managed to wrench my arm from his grip simply by taking him by surprise, and then I ran. I went down that road faster than I had ever run in my life. I didn't dare turn around in case I tripped again or broke my stride. I just concentrated on the act of running and scanned the road ahead, ideas whirling in my head.

He'll go back to his car and follow me, if a car comes, I'll run right out into the road and it will have to stop, if I see someone walking, I'll shout to them to call the police. I can't think of anything else! I can't run up to the first house I see, what if nobody's home, then I'd be trapped, I wish a cop car would come past or even an ambulance, they'd stop. Please, please let someone come along so he doesn't get me.

I was panting now; hoped I would be able to outrun him all the way into the centre of the village. Could I get to the community constable's house? But I did not get even to the first house inside the speed limit before I heard the car driving very slowly behind me, headlights off. He had run back to his car and now he was following me, quietly cruising along just a step behind me at my pace. I was unnerved by his presence and the fact that he seemed to be content to just watch me from behind. The temptation to turn around was nearly irresistible, but I steeled myself and ran on.

I was ready for something to happen; I tried to work out what he might do next. He could drive up alongside me and jump out with the knife in his hand or he could wait until I was exhausted and stopped. But would he risk letting me run right into the village? Even though I could not run for ever and he had the advantage of the car, I would have a better chance to get away from him once we were in the residential area.

. . .

What happened next took me completely by surprise. The engine sound increased, and the car hit me from behind. I fell forward on my left side on the grass verge, but even as I fell, I knew he had braked at the very moment of hitting me. He had used the car to stop me, not to kill me; not yet. Next thing he was on me, hauling me upright and clamping an arm around my throat from behind. His other hand grabbed my right wrist, twisted the arm up behind my back. The hand next to my face held the knife; I could see it out of the corner of my eye. I screamed, but I was out of breath and the scream came out as a strangled moan. He tightened the pressure on my throat, and it only took him a second to force me to the back of the car. Quickly he let go of my arm and opened the boot. Before I had time to collect myself, he bent down, put an arm behind my knees and tossed me into the boot. He pushed my flailing arms down and slammed the lid and within seconds the car was moving. I was still panting and stunned by events; there was little room to move, and I was confused about which way I was facing. I moved my hands around my body to get my bearings; I was facing the rear of the car with my head tight up against the left side wheel arch.

I lay still and concentrated on the movements of the car, tried to play the road like a recording in my mind, imagining our progress through the village. Now we should be about level with the turn-off to the Cape, now we were probably going past the policeman's house. Before I felt the rise at the approach to the bridge we turned right. But which street was it? We continued at a sedate pace. I heard no sounds from outside. A tiny strip of dim light came and went as we passed under the streetlights. It might be where the lock mechanism was. I reached out, wincing as my shoulder protested, and felt with my fingertips. There was a curved tongue of metal there and I could visualise exactly what it looked like, like a fishhook. I pushed the point if it sideways and after a second of pressure it slid out of the loop it was hooked into. The lid opened a little and bounced gently as the car moved on.

Without giving myself time to think or to hesitate I pushed the lid right up, sat up and rolled myself sideways over the lip of the boot onto the road. I hit hard, one side striking the ground with a sickening crunch. But there was no time to consider damage or pain. I knew he must have heard or seen the lid flip up and he would be after me in a second. I got up and ran.

Behind me I heard the car stop and a car door slam. Looking ahead and to the sides I got my bearings; I was on the road down by the mouth of the river, where the two rivers meet. I could just see the rise of the stopbank that contains the river when it floods. I ran up the slope of the bank, down the other side and across the wet grass, then I slid fast into the water, gasping as the cold soaked through my clothes. Using a slow breaststroke, I swam as quietly as possible into the middle of the dark river, stopped and floated silently. I let my legs sink down and used my arms in slow sweeping movements on the surface to stay afloat and to swivel around to look behind me.

The wind was coming from the east and there was a gentle current. The tide was coming in, slowly pushing more water up the river. I couldn't see anyone, but the top of the stopbank gradually became clearer, backlit by the diffuse glow from streetlights and houses further back. I would stay where I was and wait hoping he wouldn't be able to see me in the dark water.

God, this water is cold, I'll leave my shoes on so I can run when I get out, I hope getting cold won't slow me down, where is

And then I saw him. A darker shape appeared over the rise of the stopbank and then the full height of him, standing on the crest outlined against the indirect light. By looking just to the side of him I got a sharper focus; he was turning this way and that, looking along the riverbank. He walked a short distance towards the sea, stopped for a minute, turned and walked back upstream and after a minute I lost sight of him. Perhaps he had gone back to his car. And where was the other man? The drug baron would call or text him and they would get together and search for me. There might be more than two of them. I had no idea what they would do, but if I stayed away from Moira's place and if she had called the police, at least she would be safe. The thought of the cold fury of the drug baron, now that I had tricked him again, was enough to make me cringe. I could imagine his ruthless brutality next time he caught up with me.

The tidal current was moving me very slowly up the river, towards the bridge and the brighter lights. I wasn't safe in the river close to the bridge where the lights would be reflected in the water, and I could easily be spotted. I would stay in dark places; perhaps I could hide until daylight. I swam very slowly towards the far side of the river, trying to make no waves. The current slowly pulled me upstream and my path towards the bank became angled. I scanned the riverbank intently as I closed in on it. There was no movement on the cycle path along that side. Slowly, slowly I clambered out of the water, stood still and listened. I walked towards the sea, but on the landward side of the path to avoid my outline showing against the light limestone surface. I felt very alone. Since Nick was killed, I had gone through various stages of feeling cut off from everyone, I had ventured further and further into an existence where nobody from my old life could help me. But I had found Moira and Andy and they had provided emotional support.

The fear I felt now was in another category altogether. It was the true definition of being both alone and lonely. I would only survive by using my wits and cunning, and above all, my mental strength. There was nothing else to draw on, no support and no comfort. I knew what this man could do; he would cut me and torture me to make me talk and he would do it without flinching. And then, whether he felt that he had got what he wanted from me or not, he would kill me. I knew he would kill me whatever the outcome, simply because I had got away from him and caused him trouble.

19

After what seemed like an age of cautiously following the path, I reached the main road. I had moved in a large half circle and now I was just north of Clive where the road was straight and empty, and I crossed quickly. I could work my way across open land back to the river and reach it upstream from the bridge. I would swim across to one of those houses with jetties and boathouses on the village side. It took a long time. I walked over uneven fields, negotiated ponds and wire fences in the dark. I tripped and stumbled many times. I passed behind a few houses; one place with two lit windows, but I dared not approach it. Their front door would be visible from the road, and I had no idea where my pursuers were.

I got to the side road that I must cross to get down to the river upstream from the bridge; I heard no cars, no human voices. For a moment I scanned the road in both directions, tried to convince myself that nobody was waiting and watching. I crossed at a run and disappeared into the safe shadows on the far side. Getting down to the river here was easy. I went straight into the water, slid in slowly and silently. The water felt even colder this time. I was already chilled after walking in the cool night breeze in wet clothes. My skin contracted in goosebumps as I lowered myself into the water and swam slowly into the deep part of the river.

I spent what seemed like an eternity floating silently in the dark water, staying in the centre of the channel, using only gentle hand movements to counteract the slow current. It was either due to the interval of slack water between ebb and tide or the greater distance from the sea, but the current here was nearly imperceptible.

And then, just when I had decided it would be safe to get out on the village side of the river, there was a hard 'splock!' on the water a short distance away. I stopped swimming and listened; another 'splock!' further down. It took me a moment to realise that someone had fired a gun into the river. It could only be the drug baron or the other man; did they think I had stayed in the river all this time? Had they followed the river upstream, crossing people's properties and keeping an eye on the water? Was he firing randomly into the water hoping to scare me into revealing myself, or was he making sure the clumps of waterweed on the surface, was not a person? Or had he spotted me on the other side when I entered the river again? There must be a silencer on his gun, or I would have heard the crack of shots, not just the hard impact on the surface of the water.

Infinitely slowly I moved back to the side I had come from, away from the man with the gun. I had no idea why I felt so sure he was on the village side. And it made no differ- ence to me if he was trying to kill me or just wanted to scare me into revealing where I was. I had no doubts about my fate if they got their hands on me. I had to get away from him. I must get out of the water and make sure nobody was patrolling my side of the river before I set out across the fields again. I slithered slowly up the incline of wet mud and slick grass until I was lying prone on the slope of the bank. My head was down between my arms, I breathed in the smell of damp earth and musty river scents, intent on hiding the pale oval of my face. Fear held me in an icy grip, and I tried to control the involuntary shivers that shook me. The urge to raise my head and look up the steep slope was nearly irresistible.

Time passed. I heard nothing but the wind rustling in the tall poplars on the other side of the river and the damp sighs of wind-rippled water as it washed gently against the bank by my feet. I concentrated on keeping my breathing slow and quiet, listened for movement. The cold seeped into my bones and my wet clothes felt heavy, dragging me down. I worried that they would restrict me if I had to move fast. In my mind I rehearsed what I would do if they discovered me.

I will bring my hands down and push out from the slope and at the same time I'll bring my right foot up to give me purchase and momentum. This slope is so steep and the grass is slippery. What if I don't make it to the top in one bound? Would it be better to launch myself backwards into the water again, rather than stumble and be caught?

A violent shiver travelled down my back at the thought of going back into the cold black water. There had been no human sound since I slowly worked my way out of the water. I must get moving to warm myself up before I was too stiff with cold to move at all. Cautiously I raised my head and looked up the slope to where the night sky was nearly as dark as the riverbank itself. It had not rained for some time, but the sky was covered in thin cloud. I felt protected by the cloaking darkness. I turned my head right and left; there was no sign of torchlight, no movement.

Agonisingly slowly I got up on my knees, clinging to tufts of wet grass to stay in place. I listened again, bent my right knee and began to raise myself from the slope. Halfway through the motion of pushing up I sensed something whizzing past my head, just like when I had knelt beside Nick on the sidewalk - I was being shot at.

I could stay no longer, now he knew where I was. Whatever was about to happen I could not bear to think that I would die cowering on the muddy ground. I pushed off and leapt up the slope, toes digging in for better grip, arms bent and pumping, slightly hunched in instinctive concealment mode. I ran toward a cluster of trees, away from danger. The trees were a long way off, but the only thing that offered shelter. I ran so fast I could hear the water being sucked out of the wet ground as each foot lifted off and I reached the deep shadows unharmed. I leaned against the trunk of a tree, tried hard to suppress my panting breaths, stood as still as possible.

Gradually my heartbeat slowed, my breathing became calmer. I pushed slowly away from the tree trunk and looked back to where I had come from. I listened, carefully searched the shades of grey and black for any sign of movement. Without any sound or warning arms grabbed me from behind. A hand came around my head and clamped hard over my mouth, the other arm locked my arms to my body. I froze in the position I was in, one foot slightly raised, considered fighting, kicking back into the shins of the person holding me. Terror flooded my mind; this was the danger dream - it was like reliving a past event. I was waiting for what must come, the harm or the threat. Warm breath brushed the side of my face, and a nearly soundless whisper reached me through the sound of the wind in the trees. "Not a sound! Don't move." Was this the drug baron or his man? Did they think someone else was out here too, looking for them? Or someone who was after the money and who would try and keep me away from the drug baron for their own purposes?

Slowly I lowered my foot and nodded against the hand over my mouth, indicating that I would obey.

I felt the warmth of the body I was clasped against, his breath was slow and steady. Unconsciously I relaxed a fraction and let my weight rest against him. I was so tired! He responded by slowly moving his hand away from my mouth, and I knew that this wasn't one of my pursuers. I turned my head very sightly and whispered "Andy?"

His "Yes – be quiet!" was hardly audible. We stood there in complete silence for several minutes, still as a statue. He did not remove his arm and I relished the warmth of his body against my back. I tried to process his presence. What did it mean? If he wasn't part of the drug baron's lot, was he hunting the same bounty? Would he protect me for my own sake, or would he keep me safe only until he knew if I had the money? My heart told me to trust him, but my head stubbornly lined up the risks. But either way he was my best bet, because I knew that, whoever he was, he wouldn't harm me.

"Sorry I scared you," his breath was warm against my ear. "I had to make sure you didn't scream. Which direction do you think is safe?"

I turned in the circle of his arms and stood on tiptoes, whispered, "I think we should go upriver, south and inland. We could walk along the railway."

"Lead the way."

We moved slowly; first through trees, then angling away from the river across lumpy grass. We reached the coarse gravel at the base of the raised rail track and climbed the slope, rocks sliding noisily under our feet. Walking along the track suddenly felt risky, too exposed for comfort, high above the surrounding land.

"I feel too visible here. Let's walk alongside the track."

We descended the incline on the far side from the river and continued towards the south. The night was cloudy and dark as we moved slowly further from the river and the village. The railway curved inland, and the wind was dropping. I felt safer now. Andy took hold of my arm. "Do you think we should angle back towards the river now or continue along the track?"

"I'm not sure how far away from the river we are. They shot at me while I was in the water and then again after I got out. I think the railway comes close to another road further on – that might be safer."

"OK, but let's walk on the track again, it will be much quicker and we're so much further away now."

We climbed up to the track again and we trudged on. A few minutes later, without any indication that anyone was anywhere near, there was a strange, muffled sound and Andy fell forward as if his knees had given way. A hard crack as his head hit a sleeper. I threw myself down beside him with my heart was racing, and expected a bullet to hit me any moment, but nothing happened. After a couple of minutes, I sat up, cautious, ready to fling myself down at a second's notice. Andy wasn't moving. I knelt beside him and tried to turn him over. My frozen hands refused to grip properly, but eventually I had him lying on his back. He stirred and groaned, and I talked quietly to him, tried to make him lie still so I could see where he was hurt. In the back of my mind, I wondered why the gunman hadn't come closer to finish the job. I hoped he couldn't hear Andy's moans, but I had no idea how far a bullet can travel; the shooter could be anywhere.

And then I felt it, rather than heard it. A thrumming vibration that worked its way up from my knees, through my spine and into my skull. A train! I got to my feet fast and listened in both directions. There it was! Two strong lights, one above the other in the distance, but approaching fast. Desperate now, I knelt again and tried to roll Andy over the rail and down the slope of the embankment. But he was too heavy, my hands were numb, and the rail was too much of a barrier. I would need to lift him, rolling him was not going to do it. A sob of desperation formed in my throat. I ran around to behind his head and tried to get a grip under his shoulders to drag him to one side, but my hands were too cold, and his weight defeated me. Frantic thoughts chased through my mind. Somehow, I must protect him as well as I could where he was. I got down fast, lying prone and face down with my feet in the opposite direction from his so our heads were side by side. I had no idea how much room there was under a train, so we must both be as flat to the ground as possible. Quickly I raised my arms and turned Andy's head sideways. I slid my hand down the outside of his shoulders and gripped his upper arms as tightly as I could, but I couldn't reach far. I could only pray that he wouldn't come around again and raise his legs or his hands because I could only control the parts of him I could reach.

I turned my head sideways and pressed my nose against Andy's face. We could not get much flatter than this. I tried to visualise what the highest point was, possibly Andy's ribcage. The thought made me feel sick with apprehension, but it was too late now to change anything.

The train was closing in fast. I felt the pillar of air being pushed ahead of it, the noise was deafening. With my eyes squeezed shut I held on tight to Andy's arms and pressed my cheek hard against the gravel. The train was braking; the screech of metal wheels locking and sliding along the rails. Panic-stricken I struggled to control my twitching legs; my body was trying to break free and run for safety.

And then the train was on us. A strong buffeting of turbulence as the metal monster thundered over us, so close to my cheek that the breath was sucked out of my lungs. The underside of the train was only a hand's breadth above us and the noise was hideous; a screeching torment of metal grinding against metal. Dust swirled around us, everything shuddered, my eardrums ached with the pain of the noise. The train was slowing, sparks flew from under the wheels. The smell of hot metal was harsh, and I could taste it in my mouth.

Through this hell of noise and movement I kept repeating the same mantra over and over with my mouth and nose pressed against Andy's face. "It's all right, we're OK, just keep still, we'll be all right, just stay still, we are all right."

The train stopped. The silence was like a physical impact; a few pings from hot metal contracting and then nothing apart from the ringing in my ears. Slowly I raised my head and bumped it on something. I let go of Andy's arms and put a hand on his cheek and turned my head to look out to my side of the tracks.

Andy spoke for the first time since he was shot, and his voice was full of pain. "My hand is broken." Had I been mistaken, had there been two shots? I was sure the bullet had hit him in the leg; I could visualise him falling as if his knees had unhinged under him.

I tried to sound calm. "OK, we'll tell them as soon as they get to us. We're under a train, just keep still. They'll get us out soon." I kept my hand on his cheek so I would know if he tried to raise his head.

Now I heard footsteps crunching on shingle and men's voices. I saw the bouncing light-beam of a torch being carried by someone walking on my side of the track. Every now and then it shone under the train, and I realised that they were looking for bodies. I shouted, "We are here, just a bit further down. I can see your light."

A man's voice rose in surprise. "Bloody hell, they're alive! Quick, shine the light under here so I can have a look."

A moment later the light shone directly into my face, and I said, "I'm unhurt but my friend is injured. Can you get us out?"

The man got down on his knees to see us better. "Yeah, I can see him. Is he conscious? Can he crawl out?"

I touched Andy's face but there was no reaction. "I think he's unconscious. And even if he comes to he won't be able to get out without help."

"OK, I'll help you wriggle out of there."

"No, I'm not leaving him. I'll wait until you can get him out too."

"All right, all right - that's fine. We've already called the emergency services, but now we know you're alive we'll make sure they send the rescue helicopter. Jim, can you get on to it right away?"

I stroked Andy's face and talked quietly to him. He said nothing, but every now and then he jerked and groaned; the only thing I could do was to keep him calm. I hoped that my voice would seep into his unconscious mind and comfort him.

The helicopter descended like a noisy angel in a cone of strong light. A blast of air swept around us under the train. Within seconds there were more loud voices and stronger lights. Equipment was deposited on the ground beside the track and a man wormed his way in at right angles to me.

"Don't know how you two got away with this without being killed. Are you hurt?"

"No, I'm OK. Please have a look at my friend, I think he's badly hurt."

He squeezed in over the rail and somehow managed to wriggle down the length of Andy's body. Andy groaned again.

"Sorry, mate - I didn't mean to hurt you, but I have to find out what's wrong so I can help you." His voice was calm and competent and slowly I relaxed. Others were taking over now, and they knew what to do.

"OK - Ralph, we need to get the man out first. The girl seems OK, but he's out cold - he's got a mangled hand, must have caught it on something and he's also got what looks like a stab wound in the upper thigh. Let's get him out, we need to check that leg wound, it's still bleeding a lot. It's impossible to do anything here, no headroom."

"It's not a stab wound," I said. "He was shot - from behind, I think. I should have told you right away."

"Holy cow!" said the man. "Hey - did you hear that, guys? Better radio the cops and tell them that there's someone running around with a gun."

They helped me out from under the train and someone wrapped me in a blanket. "Hey, you're soaking - what happened?"

"I had to hide in the river." My teeth were chattering despite the blanket.

"Can you tell us a bit about who shot at your friend, so we can tell the police when they get here?"

"Someone had threatened me. They put me in the boot of a car, but I got out. And I swam up the river to get away. Then I came out on this side to get further away. But Andy found me. I don't know how he found me. We walked along the railway track, and Andy got shot. He hit his head really hard."

I could hardly speak even those short sentences. My entire body was trembling violently now, my teeth were rattling. It felt as if my bones were made of ice and about to shatter.

"Let's get you into the helicopter and wrap you up properly."

"No, I have to stay here till you get Andy out."

Two men got in under the train and I heard one of them swearing when he bumped his head. They manhandled Andy sideways over the rail and put him on a stretcher. A medic in a bright red overall knelt beside him and gently lifted his left arm. The sight of his hand was shocking, a shapeless bloodied mass of ripped flesh and pieces of white bone. The medic wrapped the lower arm loosely in a large dressing and moved to look at his leg. After a moment he looked up at me. "Did you say he was shot?"

"Yes, but from behind - he fell forward."

They lifted Andy just a fraction and looked at the back of his leg. "It's gone right through, must have missed the femoral artery - lucky for him. Let's get a line in and hook up a drip and then we'll get him into the helicopter. We don't want to hang around longer than necessary, if there's someone out there trying to kill him."

The stretcher was loaded into the helicopter, someone helped me in after him and fastened a belt round me. I was fading fast, and things were getting blurry. My teeth were still chattering, and the convulsive trembling just went on and on.

"OK guys, let's be off." The door was shut, and we lifted off. I remember nothing after that.

20

I opened my eyes and saw a white ceiling and a rail with a blue curtain. Hospital, I thought, of course. I closed my eyes. Images from the night started streaming through my mind, seemingly random and disconnected, but even as they appeared they sorted themselves into a sequence of events that made sense. My last memory was getting into the helicopter, then a blank space which no effort could fill.

Someone came in, and I opened my eyes. A nurse bent over me and smiled when she saw I was awake. "Hello there, how are you feeling?"

"I don't know, I haven't had time to find out. I think I'm all right."

She adjusted some sort of clamp on my finger, glanced at a monitor beside the bed and picked up a clipboard. "You're in better shape than you were last time they checked you."

"Do you know where Andy is, he came in with me? Do you know how he is? Can I see him?"

"Is that the chap who was with you under the train? I heard he was in the operating room for hours with two surgeons working on him. He's in another ward on the floor below this one. You can go and see him later - he won't be awake yet."

I thought briefly of insisting I had to see him, even if it only meant looking at him asleep, but I could tell that she wasn't open to discussion. Nurses and schoolteachers have a way of making their boundaries clear without saying anything much. I felt lethargic, as if my spring had wound right down. I would wait until I didn't have to fight my way to Andy's room.

"You were very cold when they brought you in, but you seem to have warmed up quite nicely." She made a note on the clipboard. "They had a temp monitor on you while you slept and you are back to normal, but you will probably feel very tired for a couple of days."

She smiled cheerfully and took the clamp off my finger. "Let's get you in the shower. You're pretty dirty - they didn't wash you much last night, the main aim was to keep you wrapped up and warm."

"I can't remember any of it. I'd love a shower." Turning over in the bed made me groan, my body felt pummelled and bruised. Under the covers I was wrapped in a soft blanket of some sort, tucked in all around like you do with a baby. The nurse unwrapped me and watched me stand beside the bed, ready to catch me if I lost my balance. I was dressed in one of those gowns that open down the back, I could feel the cooler air getting in through the gap.

"Apparently you have a lot of bruising and some cuts here and there, you'll feel sore for a while. Do you want help in the shower?"

"No thanks. I'll be fine."

She opened the door to the bathroom and showed me a plastic chair I could sit on, if I felt wobbly, and left me alone. I took a very long hot shower, washed my hair with some kind of all-purpose liquid soap and put on the clean dressing gown that hung on the door. My skin felt raw, as if it had been rubbed with sandpaper, but perhaps that's what happens when you spend hours in cold, wet clothes. I longed for big dollop of moisturiser and someone to spread it all over me.

When I emerged, the nurse had just finished making my bed. "I've given you clean sheets; your bed was like a sand-pit." She laughed at my face. "You look a lot better now – why don't you hop back into bed?"

I hesitated and she looked at me standing there in the dressing gown. "Sorry, I didn't give you a clean gown. Or would you rather have PJ's?"

I opted for pyjamas, and she got me a pair of blue-on-blue striped ones with a button missing. The sleeves were far too long so I rolled them up; that seemed to be as tidy as I was likely to get for a while.

"Where are my clothes?"

"Probably in a plastic bag in that cupboard over there. They said you came in covered in mud and soaked through, so they'll still be wet. Just stay as you are till the doctor has seen you. We'll get you a phone in a minute so you can call someone."

She disappeared briefly and returned with a breakfast tray and a phone. She plugged in the phone. "Do you know the number? No? I'll get a phone book for you."

Suddenly I was ravenous. I couldn't even remember how long it was since I had eaten last. I looked up Moira's number in the phone book and started eating while I dialled. She answered straight away, and I drew a deep breath of relief. We talked for a long time. We had so much to tell each other and, though I would see her shortly, I still felt a need to talk through what had happened after I ran out of the house the night before.

"I was frantic all night." She sounded tired. "It wasn't till this morning, when I heard it on the news that I finally knew for sure you were all right."

"But how are you? What happened at the house? What's that I can hear in the background - is someone there?"

"I've got a man here fixing the terrace door. It's not too bad, just a bit of broken wood and glass. When they broke in, I heard you shouting, and I realised you were running out of the house. I got the steps up really quickly. I heard footsteps and shouts just for a minute and then nothing, so I just sat in the attic until Andy came."

"Did you ring the police? What did Andy do?"

"I hadn't taken my phone when we went up there because I thought you had yours. But Andy came pretty soon after you left – of course he saw the broken terrace door and I heard him searching the house, calling out for us. He called the police and then he told me to get back in that damned attic till they got there, and then he took off. Our local constable got here in no time at all, and I haven't seen Andy since. I heard on the news that you are OK, but he's injured – is it bad?"

"He is in a different ward, but I'll be able to go and see him a bit later. Did they mention our names? On the news, I mean."'

"No, they just said that a major incident had taken place - armed offenders' squad out looking for people with guns, roads blocked off, two people under a train. They said a young woman and a man. I knew it was you." Her voice broke, but being Moira, she got hold of herself, just sniffed a couple of times. "Is Andy going to be all right, have they told you anything?"

"No, nothing much. He was shot in the leg and then he got his hand damaged when we were under the train. All they said was that he was in the operating theatre for hours "

Just talking about it made me shudder. The sight of that

mauled hand, as he lay semi-conscious on the stretcher with the bright light shining on him, was vivid in my memory. Remembering it now was just as bad as it had been when I stood there looking down at him, feeling angry and guilty that I was all right and he was so damaged.

"I'll come over soon. What do you want me to bring?"

"Could you bring a change of clothes, toothbrush, that sort of thing and my phone and the charger. Oh, and a big jar of some kind of moisturiser – I think my skin is about to peel off, I was in wet clothes for hours. I hope they'll let me go home, but just in case, bring the lot. God, I've just realised, I had the phone in my hand when they broke in, I was just coming out of the kitchen. I don't know what happened to it after that. I must have dropped it, perhaps outside as I ran away. Can you have a look please? And bring some shoes too in case they let me out. Everything I was wearing is covered in mud and soaking wet. I haven't seen a doctor yet, but I don't think there's much wrong with me apart from being black and blue and limping."

Moira's voice sharpened. "Limping? Why are you limping? I thought you said that you were unhurt apart from bruises."

"Oh Moira, I'm fine. Really! But I did land really hard on my hip when I threw myself out of the boot of that car. And the drug baron had already knocked me down with his car before that, so it was one thing after another. And don't rush - you must be exhausted if you've been up practically all night."

She wasn't pacified. "Just make sure you tell the doctor about that limp. They should x-ray you and make sure you haven't cracked anything. Oh, and your phone – I got side-tracked - the village cop found it on the veranda by the front door when he arrived just after Andy left. I think it's OK."

. . .

245

All I really needed now was to see Andy and then go home with Moira. Peace and quiet, and not needing to do anything at all, had never held such appeal. A young doctor came and said she wanted to look at my bruises. She pulled the covers down and poked and prodded till she was satisfied. "I think you're mostly fine, the only thing that concerns me a bit is your hip. The movement in the joint seems reasonable considering how deeply bruised you are, but we'll x-ray it just to make sure you haven't cracked anything."

"Surely not! After I fell out of that car I ran, swam, ran again, swam again and walked cross-country. Could I really do that with a cracked bone?"

"Yes, you could, but we need to know for sure. I'll order an x-ray and an orderly or one of the nurses will take you down to the x-ray department a bit later."

At last, she left and I sat back feeling irritated. Anything that delayed me going home with Moira was going to be a real test of my patience. But minutes later my nice nurse came in pushing a wheelchair and brought news that cheered me up.

"I'll take you to visit your friend now - better to do it before we start with x-rays and things. They said you'd better come down and see him, he's being a bit difficult." She handed me the towelling robe and I got into the wheelchair. Andy was in the end room off a very long corridor on a lower floor. A nurse was sorting things on a trolley just outside his door.

She turned to me. "I think you must be Cara? Well, I'm really glad you've turned up - we can't get him to settle down. He's been going on about you ever since he came up from the recovery room, fretting and nagging. And what he really needs is to settle down and sleep."

· · ·

She opened the door for us and my nurse pushed me through and left. I got out of the chair and looked down at Andy. He was breathing evenly and steadily, but his face was pale, badly bruised on one side and he had a black eye. I thought back; it was the side of his head that had struck the railway sleeper when he fell forward. His bed had a frame under the sheet lifting the bedclothes up from his lower body. His left hand was a heavily bandaged parcel and the arm rested on a support attached to the bed frame, a bit like a tray with straps holding the wrist in place. Thin tubes were attached to various parts of him. I reached out and touched his cheek. He instantly opened his eyes. "There you are!" He sounded as if he had a sore throat, but he smiled. Not his usual transforming smile, but it made me feel a bit better.

I dragged up his visitor's chair and sat down beside his right shoulder. He seemed completely exhausted. He should be sleeping, but first I needed to find out how he was. "How are you feeling?"

His eyes closed for a few moments. "Exhausted - and muddled. I'm very confused about what happened last night, there's a lot of stuff I can't remember."

"Do you remember walking along the railway, the second time we got up on the actual track?" He nodded. "Well, someone shot you in the thigh, from behind and you fell really hard and hit your head on a sleeper. You were knocked out cold and there was a train coming. I couldn't lift you over the rail - I was going to roll you down the bank, but you were too heavy, and the train was coming very fast. We just had to stay where we were."

I was not sure if he was taking all this information onboard, he looked so tired. I took his right hand in mine and gave it a little squeeze. "Are you in pain?"

"No, they've given me something I think, I feel a bit drugged. My hand's a mess apparently."

"Has anyone told you what they've managed to do with it? I heard there were two surgeons working on you for hours."

"I have lost two fingers, the ring finger and little finger, and I might yet lose the middle finger. And the rest is damaged too. It's going to take a while to get used to. They said there will be more operations, skin grafts and things." His eyes narrowed as if in pain and he sighed. "But I still have my thumb."

"Andy, I'm so sorry! But I thought you would lose the whole hand. When they got you out from under the train and I saw it, I didn't think anyone could save it."

I stopped and swallowed. Talking about it brought back the awful image of Andy on the stretcher on the ground and the sight of his hand before they wrapped it up. Remembering how I had thought he might be dying made me shudder even now. I held tightly on to his fingers, unable to hold it in. "I thought you were going to die!"

"Put our hands on my chest."

"What - on your chest, like this?" I lifted our linked hands and rested them on his chest. As soon as he no longer had to support his arm his grip became stronger. Then he let go of my hand and put it on top of mine. I could feel his heart beating.

"Ca-Cara, whatever happens I want you to promise me one thing – OK?" He had trouble speaking, his voice was disappearing. "Remember that I love you - never forget that I love you. I have ever since we went to the movies that first time. I can't explain it, but it's true - and it's important."

I leaned down and kissed him very lightly. "OK, I promise."

But he wasn't satisfied. "Say it properly!"

And I said, "I promise that I won't forget that you love me."

The nurse opened the door. "Sorry to interrupt, but I've got to take you down to x-ray now. You can catch up again later."

I slid my hand out from under his. "I'll come back when you've had a sleep."

When I looked back from the doorway his eyes were closed. His insistence that I repeated his words like an oath had shaken me. What was it that might happen that made it necessary for me to remember that he loved me? And why had he told me that, for the very first time just then? The sense of dread stayed with me until I came back from the x-ray and found Moira sitting in my room reading a book. It was a comforting sight as if a degree of normality had been restored.

She hugged me and looked at me for a long moment after she let go. "You have no idea how worried I've been - quite demented!"

"Me too," I said, and we both laughed. But we had only just started talking when a nurse came in followed by a middle-aged man in civilian clothes and a younger one in police uniform. The room immediately felt crowded and awkward. The nurse looked around as if to check that every-thing was in order and left. The older of the two men took charge, apologetic but firm.

"I'm sorry to interrupt, but we need to speak to Miss Williams now. Could you come back in an hour or so?"

Moira said, "I'll see you in a little while, Cara," and left. The older man introduced himself and his offsider, but I forgot what he had said as soon as he had told me. My mind was too busy trying to imagine what was coming next.

"How are you feeling? I hear you were hypothermic when you were brought in."

"I was very cold. But I'm fine now."

He leaned back against the wide window ledge and motioned for the constable to sit on the chair. "You sit there so you can take notes. I'm fine here."

Then he turned back to me. "We are investigating the events of last night and also some earlier incidents. There is a search going on for the man who abducted you and for the person who shot your friend - which might be the same person of course. We have a large number of staff involved and we need all the help we can get from you. I want to take you through all you can remember about what happened last night. We also need to discuss what led to that situation. We've been given some rather mixed-up information second-hand, but I would like to you to tell us yourself, step by step what happened yesterday - from the very beginning."

I hesitated for a moment. What should I start with and how much could I reveal? He saw my indecision and helped me out. "Perhaps I should start by telling you that we already know your name is not Cara Williams. You might not remember, but you gave another name last night in the emergency room and then you corrected yourself. We will deal with that later and call you by your assumed name for the time being. But first I want the facts about the abduction last night - everything you can remember, every detail. You told the emergency crew that someone took you against your will and put you in the boot of a car? And that you escaped?"

I spent a long time talking, first about what had happened the day before and then going back to the start of the whole saga. When I said that I had left Auckland to get away from people, who had threatened and beaten me, he nodded. He already knew about it, but he made no comment. If I had given my real name when I was admitted, he would already know all about me. I wondered what Benson had told him and if they still suspected me of being involved.

That poor constable taking notes; it turned into a very long story. By the time I got to when the drug baron knocked me down with his car and threw me into the boot the older man interrupted. "How did he do that? Did he say anything threatening or did he have a weapon?"

"He had a knife. He said he was taking me somewhere where we could talk. He had his arm around my throat from behind - I could see the knife to the side of my face. And he bent my other arm up behind my back, so I couldn't fight." I paused trying to recall if he had said he would harm me. "He said he knew how to make me talk or something like it. That's what he meant, anyway."

"OK, that's fine. We need all the detail you can remember. Continue please."

And so we continued through each step of that long trek through the night, until I got to the point when somebody fired a gun into the water. "What made you think they were shots?"

"Those two sounds – there is nothing natural that sounds like that, something hit the water very hard, twice. I thought he might have followed the river and maybe he saw something he thought was me. So, when I had swum back to the side I had come from I lay very, very still, waiting to see what would happen."

The man interviewing me said, rather surprisingly. "That must have been hard. Keeping still, knowing they might have you in their sights, I mean."

"It was – I was terrified. I was very cold by then. I worried I wouldn't be able to leap up and run for it, if they found me. And then I heard nothing for ages and decided to take off as fast as I could, but they fired another shot at me as soon as I moved. And then I ran for my life – I suppose it was lucky they didn't manage to hit me while I was running."

"So, there was a third shot? While you were lying on the bank?"

"Yes, I had been lying there kind of rehearsing in my mind how I would leap up that bank as fast as possible, if something happened - and run upriver and slightly inland, away from the river. But I was scared that wet clothes and being so cold would slow me down, so planning how I'd do it seemed important. But as soon as I moved a bullet whizzed past me – and I ran."

"And you're sure it was a bullet?"

"It happened to me once before, someone fired very close to me and bullets streaked past me, only half a meter away. I kind of recognised the sensation. I didn't hear the gun firing, but I sensed the bullet coming past."

I saw from his face that he knew what had happened when Nick was killed. He asked nothing else, just told me to continue with what happened next.

I described my run to the clump of trees, and how I was puzzled at why they didn't shoot again. "I think they must have been on the village side, like I thought when I was in the water. Perhaps when I ran off, they made for the bridge to get over to my side, but of course that took a while - I'm just guessing. I was hiding in that clump of trees and then someone grabbed me from behind. I thought one of them had got me, but ..."

He interrupted before I got any further. "Someone grabbed you? Tell me about that."

"Well, I was just standing there trying to get my breath back after running like a mad thing, and out of nowhere someone grabbed me from behind. He got a hand over my mouth and locked my arms down. I didn't know who it was, but then I realised it was Andy. That's my friend who ended up under the train with me. Well, I didn't realise that right away, but it was him. He was just making sure I wouldn't yell when he surprised me."

"So that's when you two joined up and then you stayed together right up until you ended up under the train?" I nodded.

"How had he found you?" He was looking searchingly at me as if he thought I had made it up.

"I don't know. We didn't talk about it at the time, it wasn't important just then. We made our way south once we found the railway. And then he got shot and the train came, so I never got around to even thinking about it till this morning."

"That's all right - we'll talk to him shortly. But just out of interest, how come you couldn't get off the track before the train came? Was he unable to move at all?"

So, I described how I had not been able to lift Andy over the rail and roll him down the embankment because my hands were so cold that I could not get a grip on him, and he was such a dead weight. And how I had lain down with him and held his arms steady to keep him still. And as I told them it struck me for the first time that I had failed. Somehow Andy had raised his hand despite my grip on his arms and that's why his hand was ruined now. It was devastating to realise that if I had managed a bit better, he would not have lost half his hand.

"I feel so bad about his hand! I was holding his arms as far down as I could, but it was so noisy and scary under the train, and he was jerking even though he was hardly conscious. And he's so much taller than I am, I could only hold on to his arms above the elbow, I couldn't reach any further."

In my mind they were a jury I had to convince, people who would sit in judgement and not understand why I hadn't managed to do better. "I tried to talk to him all the time, right close to his face, just to keep him calm. I had turned his head sideways and mine too, so we would be as low as possible. I didn't know how flat on the ground we had to be, not to be hit by something."

I broke off, tormented by the thought that if my hands had not been so cold and my grip a bit stronger Andy would probably be all right now apart from the bullet wound. "And there was so little time ..." I stopped. I knew I was beginning to sound hysterical, and I needed to calm down.

The men looked at each other and then at me. There was a long moment when nobody spoke and I looked from one to the other, not sure if they were waiting for me to explain further.

But the senior man was blunt and straight to the point. "Well, I think we should apply a bit of common sense to this idea you have that you failed. I think that if you put a hundred people in that situation, ninety-nine would have got themselves off that track very smartly and left Andy to take his chances on his own. And the one who might have chosen to stay with him would probably not have coped half as well as you did. What you did was extremely brave."

I could think of nothing to say. I was glad they thought I had done the right thing, but a hard little knot of guilt stayed in my mind. I continued the story until the end where I was getting into the helicopter, after which I could remember nothing at all until I woke up that morning.

They asked another few questions, thanked me for my time, and left.

21

The nurse came in with a lunch tray as soon as they had gone. "They took their time! I've warmed it up, hope it's still edible."

Moira arrived as the nurse was leaving my room; she must have been keeping a watch on my door. She sat on the edge of the bed and talked while I ate my lunch, then she went to the hospital café and brought back two coffees. We talked for a long time. A nurse came in and said the x-ray results were fine, there were no cracked bones, but they had orders to keep me in overnight. Moira raised her eyebrows. "Orders? That sounds a bit odd." The nurse shrugged her shoulders. "That's what I was told."

Eventually Moira left with the bag full of sodden clothes. I had just got back on the bed to have a sleep, when the older of the police officers returned. I knew the moment he walked into the room that something had changed. My sense of apprehension returned at full strength. He pulled the chair up to the side of the bed. "I just need a short session with you and then I'll leave you alone for today."

"Have you spent all this time with Andy?" I was surprised and a bit worried that Andy would be exhausted by so much questioning. I wondered why it taken so long and what they had found out.

"No, just part of it. I've been on the phone with Auckland a fair bit of the time."

He sat facing me beside the bed, his eyes on my face as he spoke. "I have a better idea of what has been going on now, and I'll need a lot more time with you, but not all of it today."

"What do we need to talk about?" Thoughts of suspicions, accusations and arrests swirled in my head. *God knows what Benson has told him about me, what have they have decided to do? And what is going on with Andy, are they arresting him for something - maybe that gun or something worse?*

He got an iPad out and looked at it. "I know who you are, of course, and why you left Auckland. And we know who is after you, but we don't know where he is now. I agree with your friend Benson in Auckland that you are in acute danger until we find the person you refer to as 'the drug baron'. And so does Sergeant Black, he is very concerned that you are properly protected until this is over."

"Who?"

I had no idea what he was talking about. He looked at me in a considering sort of way and I began to feel frightened - I knew there was something wrong. Hurry up, I thought, for God's sake, just tell me.

When he finally did, he looked apologetic and a bit embarrassed. "I know he wanted to tell you himself, but now it can't be helped. I'm talking about Andy. He is Detective Sergeant Andrew Black, and he has been undercover here on behalf of the Organised Crime unit."

I just sat there staring at him. I could think of nothing to say. My world had suddenly shifted, I could not even start to imagine what it meant. Andy was with the police and had been here undercover? Was I a suspect still? Did he suspect me? Was it all pretend?

He studied my face and let me think before he continued. "There's one thing I should tell you right away. Benson asked me to say that they no longer think that you ever had that money or was involved in any way, and they accept that you left only because you felt you weren't safe in Auckland."

That made me angry. "I didn't just *think* I wasn't safe – I knew I wasn't! Did Benson tell you about the woman they burnt to death?" He nodded and I sat up straighter. "Well, I believe the drug baron, whatever his name is, killed her. And I knew he would hurt or kill me. He is a very scary man when you are up against him in person. And he was watching me day and night, following me around. He called me and told me to look out the window - I could see his car on the other side of the street. He said he would come into my flat and search it himself because he didn't believe me."

"Yes, very likely he wouldn't hesitate to use violence. I know he assaulted you. His name is Moore, and he has a power base in the drug world. He is very violent, and he has a long history of unproven crimes behind him. We're certain that he's involved with a major biker gang, and he has contacts everywhere. Probably he didn't set fire to that poor woman himself – his kind very rarely does their own dirty work, but that makes no difference. He runs an organisation that has tentacles all over the place and he could probably organise to have someone killed at a moment's notice."

"But how did he find me? I thought I had covered my tracks really well and then he turned up here all of a sudden." I never even thought of asking how Andy had found me. Somehow the Andy issue was parked to one side with other uncertainties.

"You certainly did become untraceable. Benson said it was as if you went up in a puff of smoke. He couldn't find the slightest trace of you - he was very frustrated. They knew you sold your car, but from there it was as if you had been spirited away." He chuckled. "Benson said 'if that girl takes up crime we'll never catch her' and I must say it's very hard to completely disappear these days, unless you go and hide in someone's attic."

He cleared his throat, leaned forward and picked up the story again. "We think that Moore found you via that informer he has in the Auckland police - Benson doesn't know who it is yet, but it must be someone who's in touch with his team on a regular basis. You told Benson in your email that Moore knew everything that was going on and they have been trying to figure out who it is ever since."

"But Andy, how did he find me?"

"Completely by chance. Do you remember the constable who was with Benson when he interviewed you at your flat after the shooting? He's a Hawke's Bay boy and he was down here for a week visiting family - saw you getting off the bus in Clive."

"Really? That sounds incredible."

He looked amused now. "I agree completely – amazing coincidence. If you put it in a book nobody would believe it, but it's true all the same. He was coming out of the shop with an ice cream in his hand and despite your altered appearance he recognised you. Benson said he had been quite taken with you when they interviewed you. He followed you on foot to the Bed & Breakfast place and then he called Benson. And Andy Black was sent down to keep an eye on you."

And now I saw the connection. "So, Moore's police informer knew that I had been located and told him where I was?"

"Either he heard that the constable had seen you or else he found out that Andy had been sent down here. We'll

never know for sure, but it must have been one or the other
of those things."

Finally, we were getting to the issue that lay like a ticking
bomb in my mind. I was so tense I felt sick. "So why did
Andy not arrest me as soon as he found me? Why did they
leave me alone for so long after sending him to spy on me?"

He rubbed his chin and looked uncomfortable. There
was something he didn't want to say outright, and I knew
what it was, so I said it for him.

"They sent Andy down here to wait for the drug baron to
find me, didn't they? They knew there was an informer, and
now I was the bait, and they hoped the informer would tell
Moore and he would come after me. And then all Andy had
to do was wait for me to be hurt or killed and they'd have
their evidence against Moore. And possibly the money too if
they thought I had it."

My voice was full of bitterness and my heart was a cold
rock in my chest; I could hardly breathe.

We looked at each other in silence for a very long
moment. Then he put his iPad on the foot end of the bed
and moved the chair closer. "Look, let's suspend the interview for a moment. We'll forget that I'm a police officer, let's
say that for the moment I'm not on duty."

"Why?" I was full of anger and suspicion and reluctant
to talk any more. But then he did a very surprising thing, at
least for a policeman. He reached out and took my hand and
held it between both of his. "I'm old enough to be your
father and I have daughters of my own. I know you're full of
hurt and anger right now and you think you can't trust
Andrew. He told me all about you and him and how he
made an effort not to get involved until Auckland told him
you were no longer a suspect."

He was still holding on to my hand and he was waiting for me to speak. I cleared my throat and hesitated. It was very hard to talk about my love for Andy and my confused feelings with someone I did not know in any real sense. He waited in silence and in the end, I had to say something. "Why didn't he tell me?"

"You have to understand that Andy's strong sense of duty, or ethics perhaps, made it impossible for him to show you that he had fallen in love with you while you were still a possible suspect. It's a real no-no for a police officer, he had to maintain professional distance. When you were no longer suspected of having taken the money Benson told him to stay and watch out for Moore to show up. Andy was guarding you, but he was not at liberty to tell you that. And he did guard you nearly round the clock the last little while."

"But he went to work – or was his job just a pretence?"

"He left that job. He used it as cover for being here - he couldn't just turn up and do nothing. But when you moved into your friend's place, after you pretended to leave Clive, he gave up the job. He had to be around all the time in case something happened. When you thought he was at work he was watching the place from various vantage points and cruising round checking the neighbourhood. I don't think he spent many minutes at his flat."

I would need to think through all this before I could take it in. I remembered how tired Andy had been, all the time. Suddenly it seemed mad that I was discussing my very private life with this man, who was still holding my hand,

and whose name I had forgotten. "I can't remember you name, I'm sorry!"

"My first name's Keith." He let go of my hand. "I think I'll just call you Cara until this is over because that's what Andy calls you. And one more thing – he's very worried that you will think that he has used you or not been genuine. He asked me to say this: Remember what he made you promise this morning. I don't know what was, but he said to make sure you remember because it's very important."

But I knew. I had promised that whatever happened I would remember that he loved me. My heart felt as if it was beginning to beat like a normal heart again.

Keith looked at me with keen interest. "I can see you do remember. I won't ask you what it is, but it obviously makes you feel better."

"It does - thank you for doing this for me. I would have spent a miserable night otherwise. It was very kind of you."

He smiled as if it was all part of a normal day's work. "I must go and write reports and fill in forms – the worst part of the job. I'll be back tomorrow. I think you and I and Andy need to have a discussion about how to keep you safe now that he's stuck here for a while."

When he had left, they delivered my dinner tray, but I wasn't hungry now. Too many things had happened, and my mind was trying to process it all, but first I had to see Andy. I got out of my striped, blue PJ's and dressed in the clothes Moira had left in the wardrobe. When I opened the door to the corridor a police constable got up from a chair outside my door. "Do you need something?"

I was completely taken aback. "Why are you here?"

"I'm looking after your safety until someone else comes

to do the next shift. We have orders not to leave you alone until other arrangements have been made."

"Really?" I thought for a moment. "Can you take me to see Andy, I mean Sergeant Black? He's on the next floor down."

He said he would find out and motioned me back into the room. I could hear him talking to someone through the closed door. After a short pause he knocked and came in. "I can take you down, so you can see him before you go to sleep. They don't want you wandering around in public, but I'm allowed to make an exception – just one visit."

When we got to Andy's ward there was a trolley full of folded linen in front of his closed door and I noticed there was no name in the little holder on the doorframe. My companion knocked, opened to door for me and closed it, staying outside himself.

Andy was looking towards the door, he looked pale and tired, and his eyes watched me come towards him as if he was unsure of what would happen next. I bent down and put my cheek against his. "It's OK. I didn't forget what you made me promise. And I love you too." I had never said that before and it made me feel good.

His right hand came up and held me round the back of the neck the way he sometimes did, and the feeling warmed me to the core. "God, Cara - I've been worried crazy." He kissed the side of my head, and I straightened up. "I don't know why I never thought that you might be a police officer instead of possibly a criminal."

"No, it's not very flattering, is it? I kept wondering if you would suddenly face me with a direct question, asking if that's what I was, and how I would reply."

"You've got it wrong - it was very flattering, not the opposite. Think of it this way - I made a decision to go ahead even though I did think you might be criminal doesn't that prove I feel that you are a very special person?"

He smiled and reached for my hand. The grip around my fingers and his serious eyes told me he needed to get something off his chest. I thought I knew what it was, and I had to let him do it his own way.

"I kept thinking of how you would react when you were told. It's been on my mind the whole time. This morning I was so tired and dopey, and I felt I couldn't tell you until I had been officially told my role was over. I know that sounds ridiculous, but I wasn't thinking straight. I should have told you then." His eyes were fixed on mine, watching my reactions. "I knew your first thought would be that I had used you to try and get Moore, but that was only part of the brief. And I would never have let him harm you – I spent a lot of time keeping an eye on you, both while you lived in the shed and later."

"I understand it – it's OK. It's nearly over, they just need to catch Moore and then we are safe."

I wasn't sure if I should add more fuel to the blaze of emotion we had endured today, but I felt I had to. "And I'm so sorry I let your hand get mangled – I tried really hard to keep you still..."

He interrupted me right away. "I know, I heard all about it. And the hand is a small price to pay for not being dead. If you hadn't been so incredibly brave, I would be dead now - you can't punish yourself for what happened. We could make a trade-off. You gave me my life and I gave fate my hand in exchange. How does that sound? And perhaps we can include that you try to believe that for me you were not just bait to get Moore into the open?"

"I know, I do understand. Keith explained it all to me. He was so sweet. He said we would forget that he's a policeman and just talk. And then he gave me an idea of what would have been in your mind - what you felt it was your duty to do, or not do. And he said you asked him to remind me of what I had promised."

Andy's face slowly relaxed.

"When Keith said you had asked him to remind me of my promise, everything changed. Not that I had forgotten, but it had got pushed into the background by everything else."

"So, it's 'Keith' now, is it?" I was glad to see a smile on his face instead of worry. "You're on first name terms already?"

I sat down and put my hand on his chest like I had that morning. "He's so kind and lovely. If he wasn't already married, I might marry him instead. As it is I might just have to adopt him."

"What do you mean 'marry him instead'? Instead of what?"

"Well, I don't know if this is the way other people do these things, but I thought maybe I could marry you?"

22

———

There I was, confined to my hospital room with a guard on the door. A couple of times nurses popped in, not for any reason that was obvious to me but keen to chat. One of them told me I was the first patient they had ever had who had a guard for my own safety.

"Sometimes we get people who have police or prison wardens guarding them - you know, so they can't escape, but you're more like a celebrity."

It was hard to imagine Moore trying anything in such a public setting, but it was quite comforting to know that if he tried, he would have to get past something more than a couple of nurses before he could get to me.

In the morning the first nurse of the day came in, took my temperature and pulse, fussed with curtains, checked the bathroom and seemed reluctant to leave. In the end she got to the point. "They say it was you who got the child out of the river, after that crash on the bridge. Is that true?"

I couldn't deny it, too many people knew now. So, I said that it was true and she went off smiling as if I had given her a present. My temporary fame seemed to give others far more pleasure than it did me. I got dressed and sat there waiting; reading required too much concentration and I tried to imagine what would happen next. When Keith arrived, he looked calm and collected, as he probably always did, and got straight to the point, the non-official point. "Is everything OK now? Problems solved?"

"Yes, thank you," I smiled politely at him and then I relented. "It's great - thank you for helping me to come to grips with it all yesterday. I think that helped more than if Andy had just told me himself - we are just fine now."

"That's good. I thought you'd work it out."

The guard knocked on the door and Moira came in, this time looking rested and calm. "Cara, you're looking a lot better this morning."

I got up and gave her a hug. "So do you. You must have caught up on some of that lost sleep."

'Well, now then," said Keith. "Seeing we're all rested and happy – let's go and see Andy and discuss how we proceed from here."

To my surprise all four of us trooped off to Andy's ward, even the constable came. Keith saw my look. "He's here to guard you and he's not allowed to leave off till I tell him to. Hospitals are very difficult places for this sort of situation. You might as well be in a shopping mall."

The linen trolley was still in position across Andy's door; we pushed it aside and went in leaving the guard in the corridor. Andy was sitting up in bed looking brighter than I had seen him since he was shot. I touched his hand briefly and Keith patted his shoulder and said how much better he was looking, which made me smile at Moira behind his back – we were all saying the same thing this morning.

Andy looked up at Keith. "Thank you for what you did yesterday."

"You can buy me a beer sometime," said Keith in an off-hand way, but he looked pleased in his undemonstrative way.

Moira gave Andy a careful hug, asked him some nurse type questions and had a look at the monitor still attached to him. When she was satisfied that he was getting on all right we settled down to discuss my safety. It took quite a while, but in the end, we agreed to stage a careful deception, intending to divert Moore's attention, but still allow me to stay in Hawke's Bay so I could be near Andy. Keith and Andy would both have preferred that I was sent off to some other part of the country to stay with someone unspecified, but I told them it wasn't negotiable, I had to be in Hawke's Bay for now and I was prepared to take the risks involved.

The plan that evolved was that I would stay with Moira, but I would be spirited into her house without letting anyone suspect that I was back in Clive. I would once again settle into an invisible life inside the house. Moira would continue her normal routine and Andy would obviously have to stay where he was for some time. Privately I thought that I might be able to persuade Moira to drive me to the hospital now and then so I could see Andy, but that wasn't something I could say, or Keith would have pulled rank and forbidden it.

Keith and Benson and the Clive constable would spread the word that I had returned to Auckland to stay with friends, and we banked on Moore's informant letting him know. The Clive constable would pick up my suitcase from Rusty's place and give it to Moira, but he would tell Rusty that I had gone to Auckland and that the suitcase would be sent after me.

We were all confident that Moore would return to Auckland in the hope of getting hold of me, and the Auckland police were going to keep a watch on my flat to arrest Moore if he turned up there.

"Do you know what they'll charge him with?" Andy was feeling well enough now to want to keep up with developments.

"They have a raft of things under investigation; drug importation and murder among others, but they'll charge him with abduction, assault and whatever else they can throw at him for the time being and make sure he doesn't get bail."

"Have you located the Mercedes?"

"In a way, yes. We found the holiday apartment Moore and his lady had rented in Napier, but we think she left in the Mercedes before he and his thug broke into the house in Clive the night before last. We have no details of the car they took Cara in and we don't have a description of Moore's thug. So, it's like looking for a needle in a haystack at the moment."

What none of us knew that morning was that the key, the one Lorraine had found in my flat and given to Benson, was going to change all our best laid plans and put me into more danger than ever before.

Lorraine and John had gone back to the flat and found the key under my bed. They took it straight to Benson and everyone agreed it looked like a locker key.

Benson, we found out later, gave one of his constables the job of working out what the key might fit. None of them doubted that somewhere in Auckland there was a storage facility, a gym locker or something similar with an enormous sum of illegal cash and possibly drugs and passports stashed in it.

It all went wrong for the simplest of reasons - a pre-printed pad of memo notes. The officer, who was tasked with finding what the key fitted, finally located a man who installed lockers with that type of key. He provided a list of forty factories and sports clubs and the day before Moore chased me in his car the constable narrowed it down to one of three places. He went back to tell Benson about his progress, but Benson was out, so the constable took a page from a pre-printed memo pad that he found on Benson's desk, filled it in and left it on the desk.

To: Benson From: Wilton

Regarding: The key Nick gave to the girl.

Message: Urgent

The note must have been read by Moore's informant, who thought it meant that Nick had given me a key and that Benson was hoping to get it off me. Moore's informant would have let him know immediately that I had a key that belonged to Nick. To Moore it could only have meant one thing; I was an accomplice of Nick's, and I knew where the money was. For Moore this was the best news since Nick stole the money, or cheated him on a deal, or whatever had happened. Now he assumed that all he had to do was force me to give up the key and tell him where to go and the whole thing was sorted.

And now, two days later and after Moore had failed to capture me and get hold of the key, we thought he would head back to Auckland as soon as his informant told him that I had left Clive. Nobody had counted on Moore's informant not being at work for a couple of days. The news of my return to Auckland never reached Moore, and he stayed in Hawke's Bay, still intent of finding me there.

. . .

Just before lunch I left my room with Keith, Moira and the constable. Moira and I waited in a small room just off the ambulance bay while Keith fetched his car from the car park. We exited quietly through a side door, got into his car and drove round to where Moira's car was parked. She and I got into her car without anybody paying attention and Keith followed us back to Clive. Moira opened the garage, drove in and we did the side-door routine once again, then Keith and the constable left.

To be in that house again was wonderful. We went around together and inspected all the doors and windows. Moira pointed to the repaired French doors in the dining room. "They have put in laminated glass now – apparently, it's much harder to break. But let's hope I never have to worry about that again."

On the way to my bedroom, she looked up at the trapdoor and smiled. "There's no shortage of emergency gear in the attic now. I put water bottles up there yesterday. Not that we'll need them now but I did it anyway, it made me feel better."

"It was my fault - if I hadn't gone to get my phone, we would have been safe up there." Guilt hit me again. "And Andy wouldn't be lying in hospital with his hand ruined. It's all so ghastly, Moira. I feel so responsible - as if I damaged him myself."

Moira was not buying into any guilt trips or agonising. She put my bag down in my room and headed for her bathroom. "That's not the way these things work you know. Come and have a hot bath while I make lunch, it will make you feel a lot better."

She turned the taps on and put a bottle of bath salts on the edge of the bath. "Check if you like the smell of this stuff, it's supposed to be good for aching bodies."

Then she continued, as if this was the least important

thing she had to say, "It's not your fault that Andy's hurt. It's the drug baron's fault, never forget that. He set this in motion, and kept it going, and any damage is for him to feel guilty about. Not that it seems likely that he will, he probably doesn't have a conscience. You need to learn that you are not personally responsible for everything that happens."

She left and I lay in the pine scented bath, imagining that I could feel the bruises and hurts healing in the hot water. After all that had happened to me, it was a blissful few minutes and I gradually relaxed into a state of near trance, watching the opaque window and the shadows of the leaves moving in a slight breeze outside. I was deep both in water and in thought when I heard Moira talking to me from her bedroom. "Oh, come in Moira - I don't mind."

She came in with a bathrobe over her arm. "I thought you might want to put this on and get dressed later – whatever you want." And then she looked at me lying in the bath and saw the bruises. "Oh, look at you! I had no idea - I thought you had a few bruises, but this is awful. Stand up so I can have a look."

I got up with some difficulty and turned around so she could see the damage to my hip and buttock. "I think someone should take a picture of that - the nurse in the hospital called bone-deep bruising. She said it will continue to 'come out' and look worse for some days."

I looked past Moira at my reflection in the mirror over the basin. My body was covered in bruises and scratches and red blotches, but the star of the show was my hip. The bruise was enormous and very dark, and it was running downwards under the skin like spilt ink.

"Turn around – ah yes, I thought that's what I saw." Moira motioned for me to look in the mirror again. "It's truly spectacular, but this is the interesting thing." She pointed and by standing on tiptoes and looking over my shoulder I could see what she was looking at. Much further down, at the inward curve of my buttock was another bruise. "What's special about that one?"

"I don't think it is a bruise, I think that's where the blood emerges again from the bruise higher up. Blood has continued to leak from the crushed blood vessels, deep down in the tissue - it must be a big crush injury - and until those blood vessels healed the blood seeped down and surfaced there. Like an underground stream or something. But that won't be sore, it's just blood, nothing's damaged there. The pain will be where the injury is."

I was impressed. "That does it, photos please. Imagine when it's all green and yellow. My parents will be interested to see what it looks like."

So, Moira went for her camera and took some photos and I got into the bathrobe and followed her to the kitchen. We had a very late lunch and then I rubbed Moira's arnica cream on some of my bruises and got dressed.

Mid-afternoon the local constable arrived and handed my suitcase to Moira, having no idea that I was in the house. Rusty would tell people that I was the one who had been on the railway track and that the suitcase would be sent to Auckland. Her extensive networks, and the fact that she could never resist a piece of good gossip, would ensure that the entire village would know that this time I really had gone back to Auckland.

We spent a quiet afternoon. I rang Lorraine and we had a long conversation about all that had happened. She and John had been in Shanghai for their long-awaited week away and she had no idea of the dramas that had taken place in Hawke's Bay.

"Tell me every single thing - don't leave anything out. I have to hear this properly so I can tell John."

It took quite a while to tell the whole story and at the end she only had two questions. "Do you feel safe there, at your friend's place? I mean, do you truly think that man who's after you has left and come back here?"

"I think so. Benson will have made sure that everyone up there knows that I've left Hawke's Bay and returned to Auckland. So, the informer will tell Moore and he will head back to Auckland to find me."

"OK, so long as you really feel you're safe there. And can we assume that this thing with Andy is serious?"

I smiled to myself; she was trying to sound casual, but she was dying to find out. "I think we can assume that. I've asked him to marry me." She exploded with laughter as I had known she would. "You did?! What did he say?"

"Now that I think about it he didn't actually say anything. Perhaps you should keep it to yourself in case he's going to turn me down."

Moira was in the kitchen making an asparagus quiche; I said I would come and make a salad later. When I put the phone down it was clouding over, and it was cooler than earlier in the day. I closed the window in my bedroom and curled up on the bed with a book.

23

I was half-asleep when Moore smashed my bedroom window with a large flowerpot and climbed in. Before I had time to get into gear to defend myself, he was dragging me off the bed. He got me in that same grip, with his arm around my throat from behind, as he had when he knocked me down on the roadside, and he had that wicked-looking thin knife in his hand again.

Desperation filled me, and anger that it was still not over. I managed to twist to one side, nearly freed myself and punched as hard as I could upward with my elbow. It connected with his windpipe; he gasped and for a short moment he lost his grip. I knew I had no real chance against him physically. He was a lot taller and much stronger. I ran for it, down the passage, through the living room and into the dining room. I screamed at Moira to get out. And then he was on me, before I even got to the terrace door.

He took hold of my arm with his right hand, still holding the knife in his left, and then he swung me around and got his arm around my neck again. Moira arrived in a rush, took in the scene in front of her and came to a sudden stop beside the dining table.

"Stay where you are - don't move. This fucking bitch is going to tell me where the key is and if you try and stop me, I'll cut her throat."

All at once my fear turned into a rage that burned like a bright white flame inside me. All thoughts of getting hurt or killed evaporated from my mind like mist. *How dare this brutal, cruel man invade my life and Moira's and think he can cow us and bend us to his will - I will not allow it. I will stop him, and I don't care what I have to do. I want to kill him - I will kill him!*

My fury gave me an unflinching focus. I forgot about the knife next to my cheek or the gun he probably had on him. The only thing that mattered was to prevent him winning.

I knew he meant what he said, he would cut my throat to punish me, even if he got nothing out of me. I had evaded him and tricked him and probably made him feel ridiculous as well as frustrated. Now he would have what he wanted and then he would kill me. Lightning-fast thoughts flew through my head, were discarded and replaced by others. Moira's face was a frozen mask of terror; she was waiting for the inevitable.

"Now, where is that bloody key? Give it to me, tell me where it's for and you can go."

But I knew he would never let me go and not Moira either. My only chance was to catch him off-guard and somehow unbalance him both physically and mentally. I could think of no way to do that inside, but I might be able to do it outside. And if I could get him out of the house onto the terrace, Moira would have a chance to run.

"OK, OK – I give up! You can have it and I'll tell you where the place is – where the key fits."

"No tricks! If you try anything smart, I'll slice your face to ribbons and then we'll talk again."

I tried to signal to Moira to be quiet and do nothing, but it is only in books that people can speak with their eyes. All I could do was hope that she would be a passive bystander and not intervene in any way. So, I said, as if I was beaten and had given up, "The key is in the garden shed."

Moira's eyes widened slightly; she looked puzzled. I knew she was trying to figure out if it was true.

Moore tightened his arm around my throat. "What!? Don't fuck with me! Why would it be in the shed?" He shook me hard, his grip round my throat was chokingly tight and the knife trembled next to my temple.

I spoke in a croak. "I hid it. So, you wouldn't find it - if you broke in. Moira can get it."

He actually laughed then, but it was a sarcastic laugh. " Oh no - I'm not that stupid. She'd be off like a shot. We'll go there together, all three of us. Where's the shed?" His grip loosened slightly, and I drew a deep breath.

"It's in the garden - through the doors here and out to the left." I tried ineffectually to point, and Moira gestured mutely at the French doors.

"OK lady, you come over here and open those doors and walk in front of us where I can see you." Moira got the message loud and clear; if she tried to run for it he would cut me. She came closer, passed us without looking at me and unlocked the terrace door. I could nearly smell her fear.

"Swing it wide open!" He manoeuvred me around and as Moira walked slowly out onto the terrace Moore and I followed, but clumsily. His arm was still around my neck from behind and our feet knocked together at each step; we made slow and awkward progress.

I felt very sorry for Moira then, because she had no idea if I had invented the story about the shed, and she did not know what she could do to help me, or if she should even try. It must have been awful. I knew I had only one chance now and I had to get the timing absolutely right. Any hesitation would just make things worse and if I got it wrong disaster would follow.

We got to the edge of the terrace, with two steps down to the lawn. Exactly when Moore had one foot still on the terrace and I felt he was about to transfer his weight to the other foot to step down, I flung myself violently to the right. I used my entire body weight and put as much momentum as I could into it. Both my feet left the ground, and I used my whole body as a swinging weight, like a wrecking ball. I knew I risked getting the knife into my face or throat as we toppled, but it was the only way I could take him by surprise. My rage still burnt with a bright flame. I was going to get the knife and kill him.

We fell down the steps to the lawn in an uncontrolled tumble, and his grip on my throat loosened immediately. Instinctively I rolled away from him, tried to put some distance between us so I could get up and fight. A high-pressure arc of hot, red blood flung into the air and rained down between us, splattering me. The sound he made was the most disturbing sound I had ever heard. A roar that turned into a rasping gurgling sound, intensely primitive. It lasted only a second and stopped as abruptly as if it had been sliced with a knife. I sat up and what I saw was so horrible that I still sometimes see it in my dreams.

The knife had gone deep into his neck under the jaw

and cut a gash between his Adam's apple and the earlobe. A gaping wound that now pumped ever slower pulses of blood, no longer squirting high. His eyes were wide open, looking straight up at the sky. Then the blood stopped coming. I got up slowly and a light rain started to fall.

Moira came and stood beside me and together we looked down at him for a moment, then she looked at me. "Are you hurt?"

"No. What do we do now?" My rage had burnt out and I was numb and exhausted.

She made a face, as if grimly amused. "We can't do anything for him. So, let's make sure we get this right before we decide."

It took her only moments to think it through. My mind was empty, my energy depleted. I simply stood there and waited.

"I'll go and check if there's a car outside in the street. Wait here." She was back in seconds. "Nobody there - bet his mate is in the street behind or around the corner. Come inside."

I stood mute in the kitchen while she dialled the emergency number. "I need to speak Inspector Keith Somebody at the Napier police station, very quickly. He will know what needs doing."

She listened for a moment and then she took control of the poor operator, who was only trying to follow protocol.

"No, I'm not going to do that. This is an acute emergency connected to an ongoing investigation. I have to speak to Keith now. We can't have police cars converging willy-nilly!"

And amazingly she got her way. They patched her through to Keith and she quickly explained that Moore was dead in her garden, and that there was no car outside. "I'm not telling you how to do things, but if you want to catch Moore's mate you should send someone quietly to the street parallel to mine, behind my back garden. Bet he's there or around the next corner, waiting in that car they had Cara in."

She listened to something he said and put the phone down. I was still standing there like a pillar of stone, devoid of initiative, too tired to speak.

"They are sending people to check out the next street and they will come here but quietly, without sirens. Keith is on his way. Please sit down, Cara - I'll make you a hot drink."

Obediently I did what I was told. I held the warm mug with both hands and forgot to drink. Police officers arrived. Moira showed them where Moore's body was and came back to sit with me. Footsteps moved back and forth through the house, voices and other noises and still we sat there. Every now and then Moira reached out and clasped my hand. And by and by I found my voice and my brain started processing things.

"I wish Keith would come."

"He is here already. He's outside on the road talking to someone."

A few minutes later he walked into the kitchen, looking as calm as ever. "Cara, are you all right?"

"Yes, thank you. Is he still there?"

"Yes, we won't move him for a few hours probably. We have to do a lot of technical stuff to make sure we have all the details we need."

"I killed him." I had been waiting for what seemed like hours to tell him. It was a huge relief to say it.

Moira made a sound of protest, but Keith raised his hand to stop her. He looked at me with infinite patience and got his pad out. "Can you tell me how you did that, please."

"Well, I made him fall down the steps, and the knife hit him in the throat and ... and cut his throat. And he died."

"OK, who was holding the knife?"

I was shocked at the question. "He was, of course! I tricked him and made him fall." I noticed that he was not making notes. "You should write it down," I said.

"OK, I will," said Keith. "Was he holding on to you or threatening you?"

"He had me around the neck from behind, like last time. I tricked him to take me out on the terrace and when we got to the first step, I threw myself sideways and we both rolled down the steps."

Keith made a note on his pad. "So let me see if I've got this right. He came into the house, uninvited I suppose? Yes? And he had you in a choke hold from behind and he had a knife that he threatened you with? Is that right? Did he say anything?"

I nodded. "He said he would kill me or slice my face to bits if Moira tried to run. Or if I didn't give him the key and told him where the place was."

"And how did you manage to persuade him to go out into the garden?"

I realised that he had only heard half the story. "He said I must give him the key, or he'd kill me. I said it was in the shed. I said I'd hidden it there in case he broke in to search for it - so we were going to the garden shed. I knew the steps down from the terrace would be the only place where I could perhaps catch him off-balance and trip him up. He's so much stronger than I am. Or he was, I mean."

Keith nodded. "Let me sum this up. Moore smashes his way into your bedroom, takes you prisoner, threatens to kill you with a knife, you trick him into going outside so you can topple the two of you down the steps. You did not kill him,

Cara. You may have wanted to kill him, but he killed himself. And you saved your life and Moira's."

Moira spoke for the first time since he had come into the kitchen. "She's in shock, Keith. I'll make her have a hot shower and some soup. I'll fix some for your men later if they need it."

My mind heard her, but I was in a bubble of unreal calm where normal rules didn't apply, and I was deeply frustrated that he did not seem to understand what I was telling him. "But Keith, you don't understand. I was going to kill him! If he hadn't fallen on to the knife, I was planning to get the knife off him and stab him to death."

Keith nodded and got up. He came around the table to where I was sitting, rigid with tension. He stood behind me with his hands on my shoulders and spoke very slowly, the way you do to a child. "Now listen to me, Cara. You are trau-matised and shocked, and we'll get a proper statement tomorrow. But Moore died in an accident caused by his own actions. Do you understand that?"

Somewhere in my sluggish brain I knew he was right, but I still felt sick at what I had wanted to do. "Yes, I know. I just need to get used to it. You see, I really wanted him to die, and I was prepared to kill him."

He shook me gently. "I know and that's OK because you didn't do it after all. Wanting and doing isn't the same thing or the prisons would be full, and the streets would be empty."

When he left the kitchen, Moira took me back to her bathroom once again, stripped my clothes off and bundled them into a tight knot and told me to shower and wash my hair. She laid the bathrobe on the edge of the bath.

"You can get dressed now or later. There are chaps in

your room taking photos of the window. Nobody will come into the kitchen unless it's Keith." She took the bundle of blood-splattered clothes and left.

I saw the blood briefly staining the water pink on the floor in the shower and then running clear. It was odd that once again I was washing someone else's blood off my skin and hair. Maybe I should have had some profound reaction to this, revulsion perhaps or regret, but all I felt just then was relief at being clean again.

I went back to the kitchen where the lights were on and the blinds had been pulled down. Moira had set the table and poured us wine. She was standing by the oven looking at something inside. She smiled, seemingly unconcerned by all the fear and horror we had been through. "I pulled the blinds so we can have some privacy - there are so many people going past on the veranda. I know it's too early to have the lights on, but never mind."

I went to her and put my arms round her and leaned against her. "You must be as shocked as I was. I'm sorry such horrible things seem to happen whenever I'm here."

"No need to worry about me, I've seen enough messes in emergency rooms over the years. But I have never before felt that someone got his just deserts by getting killed. Today is the first time I ever wished anyone dead, really and truly been prepared to kill someone. It's a very strange emotion - it makes me feel as if I have learnt something about myself that I didn't really want to know. Now sit down and let's have a wine or two and ignore the rest of the house."

"Will we be able to stay here tonight?"

"I don't know. I'm sure they'll tell us eventually."

. . .

Much, much later I was still there, still huddled into the fleecy folds of the bathrobe, with another glass of wine. Moira was stirring a big pot of soup on the stove.

I had just said, "I'm forever having hot showers and baths and drinking wine here. It seems to fix most things," when Keith knocked and came in. He looked at the scene of domestic calm and said matter-of-factly. "You two are just the most astonishing women I have ever met."

"Oh, nonsense," said Moira, still stirring her soup. "Do you think your chaps would like some soup?"

He laughed, his eyes crinkled up and he looked at least ten years younger. "I think the guys will be talking about this investigation for years. I'll ask them in a moment, but I'm sure they'll be delighted. It's quite damp and cold out there."

He pulled out a chair and Moira put a bowl of soup in front of him and he started pulling the bread to bits, as if he was in his own home. I had to admit it was not in the least how I would have imagined a criminal investigation.

"I came to tell you that we can take you to a motel for the night and you can come back tomorrow. But there is an alternative if you prefer it." He dipped a piece of bread in his soup. "With the layout of this house the way it is, we could close a couple of doors, and you two could have the bedroom and kitchen side of the house and we could continue working in the dining room and on the terrace and also have access to the hall and the front door."

"We'll need to put something over the window in my room."

Keith looked at me, as if he was surprised that I could speak. "They fixed that already. The tech has finished, finger printing's been done, and the window is boarded up with a sheet of ply."

"I'm fine staying here," I said. "But it's Moira's house."

She did not hesitate. "I'd rather be here too. One thing I

want to know, though - did you get that other man, the one who chased Cara from here the other night?"

He made a face. "Sorry! I should have told you already. He's in custody and will appear in court in the morning before we transfer him to Auckland. He was parked a couple of blocks down in the street behind this one. We'll initially charge him with conspiracy to abduct, carrying an illegal weapon, using a firearm in a public place, being an accomplice to a home invasion and carrying illegal drugs."

Then he grinned. "Plus, not having a valid driver's licence, driving a vehicle with false registration plates and having a non-functioning brake light. And you just wait till the Auckland guys get hold of him!"

"What about the blonde in the Mercedes, did she get away?"

"There's an alert out for her and it's only a matter of time until we get her – she either ditches the car or gets caught very soon."

Moira and I felt a relief that was nearly palpable; unless there was a third man, we could presume that the last threat had been removed. Keith left, Moira set out soup bowls and bread on the dining room table and told one of the policemen that the soup was keeping hot on the stove. Then we went to the other end of the house and closed the passage door behind us.

My room looked sort of temporary and uncomfortable with the window covered in ply and grey dust everywhere from the fingerprinting. Moira took one look and decided it wasn't good enough. "Come and share the big bed in my room. I'm sure we can cope after living though so much together and we'll both feel more comfortable."

We woke the next morning when Andy called. I lay in Moira's huge bed feeling warm and safe and listened to his voice, wishing he was beside me. He was burning with curiosity. "Everyone here is talking about some drama at Clive last night, but the details are very sketchy, even on the news. Are you two all right?"

I tried to keep it minimal. "Yes, we're OK. Moore's dead - it all happened here, at Moira's house." I told him a very brief version and said I would be with him by lunchtime at the latest, the details could wait.

When we dressed and ventured out into the rest of the house, we found one lonely constable sitting on a dining chair by the door to the terrace. The body was gone, the blood had been washed away by rain or soaked into the lawn and the place looked very nearly normal.

"Oh, you poor boy," said Moira who was probably only ten years older than the policeman. "Why aren't you in the kitchen where you could make a cup of coffee?"

"I'm fine, thanks. The team left about an hour ago and I've been pottering around tidying up a bit. They left a bit of a mess. And I am supposed to go back to town as soon as you're up. My shift only started a couple of hours ago, so I've not been here all night."

He left five minutes later, and we had the house to ourselves again. I went out on the terrace. The rain had stopped, and the sun was coming out. There was no sign that someone had died a bloody death on the lawn only yesterday.

Moira joined me and I asked the question that had been in my mind since I woke up. "Do you think you'll be OK living here now? Or has all this spoilt it for you?"

"Do you know, I thought about it a lot since yesterday. I wondered if sitting on the terrace on a summer evening would ever feel the same. But I decided that I can't let it spoil things for me. Why should I allow that beast of a man, who would have killed us both without batting an eyelid, to destroy how I feel about my home?"

She was looking strong and determined. "So, I've thought about it on and off and the answer is NO, definitely not. Even though he's dead now, thank goodness, I won't let him have an influence over me. And neither should you."

She was right of course. To let him continue to dwell in my mind like a toxic substance would in a way have been a victory for him. He had done enough damage to all our lives already and we needed to regain our normality and feel calm and unthreatened again. Behind out determined attitudes we knew, of course, that things wouldn't be as straight forward as that. We would have flashbacks and bad dreams just like everyone else who had experienced threat and trauma, but by looking forward and talking to each other we would cope.

"Yes, you are right - it would be awful to feel that he could still affect our lives even after he's dead. We'll have to move on and leave him in the past. I know it won't be quite as simple as that, but we can aim high."

And there we left it for the time being. I borrowed Moira's car and went to see Andy, who was sitting up and looking more like his usual self. I kissed him and commented on how much more convenient it was to kiss someone who was sitting up.

His smile was nearly back to his normal transformation level. "I feel a lot better today. Did you notice? Only one tube left."

"Are they letting you out of bed yet? I don't suppose you can have a shower with all those bandages?"

"No, not yet. But at least I can go to the toilet if I take my IV pole with me."

We spent a couple of hours catching up. I told him every

single detail about Moore's death, what Keith had said and about the conversation Moira and I had had that morning.

He took my hand. "I agree completely. We can't let that bastard have a grip on you forever. Once you have given Keith your formal statement it should be over for you, at least for now. You might be needed as a witness at the trial of that other guy, but if Benson finds a really good charge to hammer him with, drug dealing for example, they might not need you."

This was something I hadn't considered yet. "God, no – I don't want to be involved in a trial. I've had enough expo-sure for a lifetime - all I want now is peace and privacy. And by the way, I only thought of this last night in bed - have you or someone else contacted your family?"

"Benson took care of that right away. Yes, I do have family - parents, two sisters and various hangers-on. My dad is on his way – his flight comes in about five this afternoon. He said he was looking forward to meeting his future daughter-in-law. You haven't forgotten that you proposed, have you?"

"Of course, not – I've only proposed once in my life. But you didn't give me an answer at the time, so I was still waiting to hear what your answer was."

24

When I drove out of the hospital parking lot an hour later the thought uppermost in my mind was worry about Andy's future. Could he stay in the police force with a mutilated and possibly useless hand? What would he do if he couldn't? How much would he resent a change of career?

There were two cars outside Moira's house. I drove into her garage and had another look at the cars as I pulled the roller door down, but they meant nothing to me. On the terrace I found Moira, Keith and an unknown man sitting around the table with cups of tea and a plate of biscuits. Both men got up and Keith said, "Cara, this is Gregor Black - Andy's father." Even if nobody had introduced him, I would have known. He was a thirty-years older version of Andy, tall and a bit burly with black hair going grey and bright blue eyes. When he smiled and shook my hand, I saw that the transforming smile too had come to Andy from his father.

"Sit down and have a cup of tea," said Moira. "Gregor got

an earlier flight and Keith met him at the airport and guided him here, so you could have some time with Andy."

"Andrew's not expecting me till after five, so he won't worry," said Gregor. "Keith has been filling me in on what's been going on – and Moira too. I've heard about your courage in the face of danger, as they say. If you don't mind me saying, it's hard to believe you coped with all that, particularly what happened last night."

He paused and stared at me with a frown, which made me feel slightly worried. Moira noticed and looked from him to me and back again, puzzled by his look. I didn't know how to respond to that stare, so at odds with what he had just said.

"I've seen you somewhere before," said Gregor at last, "When you arrived just now, I recognised you straight away. Where could I have seen you before?"

"I don't know." I knew full well where he had seen me but hoped we could change the subject if I brushed it off. "I don't recognise you, apart from your likeness to Andy."

Moira answered for me, not prepared to let me get away with avoiding talking about it. "You probably saw her in a video clip on the TV news. She rescued a baby out of the river after a car crash on a bridge near here not long ago. They played the video several times on TV, so that will be what you're thinking of."

Keith started laughing. "Well, I'll be damned! When I came to see you in the hospital, I thought I must have seen you somewhere in town, because I felt I recognised you too - now I get it. That was you, that muddy angel of mercy who took off on her bike and disappeared down the road. If you hadn't been so damn filthy at the time, I would probably have recognised you sooner. My God, the dramas you get yourself involved in, it's unbelievable. You are, as they say, something else again."

"That's not fair - I don't get myself involved! Things happened and dragged me in, that's all. I'm not some sort of drama magnet. I used to live a quiet and orderly life. And until Nick was shot right in front of me, I had never even met a detective or seen a dead body or any of the horrible things that have happened since."

I realised that I was perhaps unreasonably upset, but somehow, he had touched a raw nerve. Moira was soothing and sensible as always. "We know, Cara, we know. You are still in a state of delayed shock, don't worry about it. Keith is just so delighted with you - I think you're this week's poster girl. I'm sure everything will go back to being quiet and orderly again very soon."

Keith was amused and a bit repentant. "I'm sorry, Cara, I didn't mean to upset you. But your resilience is already legend at the station and now I discover you rescued that child too – can't wait to tell them. You should write a book about it. Not that anyone would believe it really happened, but it would make a damn good story. And don't forget to put in that bit about the constable with the ice cream who recognised you."

We broke up half an hour later when Keith and I went into town for me to make a formal statement. "I know you're not accused or suspected of anything, but with everything that's happened I think someone less involved than myself should be present. We'll pop into the station and let someone else conduct the interview alongside me."

When we were leaving Gregor turned to me. "You know, I went and looked at a train with flatbed wagons like the one that rode over the top of you two. I wanted to see how much room there is under them, and it's not a lot. I don't know how you didn't get your heads smashed by the front of the engine." He shook his head, as if he still could not believe it. "There's a very low and solid part nearly level with the rails at the front, probably to push things out of the way if something's on the track. And then there are those safety chains where the wagons are attached to each other. Some of those hang down very low."

"Yes, I know. When they found us under that carriage the railway guys said they couldn't believe it either. I think it was because we were both lying so flat - Andy was on his back and I was on my front and our heads were side by side, and I turned his head sideways and then did the same myself."

I felt a need to explain to him that I had really done my best to protect Andy from damage. "I was trying to get us as low as possible, hoping no parts of us would be much higher than the rails. It was incredibly scary - when the engine first came over us it felt as if we had been hit, that huge heavy thing passing within a hair's breadth of us. Andy's hand must have flicked up and got smashed by some low part."

I had spent a lot of time thinking about how easily it could have ended with both of us dead, or terribly maimed. Talking about it brought all those feelings back, but as Moira had said, shock and terror don't wear off the minute something is over, and it would get better over time. The only good thing was that Andy had been unconscious most of the time, He had no real recollection of what it had been like under the train. Coping with the damage to his hand was enough of a challenge and would be for some time to come, maybe always.

On the way to town, I asked Keith about something I had been thinking about the last couple of days. "Does your wife get sick of the way you're never home? You seem to be all over the place at the most inconvenient times of the day and night."

"It's only like this now and then," he said slowly. "I think this one is very special, firstly the drama of it and that a major player on the drug scene has been eliminated. Sorry, I mean he eliminated himself. And secondly because I've got to know you and Moira and that has been special, too – a great pleasure. What made you think I have a wife?"

"Daughters of your own, knowing how to handle women, you know?"

"I'm pleased you think I know how to handle women. But no, my wife took off with a painter ten years ago." He chuckled. "And now I think of it, she achieved a complete change. First me, who was never home, and now a husband who works from home – very good."

For the next couple of hours, it was strictly business. The statement took a long time, because everything was picked apart, questions asked, details needed. It was odd to think that, until they got it all on tape to be written up by some-body, I had been the only person who knew the full story, step by step, all the details. Moira had been there for some of it, Andy knew some and Keith and Benson knew quite a lot. By the time we were finished I was sick of my own story. I walked out of the interview room thinking that I never wanted to tell it again, at least not in one session like this.

"Will I be able to get a copy of the transcript to keep?" I felt a bit silly asking, hoped he would not think I saw myself as famous in some way.

"Of course, are you thinking of making it into a book?"

He was joking of course, but I had to explain. "No, of course not. But I will let my parents read it, and maybe a couple of friends. When you try to tell people what happened, it is really hard to remember all the crucial bits in the right order. And now it's going to be written up all in one piece. And could you please call a taxi for me? I don't know the number."

"No need," he said comfortably and walked me out the door. "I'm driving you back." He held the door open, but I stopped on the doorstep. "Oh no, you must need some private time - it's the end of the day nearly."

"But we're going to the same place. I'm having dinner with you and Gregor and Moira, so you can stop feeling you have to be so independent."

And that's what we did that evening. We had a simple meal at Moira's house, spent a few pleasant hours being ordinary people and hardly mentioned the last few days at all, apart from discussing Andy's progress.

25

February was very hot, and the city never cooled even at night. We had the windows open and the fan gently turning over the bed. I woke early and lay quietly thinking of the day ahead. It was Wednesday and we had a lunch date, but otherwise nothing to do apart working on Andy's hand exercises.

Soon he would see the hand surgeon again to discuss progress and the possibility of further plastic surgery. I was amazed at the progress he had made already. His leg was nearly as good as new, and he could run again. The hand was making slow and more painful progress.

I lay on my side and looked at his sleeping face and the hand that he always kept carefully positioned where it would be least likely to be accidentally knocked by either of us. It looked at lot better than it had at the start. The scars and the skin grafts were still red and raw looking, the shape was odd-looking but much improved.

When we returned to Auckland we decided to live in my flat, which was bigger than Andy's and he sold his. I had found it very hard to reconcile the things that he had told me before I knew who he was, with the facts I learned about his real life. I had been surprised to find that he owned an apartment, because my first memory was of him telling me he had given up a rented flat to move to Hawke's Bay.

He had an unfair advantage because he had known all about me from the substantial file they compiled about me after I disappeared.

Once when we talked about it, I said, "I can't understand how you managed to keep things separate – I mean the things I had told you, which were nearly all lies, and the things you knew about the real me. Wasn't it hard?"

He thought for a moment. "No, it was quite easy. I had never met you, but I had seen lots of pictures of you and that video clip from when Nick was shot. So, the way you looked then and the facts we had on file, that was one person called Karen. The girl I got to know in Clive looked completely different and was a different person called Cara. Somehow that made it easy."

And then he smiled to himself as if he remembered something. "I used to talk in my sleep quite a lot at one stage of my life. I thought I must have done it again when I stayed over at Moira's. I thought you had found me out, but then I realised that the little signals I picked up were about the gun. Remember when you threw that fact at me as a test? My God, you are such a cool customer. I was very nearly at a stand-still trying to think of what to say."

"We are both such good liars, Andy – it's quite scary to think that I could live a life of lies for weeks without batting an eyelid."

"No, it's not scary at all. It's just that old saying 'needs must'. You didn't lie for gain or to get something you weren't entitled to and neither did I. For you it was that your survival depended on it - that was your need that must be met. And for me it was the 'need' of my job."

· · · ·

At first, I thought I would get a new job or go back to my old one, but it soon became obvious that Andy needed me for a few weeks while his hand and leg slowly got better. We had been back in the city for well over two months, and I still hadn't done anything about a job. For the time being we were all right for money with Andy on nearly full pay and all my cash cards turned into a savings account again, so we had time to consider things. The previous evening, we had sat up late and discussed what he might do, where we might live and what I should do in the meantime. There had been some talk about Andy becoming a police weapons trainer, but nothing was settled. I had said in a light-hearted way, that perhaps we should do something completely different from both our previous jobs. I had thought of this on and off since we returned to the city but without having anything specific in mind. Andy had fixed me with that intense blue gaze. My comment had triggered something, though I had no idea what it might be. "What do you mean by different? Different career, place or something else?"

"I don't know, I'm completely relaxed about it. I like change and now it feels as if we have an opportunity to have a fresh start, we're free to create our own future whichever way we like. If you want to be a sheep farmer, I'll be the farmer's wife, or if you want to be the weapons instructor, I'll do something else. If you're happy I think I'll be happy too - it sounds soppy, but it's true."

Now I lay there watching him sleep. Gone were the tensions and the sadness I used to glimpse in unguarded moments. I wondered what he had been thinking of the previous evening and when he would tell me. With Andy things never came out half-baked or at the spur of a moment. I knew I might have to wait for some time while he considered my idea and then, when he had thought it through, a plan would be presented for me to comment on.

He opened his eyes, instantly awake as always, smiled. "What are we doing today? I can't remember what day it is - do we have plans?"

"We'll have breakfast and do your hand exercises, and we're going out for lunch at one o'clock."

"OK - I'd forgotten that."

As I got out of bed the phone rang. It was a very one-sided conversation and Andy came round to my side of the bed and stood behind me with his arms round my body the way he often does. All I seemed to say was "really?" and "all right" and "OK, we'll be ready".

"Now that's very cryptic. Let me guess – someone is going to come and demonstrate a vacuum cleaner at half past ten?"

I leant back against him and smiled. "No, that was Benson. They think they have finally located the right lockers – in a disused boxing gym somewhere. Not the place where they were initially installed, they seem to have been on-sold at least once - which explains the time it has taken to find them. They've got a guard on the place, and he said we can come and watch when they open it."

"Cool," said Andy and let go of me straight away, once again in policing mode. "Are they picking us up?"

Two cars arrived punctually half an hour later. We went in one with Benson and a woman who was introduced as 'Jen - forensics'. The Boxing gym turned out to be a dingy and depressing place in the southern suburbs. Andy was delighted to see who was in the other car, people he had worked with for a couple of years in the Organised Crime and Drug Unit.

A locksmith arrived shortly after us and got the door open. It was obvious that this was no longer used as a boxing club and probably nobody had been there for weeks or months. Maybe Nick had been the last person to come here. It smelled of stale sweat and mouse droppings. The canvas floor in the boxing ring was worn through in patches and the ropes sagged.

We all trooped through to the changing room at the back. Barred windows high up, wooden benches down the centre of the room and hooks on the walls. There was a small bank of tall metal lockers numbered from one to twelve and a cleaner space along the wall where some shorter lockers had been before someone stole them or sold them.

Jen sprayed grey powder on and around the door to locker number nine and did her thing and then Benson took the key out of his pocket. He half turned to look at us before he opened the door and stood to one side so we could all see. "Holy smoke!" said the driver and everyone looked pleased and excited and started talking at the same time.

The locker was about six feet tall, only half the width of a normal door and it was packed full. Two rifles leaning into one corner, to my untrained eyes they looked like automatic weapons. A handgun and a pile of thin books on top of a laptop on the shelf at the top. Medium sized plastic boxes with clip-lids stacked on the floor beside the rifles and just visible in the back corner, a blue nylon satchel.

They all put on gloves and started a long and painstaking process of checking one item at a time. Each separate thing was photographed, put in a plastic bag and labelled. It took ages; after a while Benson turned to me. "Bored?"

I smiled. "I could stand here all day, it's like Christmas." Finally proof of what we had all suspected, the reason for all that had happened. Closure of a sort, and the comforting knowledge that we had reached the end of a trail.

On the drive back to the city Benson sat half turned around in the front seat discussing the finds with Andy. They were elated by the diversity of material they would have to work with. "Once we get into the laptop and have time to decipher those notebooks, we might be able to track his connections both here and abroad," said Benson, satisfaction radiating from his chubby face. "The OCD chaps are hoping to find incriminating stuff about the bikie gang that Moore had links to, and God knows what else."

"Did you ever locate Nick's girl friend?"

"Yeah – it took a while, but we got hold of her after she posted a thing on Face Book about her boyfriend getting shot. But she was a dead end – she thought he was a salesman too and he never left anything at her place apart from clothes. And I believe her, she had no idea. She had only met a couple of his friends from the gym, nobody of any interest to us. She called him a 'loner'."

I had one last question. "Where did he live when he wasn't at my place or with his girlfriend?"

"We still don't know. Maybe what we found in that locker will reveal something new. The girlfriend thought he rented two rooms from an elderly couple in Manurewa, but she never went there. We'll trace his travel via those three passports we found today, get in touch with drug squads in other countries. If we can dismantle Moore's empire, we'll be happy for a long time."

We were late for our lunch date with Lorraine and John.

"I don't think I've ever had lunch with people who

arrived with a police escort before." Lorraine was radiating curiosity. "What was all that in aid of?"

Andy nodded in my direction. "Ask Cara - this is her day."

"We went with Benson to see them open the locker. They found Nick's locker in a disused gym in south Auckland - after all this time!"

"Filthy place, full of mice." Andy had noticed my constant glances into the corners of the locker room, where mouse droppings lay everywhere.

"It was amazing - really exciting. I wouldn't have left even if it had been full of rats. Nick had everything there that we had speculated about - and lots more. There were passports, driver's licences, guns and ammunition. Even two wigs to match different passport photos. And a pair of glasses with plain lenses."

"Any money?"

"Heaps of money - I've never seen so much cash. They didn't take it out of the bag, but we all had a look inside. And a laptop and some notebooks. I was hoping they would at least have a look inside them while we were there, but no such luck."

"You can imagine how happy the Organised Crime guys were to find the laptop and the diary," said Andy. "I think they had nearly given up hope of finding the place."

We had a long celebration lunch and stayed late into the afternoon, talking and laughing and telling each other that this was the final thing needed to tie up the loose ends, and now it was over. But we know that things are rarely that simple, and memories of terror and trauma take a long time to fade. They surface in nightmares and flashbacks ambush me at unexpected moments. I sometimes wake up from a nightmare, in the grip of acute fear, reliving the events of those weeks. Andy says I should be proud of what I learned about myself; that I am resilient and capable of handling dangerous situations. But knowing that I'm capable of truly wanting to kill someone is a fact I would rather never have learned.

MANY THANKS

We hope you've enjoyed reading this story and would consider leaving a review, or even a rating.

These are not only much appreciated, they also help other readers discover new authors.

For more about other titles from Tina Clough, please read on.

ALSO BY TINA CLOUGH

THE GIRL WHO LIVED TWICE

What would you do if you woke up one morning and found that time had rewound exactly a year? Would you revisit your past mistakes and try to do better? Would you try to get revenge on those who had wronged you? Or would you use what you knew to get rich? When Mia finds herself in her own past, she must decide how best to use her pre-knowledge of one year's worth of events and personal issues.

RUNNING TOWARDS DANGER

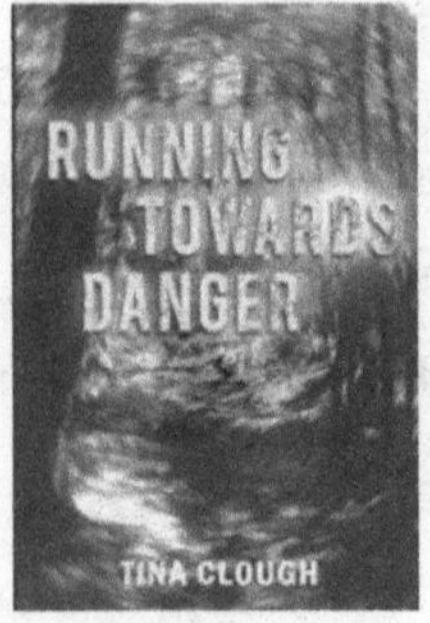

When Karen's flat-mate Nick is gunned down in front of her in the street her life is turned upside-down. Everything she thought she knew about him turns out to be a lie. She becomes a suspect in the police investigation and drug bosses think she knows where Nick has hidden a large sum of money. When her life is threatened, she decides to leave town and disappear.

Karen becomes Cara and creates an anonymous existence, severs all links to her past and adopts a cash-based way of life that leaves no electronic traces. But despite her careful planning danger still stalks her and she is forced to make dramatic choices in the face of threats and brutal violence.

Can she trust the man she is attracted to, or has he been sent by the killers to gain her confidence and find the money they believe she has?

THE CHINESE PROVERB

Book 1 - Hunter Grant Series

Army veteran Hunter Grant thought he had left war behind in Afghanistan – a conflict that left him with physical and psychological scars.

But finding an unconscious girl in the Northland bush and gradually untangling her story involves him in warfare of a different kind in his own country.

Hunter sets out to find and punish the man Dao calls Master, but he soon finds there is more to this story than enslavement. Before long he himself is being hunted by the overlord of a drug empire whose sole objective is to kill Dao because she knows too much.

Protecting her and waging war while trying to keep the police from stifling his enterprise takes all Hunter's ingenuity and determination and puts him in deadly jeopardy.

ONE SINGLE THING

Book 2 - Hunter Grant Series

Journalist Hope Barber disappears two weeks after returning to New Zealand from an assignment in Pakistan, leaving her front door open and her bag and phone inside. The police are tight-lipped about their reluctance to act, and Hunter Grant and Dao agree to help Hope's brother Noah find her. Details about Hope's time in Pakistan gradually emerge but only raise more questions.

Was Hope under surveillance?

Was she linked to terrorists?

And who is the man Hope called 'my stalker'?

FOLDED

Book 3 - Hunter Grant Series

First notes asking for help and folded into tiny origami shapes are found outside a city apartment building, then a physics textbook with tiny writing between the lines and then the woman who found them abruptly resigns and disappears. Are the notes asking for help real or is it a game? Hunter Grant, ex-army and with a pragmatic view of justice, reluctantly agrees to help find the missing woman.

Things get complicated when a high-powered lawyer arrives form the US, and shortly after his meeting with Hunter and Dao, a "cease and desist" letter arrives from the Cayman Islands. Inspector Bakker - a woman, who in Hunter's words "looks as if she would be useful in a brawl, provided she was on your side" - takes instant exception to his involvement and threatens to arrest him for interfering in an investigation.

Dao sets out alone on a dangerous mission, driven by a compulsive need to find out what has happened to the girl who wrote the notes, and Hunter looks death in the face when he decides to risk everything to put an end to the Darknet forces that threaten their lives.

THE SHADOW BROKER

It is 2026 and individual freedoms are severely curtailed, with state surveillance everywhere. State Security has a Watch List, and being on it means that nothing you do or say escapes the authorities, but does the Kill List really exist? And if it does, how would you know if you were on it?

Coded messages on a found burner phone, top-level government corruption and a shadowy mastermind who calls himself The Broker. In this climate of state control, three unlikely friends start quietly looking for connections and set in motion a deadly game of hide and seek that will change their lives forever.

Trying to uncover the truth means risking your life, and nothing is more dangerous than searching for evidence of government corruption.

LETTERS FROM THE PAST

Letters from the Past is a series of stand-alone novels where a letter from or about the past reveals something that changes a woman's perceptions of herself or of her family, and that affects her outlook on life.

These books are such fun to write, and I am always working on the next title in this series. I hope you will enjoy reading them as much as I enjoy writing them!

Tina

Having had nobody in her life since her husband died, Lara unexpectedly finds herself involved with three men. One is planning to use her, one she plans to use for her own ends, and one becomes a "friend-with-benefits" with surprising results. Sometimes a quiet schoolteacher is not all she seems at first glance.

Callista experiences an event of apparent ESP at the Okehampton Castle ruins and becomes a media sensation, but the effect it has on her life is dramatic. How do two people, one calm. one seriously claustrophobic, who feel they are poles apart, cope for an hour and a half in total darkness in a stalled lift? And can they handle the consequences?

Sofia's life is in turmoil: a difficult diva mother, a letter with a confession about a family killing and having to accept help from a man she loathes when she is injured. Can reluctant attraction turn into love?

Who is the stranger living in the empty house Miranda inherited from her grandmother? Why is he living like a secretive recluse in someone else's house? Reckless Miranda decides to confront him, and what she discovers prompts her to set out on a fearless quest to bring justice to a man who has given up hope. But is the gamble too great or a risk worth taking?

When Emma finds an old letter in a library book she is instantly intrigued, but by researching the origin of the letter she unwittingly opens the door to danger and becomes the target for threats and harassment. Nearly desperate, she takes a leap of blind faith into the unknown and accepts an offer of help from a stranger - but can she trust him?

Jamie, an ardent protester against the gigantic Vista Resort development and Leo Masters, the high-powered developer, seem unlikely to ever agree on anything. But unexpected coincidences and chance brings them together in a fragile state of mutual respect. Will courage and kindness resolve the situation, or do they need help?

After a bizarre accident with ESP overtones, the media haunt Arapera. But can she trust an offer of help from a man she has only met once? Or will she regret it for the rest of her life if she doesn't take the chance? Sometimes life is a knife-edge balance between staying safe and taking risks, and there is no way of predicting if the gamble is worth it.

When crime-writer Saskia finds an unconscious stranger, she has a strange and strong emotional connection. Pretending to be his cousin and with no thought for the consequences, she spends weeks at his hospital bedside. But what will happen when he wakes and discovers she has invaded his life, breached his privacy and made crucial decisions on his behalf?

ABOUT THE AUTHOR

Tina Clough grew up in Sweden and now lives in New Zealand; dividing her time between writing fiction and translating and editing medical research papers.

Between working and writing she looks after an acre of fruit trees, vegetable gardens and roaming hens.

Apart from reading her interests include photography, wine, growing organic vegetables, making jam and kayaking.

www.lightpoolpublishing.com